Shedding the Metaphors

Shedding the Metaphors

From the Amazon Bestselling Author
Nandini Sahu

BLACK EAGLE BOOKS
Dublin, USA | Bhubaneswar, India

Black Eagle Books
USA address:
7464 Wisdom Lane
Dublin, OH 43016

India address:
E/312, Trident Galaxy, Kalinga Nagar,
Bhubaneswar-751003, Odisha, India

E-mail: info@blackeaglebooks.org
Website: www.blackeaglebooks.org

First International Edition Published by
Black Eagle Books, 2023
Reprint - 2026

SHEDDING THE METAPHORS (Short Stories)
by **Nandini Sahu**

Cover Art: **Anil Tato**
Interior Design: Ezy's Publication

ISBN- 978-1-64560-348-1 (Paperback)
Library of Congress Control Number: 2023930898

Printed in the United States of America

to
Parthasarathi, my son.

Contents

PREFACE
Shedding the Metaphors

I am a writer of many moods, and my toiling the soil is a montage of varied anxieties and celebrations—of classicism and modernity, of fundamental responsibility to society and idealistic love, of proclamation and repudiation documented for the self-esteem of the humane. I am a writer speaking for the virtue of pure human heartache, the creative consultant of the written word and the sacredness of my individual belief systems, stemming from my social beliefs and traditional knowledge systems. My creative fiction is my social-mobility-platform, with the agility of love's touch, pungent through my mind's wanton complexity. Precisely, my stories do not preach at anyone. They wish to simply gather you together and grip you, sans any verdicts.

Now I realize, one sheds all metaphors when life comes to a full circle. It is a new beginning, being inclusive, empathetic, universal, accepting, reconciling and persistent. At such a landmark, one stops misconstruing and misapprehending. Now life is about evasion of delusions and reception of the present time in its multiple shades. Now one is complete, it's a commencement, at the same time it's the end. It's the mode of *nirvana*, abyss, all-inclusive, nihilistic, irrationally-rational, non-judgmental, romantic. It's difficult to contain all such finer metaphors of life in one living, thus, shedding the metaphors and shedding my Id, Ego and Superego, now I am the *Brahma*. Now I am a clean slate, I write with an all-embracing rhythmical imagining, like an enormous river that conveys in its curve plentiful tributaries. I decline no knowledge, discount nothing, endeavour veracity in its enigmatic complexity. Precisely, I am shedding all the metaphors attached to me in the past, present and future. Like T S Eliot, I sing,

"Time present and time past
Are both perhaps present in time future,
And time future contained in time past.
If all time is eternally present
All time is unredeemable."

After I penned down all my stories for this collection, I decided to write the Preface, which, I prefer to title as 'Shedding the Metaphors'. Here, I am reminded about an incident that happened in Pondicherry a few years ago. I was on a trip to the Auroville, sitting and chatting with Padmashree Late Professor Manoj Das. One of his fans who happened to be a writer himself, visited him in my presence. He requested Manoj Das Sir to write a Preface for his upcoming story collection. Sir had a kind yet articulate smile on his lips, and he said, "Why do you need an introduction for your stories in the first place? A story should speak for itself!"

How pertinent a comment that was about the art of storytelling!

But yes, when a story crosses the boundary of mere 'story-telling', and it becomes a part of a reading culture, not just oral, and then even of the arena of translation for the benefit of readers from other cultures/languages, perhaps a Preface is a welcome presence in a text. French philosopher, sociologist and historian Michel Foucault's text, *What is an Author*, considers the relationship between the author, text and reader arguing that the author is only a certain purposeful opinion by which one confines, discounts and selects what to read and what not to. The author is the socio-political figure through whom the reader creates symbols and methods wherein one faces the anxiety of the creation of a restricted meaning. If that is the case here, then I would safely go with Khaled Hosseini who believes, "Writing fiction is the act of weaving a series of lies to arrive at a greater truth."

My bigger concerns, when I write stories, are the symbolic and the symbiotic connections between unworldliness, religion, theology, art, and more obviously, similar connections between language and literature that strive to interiorize men, women and nature. The symbolic connections between human and non-human play a rare enough role to show the greatest importance of time, place and people. Thus, it is apt to read carefully my stories of feminine adept, and understand how I feminize nature and naturalize women. It is my empirical and experiential connection, which scrutinizes age, sex, race, class and colour to shelter the naked empirical evidences—talking about subjugation of women and nature as well as mental health of men and women and the jeopardy thereof. The characters, major or minor, ever created by me, fall sick, fall in love, have mood swings like Nature, suffer both physically and psychologically or accept death without fuss. Certain others encounter difficult situations; however, it is dangerous and rackful because they have already waged a war against iniquitousness in human civilization. They live an unannounced, unconventional, prodigious Renaissance. And they aren't tone-deaf to cultural moments.

My characters endeavour to probe into the epistemological connection, into the art and the science of knowledge. This construction often is contingent with the apprehender of nature and nature of the apprehender. Here, in this connection, it seems to be an exception to me as a writer-teacher-folklorist-poet-theorist who is keen on creating a nature-versus-culture dichotomy to allow my readers to practice critical schemes. Writing is the home for me where I am completely honest with myself and the universe. It's my only way of expression. Because I know that nobody can take away your writings from you, no one will judge you here. Personally, writing helped me when I was in denial, when I was delusional and unmedicated for issues that needed attention. It's easier to write the truth than saying it aloud. My writings are my immense creative domain, my superlative agenda.

One is halted and probably further dazed by the political connection my characters create in their demeanour – they are rather connected with the grass root political movements, essentially social and anti-war crusades, anti-militarist and anti-capitalist ideas to rationalize and corroborate the significance of the society, civilization, the country and their application to present-day problems like health, peace, harmony, science, technology, developmental schedules and above all , anti-nuclear politicking. The final and the very fair connection is the moral assembly which more explicitly pervades to study ecological conscience to change both theory and praxis and the exercise of those values. Relationship (read, 'love') ethics in my stories is the ecofeminist ethics of attention and apposite reciprocity. The most appropriate construction is the theoretical involving and evolving of my characters, which is also delimited to some kind of environmental ethics. In the stories, the women-nature networks contend with each other, maybe because of time-space complications! The characters of my stories are mostly people around me, or people who I met far and near. When I am curious about someone's story, am pressed with the urge to talk about it, I pen it down, by imparting my character traits, my femininity into my fictional female protagonists. At the cost of sounding personal,I pour my image, my personality into them. Thus, the narratives sound autobiographical, whereas in most cases it may not be so. A few stories in this collection, like 'Being God's Wife', 'A Very Different Story', 'Alternative Masculinity', 'The Juvenile Love Letter', 'The Wild Stream' and 'The Elusive Orgasm' have autobiographical elements though.

My stories are intricate as I play around the complex human emotions.

Translating my thoughts into multifaceted stories with composite characters from my primary imagination into my creative medium through a radical, euphonic language like English has been a cerebral challenge. I lived with the layers of my personae, marvelled at their glory and despondency with aplomb. As far as my understanding of translation, transcreation and transliteration as art and science goes, it is simultaneously a theory, practice and an evaluation. It is a cultural discourse, an artistic designation for bringing home a culture. It is a discourse analysis, an analysis of the text beyond and above the sentence. It has to deal with the semiotic meanings, hierarchal words, interchangeable terms, figurative speech, imperative speech, puns, semantic adjustments, neologism, personal phrases, eponyms, heterogeneity, restructuring, testing, reproduction and such other hermeneutical issues. It was a beautiful experience for me to create an illusion of the authorial presence in the text while translating my thoughts into black-and-white. My preliminary and operational strategies were clear to me, and the end result was the text,

Shedding the Metaphors. When I talk about translating my thoughts, I am also obliged to mention here that twelve stories from this collection have already been translated to Hindi, and the Hindi story collection is under publication.

My recollections are fluent, without rinsing any tension. My redemption is my own creative writing. I have used mythology in my stories, my private mythology. Everyone has their private myths from which s/he gets her/his inspiration.

I express my deep sense of gratitude for my erudite publisher, Mr. Satya Pattanaik and his team member, Mr. Ashok Parida, for their faith in me, and of course for producing my stories with grace and poise.

Gratitude and love for my family and friends, teachers, colleagues, students, readers, admirers, critics, editors of journals who have published some of these stories, and of course my son, Parthasarathi, for being there for me, always.

For me, *the personal is political.* My quarrel with the self and otherwise is rather a reassembling and uniting war cry, a clarion call, like that of the slogan of students' movement during the second-wave feminism of late 1960s. I write social mobility literature, I do that with clear intentions. Mahasweta Devi writes in her Preface to *Shrestho Galpo,* "I had never had the capacity, not the urge, to create art for art's sake. Since I never learnt to do anything more useful, I have gone on writing. I have found authentic documentation to be the best medium for protest against injustice and exploitation." Like her, writing is my personal agenda, and it is my political agenda too!

Nandini Sahu
www.kavinandini.blogspot.in
kavinandini@gmail.com
nandinisahu@ignou.ac.in
www.nandinisahu.in
9811991539(M)

A Very Different Story

"Human bonding is the most difficult thing to fathom Meeta! Every relationship has to be nurtured, else it won't persist."

She just nodded her head.

Her questions were simple, her thoughts, innocent, unlike mine.

Her question was, when she didn't need anything in return, where was the question of survival of the relationship, for that matter?

All these years, she had been a willing prisoner in a trap, without a word of complaint, without anything that she can call her 'personal need' or 'demand'. Now for the first time, ever, she wanted to breathe some fresh air. Was it too much? Was she asking for something unpardonable? Impossible?

She was, in a way, 'happy' in her thirteen years' marriage, and then we met. She had been sitting quietly in that Creative Writers' Workshop, though she seemed to be quite chirpy at times, laughing with ease and eyes gleaming with, well, love! And I was, like everyone who met her, kind of unconsciously taken in by the soft, quiet, sensuous face. It was a gorgeous face, with a couple of dimples on cheeks and eyebrows that met at a small dot of *bindi* to bridge over her transparently emotion laden eyes.

We exchanged a few courteous words, but that was about it. Her eyes glittered in a way that I cannot take, so I mostly avoided eye contact. She said she liked to sing, cook, read, write, smile, and I noticed, she giggled like flowing water. Through the following months, I learnt, she liked fish, liked to wear short skirts and knee-length frocks with high heels, showing her sensuously slender legs, and liked to meditate on the green hillock in front of her house.

I am not sure when I started relating to her,but I was sure I was very comfortable in her presence. I knew soon enough that this was the person I was looking for all my life.

Instincts never lie.

She was a renowned writer in her own rights, but was extremely down to earth. In course of the day's work, I had to introduce her to the audience, and I did that to my heart's content, mixing facts with meticulous choice. There was this power point ready with the minutest details of her creative oeuvre, that focused upon the prodigious work she had already accomplished at quite an young age. As I was speaking and as the audiences were looking on, she was visibly embarrassed, looked down, biting her nails. When I stopped and faced her scarlet face, she just whispered, "Was it required?" There was this delectable mix of feigned anger and ill hidden feel-good in her eyes. But the *bindi* bridge only made the frown sweeter!

I guess, I fell in love, at that moment, with the unpretentious girl. I guess, unknowingly, another bridge was built between us that moment.It became the most cherished relationship for both of us, a relationship which became a work in progress forever.

She had all the qualities I seek in persons that make them my friends. Well, people who simply turn out to be just like me, not at all goody goody, with a great sense of humour, someone who would start singing or dancing when I sing love songs, someone who would say "let's go!" when I suggest some crazy thing, like leaving the car in the parking and travelling by metro or catching up a movie at odd hours.

To be precise, she was absolutely wild, with splotches of naughtiness in the eyes. She was the craziest person I had ever met. And then, she was a queer mix of elegance, edginess, composure and versatility as an individual.

But love seeks qualities more than fun or elegance, right? Right.

Madhvi had qualities even she didn't know that she had. We were of the same age-group, but she was the mature one. She was someone with whom I could be as romantic as a Bollywood hero, as stupid, as insecure, and as good or bad as I wanted to be. There were no judgments passed. I wanted her to be my mistress in youth, friend in a mature age and nurse in my old age. But we always do not get what we desire in life. That was that.

She accompanied me, quietly, in a long-distance relationship, for past twenty-five years, sharing my worries about my life, sending me messages, letters, helping me with my work, sharing her creative writing with me, and her pleasures and pains. She has been through the thick and thin with me throughout life. I was not just her fair-weather partner, I shared her life. And she, being a student of literature, read and understood everything conceived and envisioned by the great minds, and she did apply those to her life. She lived a life of contentment in the midst of all paucity.

After her, there was no one else. No other woman in my life. Before her, I had a broken marriage.

That day, after the valedictory session of the creative writers' workshop, I was asked by the organizers to drop her. Past few days, we had exchanged a positive vibe, talked through our eyes if not words, and I had missed little about her, starting from her formal suits, casual *salwars*, deeply sensuous saris, silken hair,from her finger tips to the toe-nails. Well, that's a separate issue that she could hardly notice that she was being noticed prudently. She was a tom-boy, as she said, or she liked to think so.

That day, I could hardly wait for the morning, because I was supposed to drop her in the airport. That night I sent her a few text messages, stating about the best restaurants in town and the best places to shop. Her response was a simple "thanks." I wondered, was I getting too personal?

But she was unpredictable, as I had rightly sensed. She sent me a message late in the evening, "I depend on you. Please be there in the station at 3.30 pm." It was more than I could deal with. But as always, I knew how to suppress my feelings and made an impassive expression when I met her.

She got down from the train with a huge Samsonite bag which she wanted to carry herself. I had to literally snatch that from her. I had taken print outs of her air tickets, thinking she might have forgotten to get those; after all her last two days were hectic, she had delivered quite a few lectures in two days. At a later stage she told me that she liked that gesture, and thought I was very caring.

I loved to see her in her work-mode, I admired her professionalism, appreciated her achievements. But I never told her what I loved about her passionately. Slowly, unconditionally, she had become the woman of my dreams, past few days. I was surprised with the things life showed to both of us, at the ripe age of late thirties! She was one of the most delectable creations in the world; full of womanly magnetism, gifted with an unobtrusive yet full-bodied sexuality and divine passion.

That day she was at ease, also a little skeptical. Her lips locked but lively, her smile faintly askew. Her complexion was coppery, expressions captivating. I was extra cautious to make her feel at ease in my car. So I opened the car windows as she got in. She was in one of her tomboyish dresses, a pencil fit cotton pant, a beige coloured cotton full sleeved top, light make up, supple skin and a transparent smile. She instantly closed the glasses of the car, to my surprise. At a later stage when I asked her how could she do that, she said, a woman can look at the eyes of a man and tell if he is a gentleman.

Well, I was her 'gentleman'.

It was one of the finest long drives I had ever had till date. She kept her large Hidesign handbag on her lap, may be to avoid my eyes looking at her closely, to 'protect' herself! Or maybe, that was her habit. After some casual chit chat, she said she was disturbed by the blower, and switched that off. Only the A.C.And a calm ambiance inside my Red Wine Alto. Aha!

It was pure bliss!

She didn't like the silence after sometime, and told me about her job, her colleagues, son, her formative years, her personal library, her future plans, her growth as a creative writer, her love for theatre and music.

She was the chatter box, that way. At a later stage I told her, I had coined a verb about her ways that day, 'tom-tom' — a stylish girl who walks fast, talks faster, her hair bounces when she walks, and she moves like lightening. She laughed and laughed.

I was getting a new surprise every moment--was this the person whom I didn't even know a few days back, whom the world assessed to be the supreme egoist, who hardly spoke to men and who inspired awe amongst the women folk!

For me, it was not the everyday talk, it was a very special day. She told me later that at that moment she was wondering about the man sitting beside her who sensed poetry in her casual talk, who was excited about every small thing that she told in the workshop. Whom she sent a message on landing at his city, "reached the city of joy!" And he texted back, "welcome to joy!" And who was like a shadow beside her for the past few days. She had guessed it all.

But she was still the 'sternie',the formal,well-mannered girl that I was trying to remove from her person, don't know why. She said, "I troubled you! You have to drive me to the airport on a Sunday!"

"Oh really?Then please get down and take a taxi!"

"Oh my god! So rude! You are asking me to get down? No... I won't."

We laughed, we joked. Later on, she told me that I was the first man who made her laugh so much. And I was the first one who didn't flatter her by putting her on a pedestal, neither worshipped her. She liked that. I was the first one who had caught her, the elemental, silly, simple girl, red-handed. How could I tell her that I hated the Elizabethan sonneteers for making divas of their flesh and blood beautiful women!

And I had actually caught her unawares.She was gazelle-like. And she, too, caught me with my every Bengali's sense of a catastrophic poet, a tragic hero. With me, she felt her girlie feelings, hoary feelings, lyrical and melodious feelings.

I happened to ask her about her family. We had enough time.

Some little thing stabbed her chest and moved inward, towards her stomach. But she decided to open up, and categorically, patiently, told, she had never opened up before any man, and that she had only a few female friends who knew about her personal life. Being a public figure, she was cautious. I still remember what she had told me, fixing her watery gaze on the horizon.

She was from a lower middle class family with very high dreams about a career. Her parents got her married off to a wrong person at 23, and she became a victim of domestic violence, marital rapes, jealousy, male ego and physical abuses for a few years. During pregnancy, she managed to qualify a fellowship and did Ph.D. After her son was born, she shifted to another town and then, gradually, to Delhi. She got separated from the mentally challenged husband within a few years of her marriage.

In the meantime, she and her little son got close to another family; the only son of the family was a support to her son during his formative years, and he was a nice man. Her son was totally dependent on him, and she had a good rapport with him. Thus, they decided to marry. Anyway, destiny does a raw deal with some people, and she was one such woman. The second husband was far from understanding her aestheticism, emotions, was far from literature; he had never had any physical closeness with her, and perhaps his sexual preferences were different. But she had no desire to complain, because she wanted peace at home, peace for her child, who loved him very much. And thus, now she was lonelier than ever in a marriage of appeasement, convenience.

It was in her tender, faintly panicky way that she

spoke her words that I knew, she was a wounded person. That, her feelings were real, immense and enduring as the sky, and that it would someday engulf me. It was the kind of love that surrounded you with an optimal loop. Either you tore free or you waited and endured its meticulousness even though it clasped you into something lesser than yourself.

There was silence, torn-apart silence.

She broke the silence, changed her mood, and asked me about my family.

"That would need a bit of personal talk, again. My wife lives with my son in another city, working there. She was my childhood friend, but after a few years of marriage, we discovered that the marriage wasn't working; I mean we were not compatible. So we thought we can give it some time, and live in separate places. Now my son comes to the town to spend some time with me and my parents during his vacations."

"Do you love her?"

"No."

I was surprised at her frankness. Love was in its own place--that had turned a mirage in life, but there were recurrent memories of younger days that somehow somewhere gave me the shivers to think of pulling out. The mind was kind of torn between present solitude and past memories that seemed ineradicable.

"Then why don't you think of a way out? You deserve a good life!" Her tone was nonchalant.

"Is it that easy? Can you do anything to change your present state? We have children who need both parents!"

A long silence, again.

Not being in love with spouse, crying foul about her, is a strategy used at the beginning of every extra-marital relationship, which most men use to allure a prospective partner. But she was too simple to doubt that a stranger like me could also be using this technique to impress her. She believed her instincts, and instincts never lie.

I took her to a coffee shop, we still had an hour.

We tried to keep our moods light and smile, share light things.

I observed the beauty, the fragrant jasmine, from a distance. She was engrossed in herself, making phone calls to her family, and waiting for me.

We had coffee, *pakodas*. It was time. I had a bottomless feeling, and I wanted this hour to linger.

In front of the airport, we shook hands cordially, and parted. Like *partners*.

I remember, this was the last I saw of her. An intense look into my eyes, perhaps her eyes were a little moist, little glittery, and she had a charming smile lingering on her lips. A smile that can disarm the deadliest terrorist and make him fall in love with her. I could see her transparent skin and attractive body. For a moment, I was tempted to touch her chin and ruffle her short hair. But had I done that, I won't have been the gentle lady's 'gentleman' anymore, and life would have been different.

So the flamboyant man stopped himself. And went in the lady, the lady of his dreams.

I walked along, of course outside the airport, watching carefully a casual she. Lost in herself, queuing up with the other passengers.

Suddenly she caught the sight of me following her surreptitiously. She got distracted, looked back several times, and almost lost her way.

At a later stage, she told me, this was the moment when she was surprised with herself, because she couldn't dismiss a feeling for me that she never had felt before for anyone. An aspect of her knew at that moment that I had already possessed her. Had tugged her heart from her without any agreement, a transaction no other man had ever endeavored.

She was no more visible. Her luggage checked in, she went inside. I sent her a few messages, thanking her, instructing her to have food and water, take care of her hand bag and the laptop. Then I wrote her about a female character of Tagore, who had always inspired me, on whom I had been writing research papers, and who was her namesake.

Now the lady writes, "Oh...I love my name a little more now."

Was I dreaming? Was I thinking the unthinkable? The impossible?

I drove back with some dizziness in my head. Mind and body declined to cope with each other. After two hours, when exactly her flight landed, I got a message, "Reached. Cold. Raining." And I messaged back thanking her again, wishing her safe home.

Two days passed. Madhvi was in the back of my mind, most of the times. Her smile, her story of struggle, her optimism,her ambitions, everything about her appealed me. This was love at a mature age. So it was no infatuation on my part, I was sure, wondering, must she be thinking of me as much? A part of me desired her to get back to me, be my friend; and a part of me almost knew that she will forget me. After all, the celebrity goes to many places to deliver lectures, she meets new people everyday. She has to forget people and focus on work, which was justified. I was feeling low, missing her, hoping against hope that she would get back.

After two days of silence, she chose to open up. "Something is at the back of my mind, haunting me all the time. Don't know what! Can you tell me? You understand my mind well."

Oh my god! What was I going to write? Given her reserve nature, she must have thought a thousand times before sending this message.

"This is really serious. Someone haunting the mind of a beautiful lady?" I kept it simple and funny, pretended not to understand.

We exchanged a few more text messages that day. At the wee hours of the night, she wrote, "Prof.Madhvi lying on the sofa at this time without a book? Bad,bad,bad." I understood. And this time I categorically conveyed that I understood.

Pathos and humour were the two qualities amalgamated in her character curiously; she became the object of my interest, research, analysis, thought, love and meditation in the coming days, weeks, months and years. The love of my life. She would send me her creative writing and research papers for my comments. I was kind of hesitant to begin with. She was an established writer and I, after all, was a nondescript academic. There were thoughts like how would she take my suggestions or even corrections at times. I was often at a loss. But gradually I began to realize that I needed to do my part in all seriousness. She had that tremendous faith in my competence which no one had. She found me "outstanding" in my writing, speech and critical judgements, which, rather, put me under some kind of mental pressure. She said I had a kind of intelligence which was raw, primitive and original. She felt her mind became more sharpened and focused after each academic interaction with me.

In return, I started parenting, protecting and pampering her and getting possessive about her.

We had slowly stopped, being 'she' and 'me', we had become 'us'. Every one hour, or even less than that, we exchanged messages throughout life after that. For example, I always knew what she was doing at any given moment, 2000 kilometers away from me. Her telephone was a stand-in proxy for myself, as though my absence never mattered. What was she wearing on any particular day, what had she cooked or which nights she did Reiki, I always knew.I read every poem and story she wrote after that, I read and commented about every interview and lecture she delivered last twenty five years. I was on the phone all the while during her son's twelfth board results, college admission, house warming, her every illness and her son's wedding. I took personal care of every small detail of her life, but from 2000 kilometers away.

A long-distance-relationship, which was soul-to-soul. She had lived all her life with secrets. An apathetic life, looking at her existence on the rearview mirror. She was a fundamentally solitary being with an abysmal hole about her soul. Slowly, I became the vessel into which she poured all her loneliness.

She had tried to meet me only once, after three months of our last meeting. I committed a blunder by telling her,"You need not promote me by inviting me to places where you are the chief speaker or chief guest." She decided never to meet me after that. *NEVER.NOT EVER.*

Her character was multi-dimensional. Every day, each message, each e-mail, every phone call revealed a new shade of her personality before me. One week, two weeks, months, years rolled on. Long twenty five years, but the lady decided never to meet me.

Once I told her, "I love your name, but I would prefer to call you Meeta. My Meeta, *morameeta,* my friend for life."

She was very happy,my Meeta, my Jasmine, my *mmm.* That was how she would respond over phone when she would be in her elements. Her simplicity, innocence, childlike qualities amazed me. She would be overwhelmed with the smallest expression of love, like Robert Browning's *Last Duchess.* She would blush with my modest appreciation of her. But her success hardly exited her; she accepted her achievements nonchalantly, dispassionately.

Meeta's senses were active. "I am very smell conscious. Smells decide for me."

"But I am like a piggy at the end of the day! I travel by public transports for 50 kms a day dear, and you only travel by your car. You are jasmine and I am piggy."

"Piggies are cuties too. I love a cute piggy."

I made her laugh, a lot, by laughing at myself.

"You know what the four essential qualities of my man are? He must be sensitive and honest. He should appreciate art, literature, culture and music. He has to smell good. And he MUST make me laugh."

Ahh! What simplicity! She was rich, successful and beautiful. But her needs were far from that.

Once I sent a few smileys to her in a light mood while teasing her, and she messaged back, "Why are you laughing at me?" And when I wrote a few words in capital letters, she wrote, "Are you shouting at me?" What sensitivity! Apparently, she came from a family where it was initiated into her that a girl must not shout, her speech should not be loud enough to be heard in the other room. She couldn't bear noise, violence of any kind and ruggedness.

That was my Meeta---hypersensitive.

That day I sent her a message, "Somebody I didn't

know much, told me some time back that she came across me as a spirited person."

"And that spirited person transmitted his spirits to a 'spiritless' person. Now she badly needs his counsel and help."

"Spiritless? Help? Fie on those words. You are broad-shouldered, how dare you think like a weakling? Buck up. It's equality after all Meeta."

At her slightest wish, I was willing to move up to the end of the world. But Meeta dreaded any kind of change. He phone number was the same for decades. Her favorite colour was white, always. Favorite singer — Lata-ji; her best friend and lover, me. Forever. She didn't want her family to suffer because of any of her decisions.

"I want to be a part of you, but I can't shift my responsibilities to anyone. If you want me to leave everything and run to you, I can't fight that. I can't say 'no' to you for anything sweetheart! I need you so selfishly. But please don't distract me from my responsibilities. If I do that, you will never get the woman whom you love, I'll be a lump of remorse, hurt, regret, and that will transform me."

But I never wanted her to be anything other than what she was. The itinerant, vintage, classic, modern woman, who was innocuously unselfish. That was the paradox. If it had not been for her, I am not sure if I had been what I am today. In her letters and messages, she gave me a universe, and made me a comprehensive unit, which had been scattered into pieces. And she said, I made her an organic whole, adding the bits and pieces of her. Even when we were not in our conscious minds, we could feel each other. We had always been there for each other. We spent our youth together and grew old together, completing each other. She touched my core, without touching this body, ever.

She had a family with her, and she was sad that I had no one with me. But she was my constant companion, in my sleep and wakeful hours, in my heart and soul. She made me understand the real meaning of love –through her I got to know that even love exists!

But we never made this love a public affair. Never told about our heartaches to anyone. Never met, never parted. But still, all the while we were broken hearted. We had decided never to underestimate the telecommunicated flash of trivial news in our academic circles. Prof.J B Parit could write fifty research papers a year; DU would introduce four years BA Honors course ignoring the students' protests; there would be ten new central universities in the country and fifteen new IITs; and that would not cause a bump in our consciousness. But Prof. Madhvi Srivastava, the celebrity writer, seen with Mr. A , B or C – well, that was national news material. Breaking news! News to be talked of in seminars, university corridors, news to be cooked with spices and made tastier with every news reporter. So,we made it a point that no one on earth knew, for last twenty five years, that Prof. Madhvi Srivastava, the arrogant, full-of-attitude (sometimes I teased her as *Ms.Atti!*) writer, was actually my love, whom I called *'Pugli Meeta'*, the simple and sensuously elemental woman.

Meeta had this classic, unalterable habit of jumping into conclusions-- "you don't love me. You have no time for me"-- at the drop of a hat. There would be days when I was sandwiched between two fatty aunties in a local train, and then the girlie would call up. With a lot of difficulty I reach my pocket, take out the mobile and say, "hello!"

"God, you are always on the roads?"

"Hello….can't hear you baby!"

"Oh pleeeese! Why are you shouting? Are you addressing an audience?"

Then there's no network.

By the next two minutes, she would have sent me a message, "You don't love me. Don't ever call me. I am not your Meeta…"

The sulky-silly-girlie reminded me the Bangla song, "O go meeta, moro sudurer meeta..",or an Odia song, "Mo priya tharu kie adhika sundara…" which I remembered since my Bhubaneswar days where I spent my early youth.

And then, the next five hours I would spend sending her messages from meetings, academic councils, school boards, bathrooms, and 'pataofy' her, flatter her, flirt with her. But the silence between us during her katti(not-talking) hours seemed like a perpetuation of our relationship.

"Meeta, when on talking terms, my words hurt you. When not,you are sulky. It's not about who is right and who is wrong but about what's the best way. I definitely do not want to be your nemesis.You are a good human being, an accomplished person, and already have enough troubles in life. Please talk to me".

Then, at last, the lady would be pleased to take my call.

My days and nights were beautiful. She made them beautiful. I was in love—truly, madly, deeply.

Once she took my calls, she would open up, petal by petal. She had this tremendous capacity to express all her feelings in words. She was my Muse. I turned more respectful to her poetry with each poem she wrote, with such ease and eloquence. She was the one who thought that she would die with a book on her chest. I would sometimes appreciate her poetry in high-sounding words to elevate her moods. She wrote, "No,don't talk of poetry.Well, I read a lot of classics; but modern poetry? Half of it goes above my heads—I mean not the words, but what makes people ruminate with an armada of adjectives, I don't understand. I wish the scorpion of some rationality will bite the back of these poets. You modern poets, you just sniffle. Take my handkerchief laden with chili powder."

Funny indeed. *Funny Meeta*. A funny girl with a runny nose.

We shared every small detail of our days. Once she wrote, "Just now I took a lecture on Dover Beach with our M.A.English students. Remembered someone who swears his love for me with this lovely poem!"

"That's one of my favorite poems Meeta! It talks of love as inclusivity and thereby a panacea. Lovely last lines. I see life as literature. Truth is, literature gives me courage to stand up after every lost battle. Most are self-defeats."

Unlike me, Meeta was very much a self-motivated person. She said, if she had the mood, she could fly miles with just the blow of wind. If not, a thousand horses couldn't drag her even by an inch. But during her creative hours, she was impenetrably serious, quietly contemptuous. Once I sent her a poem to interpret for one of our courses; she did that in a few minutes and mailed me the critical interpretation. That was lovely! "Oh! Meeta at her best, as always. Powerful. My interpretation is no match."

She was restless if she forgot anything, say, the name of an old friend or the lyric of a Lata Mangeshkar song. To her, it seemed awful to lose a memory. She had the face of a young girl, untouched by motherhood. Meeta was a poem herself, deep, fragrant, melting with the words of love I whispered into her ears.

Her husband was never interested in sex, and her only child was from the first marriage. Thus, she shared her room with her son, till he went to a hostel to study fine arts. Even before that, her son would be put to sleep at 9 pm. Meeta had sleep-disorder, insomnia. She would hardly get sleep for two hours continuously. Her husband was more of a companion than a lover, he was engrossed with his career. She had adapted herself to his habits of having an early dinner, watching T.V. while eating, and then closing their doors by 9.30 pm. with a quick good night kiss. He would snore within no time, and she would chant a hymn for her son to sleep, or tell him a bed-time story. She was an exceptionally good mother. Being a strong moralist herself, she would teach positive values to her son in the most creative way. She would cook his choicest dishes, teach him with patience, and be his friend, philosopher and guide. After her son slept, she was left alone, with her books, study table, bed light, mobile, laptop for company. She would struggle to get some sleep, but rustling inside her was another person who wanted to be smelt in her neck, caressed, coddled, felt under her skin and loved, be carried away. Night after night she would lay there on her lonely bed, in her lovely night suits, hair blowing in the wind, watching the birds, clouds, stars through her bedroom window, thinking of me. One night she sent me a haiku:

"*My sleep and sleeplessness*
play hide-and-seek.
Is someone awake in me?"

This is when we started talking during the midnights. The background music would be the buzzing of the A.C. or the snoring of her husband.

First few days we talked of our days, work, creative writing, children, our fights and patch-ups. Once I requested her to sing over phone, and she went on in her melodious, sensuous voice. Till I was teary eyed.

What is she getting in life? She is so full of love, her heart is like an ocean of love and she can drown a thousand ships in it. And she is not even getting a lonely ferry to explore her!

What is the barrier to freedom that had been shaped up to block her feelings? Why are the walls of culture blocking open and natural relationships between men and women? Why there is no intimacy and eroticism in relationships? Why sexual preferences aren't talked of before marriages?

One night she wrote, "Not getting sleep. Listening to *Raag Handol* and *Raag Doot*; working on the computer."

"You have worked enough. Rest now."

"How to get some sleep? Tips please."

"Isn't it hypocrisy for one to whom sleep comes as rest from thought and heartache to advice ways to fall asleep? Maybe take a book of your choice and tuck into bed *nosey* girl! Do you mind someone playing with your fingers when you are reading yourself to sleep?"

Silence.

Next morning she wrote, "Slept in fragments. Thanks for playing with my fingers and putting me to sleep. There is a drowsy numbness in the body."

Meeta had accepted, eroticism had no place in her clean, disciplined life. There were books, designer furniture, extensive wardrobes and big cars in the household. There were maids to take care of her, campus kids to party every weekend, husband to invite friends over a drink on Friday evenings. T.V. programmes to follow, cricket to debate over, relatives to make phone calls or come over without notice.

But there was no eroticism. There was no talk of sex. It was the forbidden topic to discuss or ponder over. *A woman who needs sex and asks for it, is definitely a slut.* "Woman...dare to call yourself a slut!"--she was

told. It was dribbled into her ears by her husband, loud
and clear. He had passed an ordinance, unwritten, that
my name was a big *NO* at home. Her husband had too
utilitarian a mind, he was extreme in everything. He
was, indeed, a prisoner of extreme narcissistic self-love,
self-righteousness. He said, he loathed the senseless
viciousness in the lives of many families around. As if
there could be sensible, thoughtful ones! Perhaps there
were; he had discovered a way to be sensibly irrational
towards his wife. That's how she was *deprived* of the
basic rights of a woman. He ridiculed the idea that a
woman needs to be pampered, celebrated.

On the contrary, I admired her during our late night
calls; precisely, I celebrated her. I convinced her that it's
no sin to be erotic. That is the root and the instinct of this
creation, after all. My admiration was genuine, she knew.
She basked in it, immersed in my desire, let my whispers
sway and swindle her, and in the catch of those moments
she fell in love with me over and over again every time I sent
an erotic text message, an e-mail, or whispered a word of
love. After a night of virtual love-making, she would wake
up in the morning, refreshed, relaxed, smiling, awash, her
face flushed, skin pores open, eyes glowing with desire.

Those days, she told me, that she was pleased with the
way she looked and felt. She felt light, warm and feminine
in my hands. For her, I was a virtual-reality. And those
days, she always smiled; I was hanging like a silver smile
on her lips. She wanted to swim naked in the pool of desire
that I had designed for her. She wrote, "Your eruditions
convey such tenderness, generating a world that comprises
only the two of us, that I get oscillated. The passionate ache
that touches me through your words makes me ascertain
things about me that I hadn't recognized till this time."

Once she told she remembered my smell that she had felt sitting beside me in the car on that day I went to drop her in the airport. It was the clean, soapy, warm, fundamental, civilized smell of a man, who was erotic. God!! She knew how to juggle with words. Her words, only words, kept our love alive for more than two decades! Just three hours of togetherness and she could keep the flame burning forever – only with her words!

A river of words flowing between two cities, two lives, and a river of soft kisses, smiles, tears, letters, messages, e-mails, vibrations, heartaches.

But the love was far beyond physical. Loving me was, for her, pure devotion, like Mira Bai's.

For me, she was extremely graceful whom I never wanted to dominate, yet she loved to be completely conquered, in the exact way she wanted me to make love to her. With my whispers, breathing, soft kisses in quiet nights from 2000 kms, she told, she got orgasms. It was such a pity! A beautiful, aesthetically sensuous woman, who had committed no sin, had never experienced an orgasm in life! Though she had a child, she had never had a thing called 'making love'. Perhaps her body responded to one of those marital rapes from the first marriage, which resulted in the pregnancy. All the time she pondered about me, and asked me once if the orgasms of the mind were any different from the physical, real orgasms? All I could respond to her innocent query were, two drops of tears.

Now she had started counting on my curious power. I had taken possession of her, in her elemental self.She was in a way frightened with what she had with me. A major part of her 'self' was with me, and the other part belonged to her family. Both the parts were definitely at odds with each other. With the incremental weakening of the body, I thought our minds would also give up. And the "passing phase" would be over. But that didn't happen to her.

Closing her eyes and thinking of me, she would smell oceans and raw sand, could hear the tribes singing and dancing from the remote villages, could see the Buddhist monks crossing bridges in saffron robes, chanting, "Buddham sharanam gachchami." Then she would murmur softly, huskily, into the receiver of her phone, "Oh dear....I am lost". At that weak moment, I told her, "Meeta, why are you living this life that lacks romance, eroticism,our kitchen romance, and me? Why is this damn sense of responsibility killing you? Why are you destroying yourself? You are a beautiful woman, the goddess of love and your kind of a woman has to be celebrated, not deserted like this!"

"Why don't you take me out of this, if you can? I had been leading my simple life of home and hearth. What made you create this havoc? Why did you do this to me? Why?"

There was silence at the other end. I could sense, she was weeping noiselessly, that she had rolled her head away from the phone to do it.It saddened me, because it revealed before me Meeta's indigence, anxiety, fear of isolation, her horror of being marooned, abandoned.

Then there was a silence for three days, three days of torture for me and my Meeta. For the first and last time in life,complete separation of three days with Meeta.

I wrote, "I am no good if my message doesn't lighten your face, doesn't enliven your heart, doesn't give you a relaxed mind. I am no good if a long gap doesn't make you fume and it only causes chest pain. I am no good if I'm not a positive change in your work and play, cookery and music, Reiki and red-wine. Rate your love beautiful!"

"We rate something when we have a choice, perhaps.

But I have no choice. You are the only one, good or bad. So, be good."

She was simple and straightforward, always. I used to call her,'*the goddess of small things.'*

Small things overjoyed her. Small pains immensely pained her. She would catch hold of beggar women in the red lights and try to settle them down through NGOs, scold them for using their new born babies to beg in the sun. She thought the world was like her. The day the President of India had a visit to her university, the daily wagers and the rode side vendors were detained from coming to work, resulting in a day of hunger for them. She wrote, "I am ashamed that I am a bureaucrat in a place where 'human right' is just a phrase in the dictionary. I am more ashamed and helpless, because I can do nothing about it."

She was not just the poet of a few words, she was a social activist, taking care of the children of her dead domestic help, funding the education of slums children.

During one such conversations,she told me that she will quit her job after her son is independent and do her bit to uplift the girl children, the victims of rape and domestic violence and the differently-abled. That day I respected her more. She wrote, "I feel restless when I see these women, and specially the children, who don't even understand that they are sexually abused! Things like my house, my cars, my books that bring me so much glory, the luxuries I have – all seem meaningless when I see so many women victimized every day like street urchins. When two/three year olds lay there outside the PVR Cinemas and near the Saket Select City Walk mall or try to sell a bouquet to me, I hate the system. They don't deserve so much hurt. Someone should tell them their rights! Someone has to fight for them. Babu, it's like I am gearing up for something greater, moving towards a road not taken. At one point of my life, I'll be leaving everything and take to the streets. And for the needy, I will design a shelter home, a public library, because only education can enlighten them.And then,I'll also introduce a publishing house for the budding talents. I need your support in all of these."

Ambitious,indeed.

The lady was ambitious in everything, starting from her elaborate menu for any guest at home to helping the needy and creating a public library for the access of the mass. Her writings addressed ground-breaking issues that characterize lives. Existential issues of the marginalized.

She would address me as '*Babu*' That was her way of pampering me. I was the only one who could convince the Pegasus to do something – from opening a savings account in her name to getting a medical check-up done. Otherwise she had the ill fame of being the most disobedient when there was something related to her.

One night during our pillow talk hours, she sent me a message, rather a poem:

"The night has stretched out
afresh watershed for me.
It squashed my eyes of slumber
And packed the hollows with blubbering
and said
'you have been acquitted
of all offences, and hereafter
you are at liberty
till eternity.
Go somewhere you wish
Rouse do benumb.
The entrance to reveries
is padlocked."

I was sad, very sad. I wrote her back,
"Expanses have not yet twinkled, Oh *Meeta!*
The delusion dynasty is quiet and benign.
From the bonfires of fiascos and disillusionments
let the legends of the approaching new beginnings
remain inexpressible."

She called up, voice all choked up, sobbing, and asked "Why inexpressible? Can't you just open up and tell me? Why can't you be simple, be boy, be elemental? Why do you throw your philosophy upon me all the time? Am I just your 'duty' without any attachments?"

"I don't look back where I have no attachments. Never do a thing that's only duty. You never thrust upon any duty on me. I would just be grateful if you accept that my hurts are a part of me and give me time and compassion to stand on a surer ground. Without that I am a piecemeal. You want commitment from my eyes, hands and all or the person who you know cares for you and wants to go on doing that?"

But she still wanted me to define our relationship.

"A young Madhvi let herself be had to a husband in a marriage she couldn't question. A grown up Madhvi keeps questioning a man who wishes good for her, asking for definitions when he confesses he is trying a way out of bends in life. A mature Madhvi will perhaps realize that love and commitment have many forms, as does assimilation. Truth shall prevail."

She was uncontrollable that night. In fact every time we spoke for more than an hour, she was sure to cry, over something or other. Then I had to console her, love her with utmost dedication. Yes, I had become a dedicated lover in life, if not anything else. Courtesy: Meeta. And she could kill me with her conversational ease. Her tears were contagious. I am not ashamed to admit that being a man, even I have shed drops of tears so often over something or the other she told. Men don't cry, they bleed, inward. Like, the other day she asked me, "Babu, have you read Virginia Woolf's '*A Room of One's Own?* I am going to write another one, '*A Table of One's Own'*."

"Why baby?"

"You know what, I am from such a large family that the two tables we had at home were for my eldest and youngest siblings. The dining table was for Baba. So throughout my childhood and youth, I craved for a table, but never got one. I had to write lying on my tummy on the floor,or leaning over a plywood placed on my lap. Now there are tables in my house, one for my son and two for my husband for his laptop and files, even there is one kitchen table for my maid, but there's none for me. I bought one exclusively for myself, but that too is encroached by both of them. *Hehe.*"

How could she laugh over this issue of identity politics? This was such an existential problem to be taken lightly!!

She had this tremendous capacity to hide her pain and smile, laugh all the time. She was actually two people. The one whom the world knew--the serious academic, creative writer, glamorous, practical, adamant, jovial with friends, helping and caring Prof.Madhvi. Then there was the other one – elemental, romantic, emotional, sensuous, true, honest, ready to capitulate and vulnerable, my Meeta. I knew that the second one was exclusively mine, but I always wondered, how could she manage to be two people? Especially the first one who was not her real character?

And she was yet another person when she was drunk. I loved to hear her when she was. She loved red wine. She would giggle after the second peg. Then call up to tell me absurd things. I found pathos and humour mingled in her temperament. I could perceive her perpetual agony coming out of her when she would giggle and tell me the funniest things.

Once I asked her, when she was drunk "What are you reading today? I mean what academic work you are doing?"

"Oh my god!You always want me do something? To be someone? Why? Tell me, why?? I am *nothing*, I want to be *nothing*, just *nothing*! Do you understand?"

"Yes baby, please be *nothing*."

"*Nnotthhing*, right? Just *nnotthhing*.You got it?"

I always gave her that space, to speak her mind. To open up. And she would inevitably sob at the end,shed tears, blow her nose,(she said she wanted to wipe her *nosey* on my shirt!!) and talk like Hema Malini. "Hema Malilni is an awful actress, you see; of course she's beautiful and a great dancer. When I cry, I sound like her. Pathetic, melodramatic. *Hehe.*" But I thought, if she was in a gloomy mood, her tone would be like the tragic heroine Meena Kumari in *Saheb, Biwi aur Ghulam*.Sometimes she sounded like Madhubala when she was in a high, after drinking wine.

Winey Meeta.

"You know Babu what happened today, someone continuously stared at me in the market. I moved away, but he still continued to stare; everyone could visibly notice my discomfort. So what I did--I covered my face with both hands, and then opened my palms in front of him, playing *peek-a-boo*! People laughed and laughed, and the uncle ran away."

This was my Meeta, *Pugli Meeta*.

But she had the strong opinion that a woman dictates the way she likes to be treated by men. She has to uphold her self-respect.

She had a problem with the words 'uncle' and 'aunty'. It seems in Delhi, everyone would call you aunty, irrespective of his/her age, looks, weight and height. "If you are seen with a child, you are aunty-material for sure. The other person might be older than you! But if you are roaming alone, you are an *item* for Delhi men; you might be a mother of two."

"It's ok baby, you are a sexy-aunty."

"Shut up uncle!"

Some nights she would just shut all her windows and not respond to any of my messages. It was time to worry then. I knew that she was a night person and most of her writings were done late nights. I would make one last attempt at 1 AM, "If you were working, I infer you have been at peace. If you were into talks with your husband, I shall see hope, though it may not be immediate. If you have slept, I am happiest for my grown up baby. And if you have been sulking, that leaves me sad with a sense of inadequacy."

"No, doing nothing specific. Missing you."

"Then call after three minutes and talk to me for seven minutes."

"Your timing is weird. You are just mad."

"How do you know about my *timing*?"

Then she would blush and remain quiet for some time, then send just three dots as a response, and in return I would send some messages that gave her a high. And would make her open up.

"Meeta, good that your mind has let you open up,

beyond *isshhh* and *yuck*. You need to know how adorable every single pore of your body is."

We had an e-mail account which we both used to exchange letters or chat. Her husband was a tech-savvy person. Once he hacked the password of that account and read all correspondence between us, and made a hell out of it. We couldn't understand, what had been robbed of him? What had been taken away from him by me? Her commitment? No, we weren't committed; rather we had decided never to meet in life. Sex? No, we never had real sex, neither was he sexually attracted to her. They never slept on the same bed, anytime. We discussed literature, life, love, eroticism, philosophy, which was beyond his understanding. So we could hardly understand the reason behind his insecurity. Perhaps he was basking in the glory of the puritanical old world values like purity, chastity and loyalty, expected only from women. The purity-pollution debates, age-old, were deep rooted in his mind. He demanded commitment, chastity and purity from her, without fulfilling the 'duty' of being the man of her life!!

She would put together her appearance and put a smile on it, hiding tears, when in public. For her, her husband was never existent. He was, as if, someone belonging to a previous life. Their rapport had become flimsy, volatile and elusive, as if a pigeon-hole with a tag, *'switch with caution!'* For them, the olden days, when they had met, were some unfamiliar land. He was more interested in moral policing rather than giving her love, that she deserved. And Meeta spent the best part of her life justifying herself, that she hasn't wronged him by loving me, because she never got emotional bonding or physical closeness from him. And that, he was behaving paranoid; he should not jeopardize a good relationship by being blatantly suspicious, because I wasn't snatching anything that he possessed.

That night, she wrote one long mail from our personal account – that no one can ever snatch the beautiful memories I have given her via those letters even though she would use that mail no further. She actually did that; she never accessed that e-mail account anymore. She knew that the husband read that last mail as well.

Ziddi Meeta.

Later on, she complained several times that she missed my long e-mails, missed our engagement with words. She loved my long letters.

"Please send me *loooong* mails Babu!" She would sms me.

My letters were complex, her's, simple. She loved my critical thought and approach. She would tell me, "Babu, even though I have achieved far more than you, but academically you are excellent. You are much better than me. It's just that, you never realize this."

"Oh come on! Don't compare."

"No, I am not comparing. But we can complement each other. As you say, we are the members of *'Team-Meeta'*-- membership closed with just two people! "

Life was smooth; no one could stop us from communicating. From loving blindly, passionately, irresistibly. After all, we had accepted that even though tough times leave us brooding, they also bring out the essential strong self in us—resilient, will-powered and indomitable. They also show that life isn't any fairy tale, yet it's worth living to prove one's mettle to oneself. Because Meeta strongly believed that our gods are our own making. Taking their names is just giving palpable shapes to our innate resoluteness. Her teaching, research, her engagement with words kept her going.Every day she was going from crest to crest, scaling peaks with aplomb.

We had our share of fights too. If I was too busy to send her a message for an hour, she would complain. There were many times that I forgot to inform her every detail of my days. She was annoyed. "You know what, I expect at least a blank sms from you every one hour, just to tell me that you are missing me." I used to tease her that she suffered from IRDD (incurably romantic disposition disorder!)

"You pretty well know what kind of life I have Meeta. Our lifestyles are different. You don't use a public transport and I do that. You have holidays, vacations, but I have none."

That led to an argument, and then the lady was flooded with tears.I always felt guilty that I made her cry so much. I never wanted her to shed tears, but she always ended up crying.

Was I pulling her heartstrings to much?

"I curse you, Babu, that if someday I die, no one will inform you. Who knows that I love you? No one. You'll get to know of my death at least ten days after it happens."

"Please stop it. How can you be so selfish?" Then it took me an hour to get her back to normalcy.

I used to get bouts of my painful past sometimes and spoil her moods. She never wanted me to talk of the past and told me it's 'boring' to carry the baggage of the past. I retorted, "That boring is harsh.I know you'll be put off, but just because the past isn't present, that doesn't mean being oblivious as if it never existed. There are greater memories, people and hurts given and received. Accept me today and you accept one whose yesterdays have shaped today's. It will be sometime before they are relegated to memory. Your call—Prof.Madhvi or Meeta?" But then,she was upset and silent,and I had to boost her up. I wrote, "I am no kid like you to pout lips at every small thing. One of the basic reasons why I respect you is your indomitable spirit. I would have crumbled long back given your kind of ordeals, leave alone reading or writing. Over-sensitivity is my bane."

After every fight, she would come back to me. I thought, she should resent me some day for the tightened boundaries of my existence, for being the reason of her best years being drained away from her. Were there days when she wanted to be free of me? No, there weren't any. I was always wrong.

And I would write, "Meeta, life has taught me certain things. There is no religion but the voice of conscience. Do right action, irrespective of short term consequences. Forgive wrong doers, but take lessons from wrong done; one doesn't have a right even to expose oneself to repeated wrongs. Nurture things one holds dear, even if reciprocity in material terms isn't possible. Finally, each one is a lonely planet. I apply these and search for no further meaning or casual connect in life."

"Oh my God Babu! I'll take seven births to be as *gyani* as you; I mean intelligent!!"

The very fact that we were in love, kept us alive. From thirty-nine, we got to forty-nine, fifty-nine, thus, we grew older together. She would murmur my name hold her breath, and wait for an echo, almost sure that it would emanate one day.We understood well that we are all condemned to be aliens to each other, forever stuck down in isolated glass vessels and then we call it as the 'self'. Still, the 'selves' of me and Meeta were never at odds with each other.She told me all about her life, her family and friends, relatives and colleagues over those decades, as though I had known them all my life. As though she and I had grown up together, gone on family holidays and summer camps to the seaside where we had made sand houses and touched each other's' fingers under the wet sand.

As I said earlier, I commented on each piece of her writing all these years. I selected the best picture among all the pictures she had mailed for a girl for her son. Her son wanted her to select the girl for his wedding, and she wanted me to do that. Eventually Siddharth married her! I selected the cover pages of her books, read each piece of interview she wrote, suggested colours for her saris and interior designers for her home.

I was constantly present in her life, through thick and thin. Elegance hailed upon her, with age, as though it were a genetic dexterity. She grew old and elegant, like fine wine.

* * *

Suddenly my world seems to be shattered today; there is an unknown fear lurking in the mind. Because, like Meeta, I haven't mastered the art of pushing the envelope and taking life in my stride.

Today is Meeta's 65th birthday, and she has not been taking my calls, not responding to my mails since a week. Whom shall I ask? Is she out of country? But she always informs me; in fact I plan most of her trips.

So why is this long silence? I can't take it. I know none of her family members or colleagues closely so that I can just call up and ask about her. Neither do I have any other number. She's completely inaccessible. I am worried, upset.

Is my Meeta unwell and doesn't want to inform me, like she did the last time?

The calm between us looked like a perpetuation of our bonding. We were like two leaves of a plant propelling miles away from each other by a fierce wind yet assured by the deep intertwined origins of the plant from which we both had dropped.

* * *

Someone in the department was reading out an old news from Delhi, reprinted in a newspaper in my city after a week.

"Distinguished poet and social worker, Late Prof. Madhvi Srivastava, has expressed her desire in her Will that her house may be converted to a Home-for-the-Differently-Abled. She has dedicated her library and her publishing house to the public and both of those are now looked after by her son, Mr. Siddharth Srivastava. Prof. Madhavi passed away on 17th of this month by cardiac arrest, after being treated in Moolchand Hospital for three days. We pay our deep homage to the departed soul."

I was devastated. There was a throwing up pain in my head. I was just going out of the staff room when the office peon handed over a packet.

I went home, quiet.

There are so many poems and a letter, written in her neat hands, which perhaps she had given Siddharth to post; for the first time any third person coming between us. I read one:

"I am a bud, pulled
off the branch.
Where is my redemption?
I am Mira.
Oh Krishna! You are elsewhere
in the thoroughfares
in your chariot.
My feet stirring to a conduit
unversed

but the tap-tap of each heartbeat
every string of my being
constrained in the sludge
of the artery's ribcage.
Amend me
like a lime stone sculpture.
Place me in your familiar city."

I sat quietly for a while, the air around me thick with discomfort and my awareness of all the time lost, all prospects squandered away.

And then this letter. My eyes are blinded with tears.

"Babu, my dearest one, when I cursed you that you'll get to know about my death after ten days, I never meant that. I am dying. I can make a phone call now, can ask Siddharth to call you. But let this love remain veiled even now. You have given me a beautiful life. Years back I met you with vacuum in my eyes, and you filled that with your love. Time is flying away, snatching my breaths. I am receding, like river waters, like mountain tops. I am going back, like the water bearing clouds. Now I am defenseless. Why do I still remember my compassionate lover when I am free of every desire? Thank you, for giving me such a beautiful life. You have been to me--my life, love, happiness. Will you drape me in your arms, at least now?

I am sorry ,you need me more now, because you are going to retire this year. Don't feel lonely. Live a good life. I am sending you some of my incomplete research work; complete the work, as you have always done. Then these are some of my poems written last few months. I dedicate those to you. You can compile all and publish my fifteenth poetry collection posthumously. Now that I am leaving, you can come to my city, see my home that you have designed, see my publishing house that I created under your guidance. See the children, the disabled and the deprived, who are living happily in our Home and using our library. Touch my wardrobe, all my saris are familiar, aren't they? Give those away to the needy. I am sending my floral yellow-blue suit, your favorite, for keep-sake. I haven't washed it even after wearing if for a couple of times as you wanted it to retain my jasmine flavour. And then my grey slippers, that I wore for past thirty-five years; you know. I had those even before I met you! They are yours.

I had never been completely *Madhvi,* or absolutely *Meeta.* I spent an entire lifetime thinking about my identity; but somehow I learnt to live this hyphenated life organically. But let me tell you, since I met you, the 'Meeta' sensibilities have seeped into my identity and personality. I have never been paranoid about 'Madhvi' or 'Meeta' losing identities because of each other; you never let that happen.

Today I am far in the expanse, amid a cobalt stroke of sprays; in front of my eyes, a golden haze. I still hark back to you from a sky of molten gold.

Yours forever, Meeta"

Alternative Masculinity(?!)

We surely were annoyed, rather uncomfortable, looking at the PDA of the middle-aged couple.

Dr. Harihar Panda and his wife Mrs. Savita Panda were my guests that evening, along with two other friends from Odisha—Dr. Manas and Dr. Shubhra. All of them except for Savita were in Delhi to attend a conference. Manas and Shubhra were my old friends, I invited them over dinner after the conference. Harihar and Savita came along; in fact they got self invited and I didn't mind that, because the four of them had come from Bhubaneswar as a team. I had booked three rooms in the university guest house for them—one for the couple and two for the other two.

Savita had nothing to do during the day when her husband and his friends were busy in the conference. She was restless and very worried about the food, medicines, etc of her husband. She always remained worried about these trivial matters--- like many housewives—starting with what he should wear any given day to how much tea he should consume in the evening. Should he apply oil on his hair today? What if he catches cold by a head bath? Should he eat chicken more than once a week? What if it upsets his stomach? Is he talking too much on the mobile? He may get a migraine, so the phone should be switched off. And why is he taking such a long walk? It's windy today.

Their children were settled, grown up, and the sixty years old wife's only concern, focus, topic of discussion, life, love, happiness, worry--just everything--was her sixty-plus husband.

Throughout the past couple of days, we were noticing Savita's overwhelming care and concern for Harihar. Initially, we found it cute. But later, we were annoyed, as expected.

My friend Manas was a writer, an emotionally charged, intelligent person, somewhat close to my heart. Shubhra was a chirpy, witty, pretty woman; she was most talkative.

That evening, my friends got introduced to my son Sonu, a humorous, intelligent and sober teen. They were happy to receive his hospitality. I had cooked quite a few dishes for them, and the guests thoroughly enjoyed the food. We chatted about Odisha; in between Manas talked about his new stories. He knew I loved his stories, he wanted my complete attention, which I, too, was willingly giving. Shubhra was keen on knowing every detail of my friendship with Manas—when and how did we meet? How come we were so compatible with each other despite his having a happy married life in Odisha; and neither was I his lover or anything like that. She was trying to understand this special bonding.

Harihar was eager to get the attention of me, his hostess; he tried to give his opinion about everything around, talked about his achievements, his admiration of the excellent life I had made for myself in Delhi. In between, he never forgot to praise each dish I had cooked; and I had to thank him politely every time he praised. Overall, it was a pleasant evening.

Beyond all of these, oblivion of us, Savita was in her usual fidgety disposition – checking and serving food on Harihar's plate, chiding him for eating more of one dish or less of one, restricting his intake of coffee after food. She even asked him if he washed his hands before food.

I requested, "Madam, you please eat, Sir will help himself; if he needs any help, I'll look after." I guess as the hostess, that was my duty.

"No no!! How can he eat if I don't serve? I'll eat later; as such I had a lot of snacks('snakes', she said) in the guest house when you all were in the conference. "

Shubhra has this crooked, uncontrollable sense of humour, which will make anyone laugh. She said, "arre Savita madam, do you always take care of Sir like this? Is he a domestic animal?"(she actually said, *'gruhapalita pashu'!!*).

Unbelievable!! Incorrigible Shubhra!!

I couldn't control my laughter, nor could Manas and Sonu. I rushed to the kitchen to laugh in the plea of getting some pickles. In the kitchen,while laughing my guts out, I remembered Shakespeare's Lady Macbeth. Lady Macbeth said, "unsex me today". This statement paralleled negativity to manhood and power. Was this her reverse feminism?

Was this over-consciousness Savita's reverse feminism? What a drama queen! I joined them back with a desire to see a little more of domestic drama, I must confess here.

Dr.Harihar, who was an Associate Professor, and was waiting for his CAS promotion to a Professor's position, of course did not like this 'domestic animal' adjective. He had to make his stand clear.

By then, Savita had started eating, relaxed, after feeding her husband to her heart's content.

Harihar cleared his throat and said, looking at me, clearly avoiding Shubhra, "Madam, do you know, Savita is the most loving and caring wife I have ever seen. She takes care of everything. From morning to night, twenty-four into seven, she is there for me. She takes care of my home, my children, me. She cooks, cleans the house, arranges my shattered books, shabby study tables, irons my clothes, feeds me. I simply depend on her for every single thing. In fact, for every small thing I need her."

Savita had a beaming smile on her lips. "I even make him wear his dress. Else this mindless man would go to his university in his underwear—he is so offhand." Announced Savita proudly.

"What the …!!!" Shubhra was unrelenting. She wanted more spice for the dinner table. "I mean, Savita Madam, do you actually make him sit on the chair semi-nude, and do his *shringaar* before he goes to the university? Every day?! "

"Oh yes! Definitely. I even give him a bath every morning. I have been doing that forever!"

I looked at Harihar covertly,scornfully to see if he was feeling embarrassed. But he had a blank, nonchalant expression on his face. Like the Monalisa painting. I couldn't understand what exactly was he thinking at that moment of humiliation.

Savita got up, washed her hands quickly, and came back to her husband, wiped his mouth with her dupatta, arranged his scanty locks on the bald head, set his shirt collars right, and sat closely beside him, in the most lovey dovey position, making all of us uncomfortable.

Sonu is one more witty boy here. He added, "Wow uncle and aunty! You both are young and happening, like characters from a Bollywood film." And then he left the dinner table,laughing, went to his study, to my utter relief. I didn't want him to watch this family drama of Savita-Harihar, neither I wanted him to give his expert opinions.

Seeing my awful discomfiture, Manas tried to change the topic. "Leave it Harihar bhai and Bhabhi. Let's plan something. Shall we all go to Agra, Mathura, Vrindaban over the weekend? We have our flight on Monday morning, so the weekend can be utilized with Madam and Sonu. All of us can fit in a bigger cab."

I thought, *thank God!The topic changed.*

But no! Savita and Shubhra didn't stop there.

"So, Savita Madam! It's most impressive that you help your husband so much! My husband will give me a divorce if he sees your example…haha!! What else do you do for Harihar Sir?"

That was quite an ego booster for Savita. "I got married to *him* when he had just passed his Masters Degree and was newly appointed as a lecturer in a government college. He was lazy-number-one from the day one, I could see that. He did not have the training to pick his wet towel and put that in the washing machine, neither did he know how to make a cup of tea. I took charge of him. Ask him, I am the one who made him do his PhD, I am the one because of whom he wrote his research papers and books. Because of me he got his promotions. Tomorrow if he is promoted to a higher position in his workplace, it will also be because of me. Minus me, this man is a big zero."

"I see…". Shubhra was enjoying the conversation with a crooked smile, and in between winking at me and Manas.

At least now I expected Harihar to object to the discussions around him and his career. But he kept quiet. Nonchalantly he took two *rasagollas* in a small bowl. Savita quickly removed one from the bowl, and looked at him like a disciplinarian Principal ma'am of a primary school, chiding her naughty pupil.

Harihar pleaded for one more *rasagolla*, with a guilty smile. "No!! You cannot eat more than one."

Savita went on boasting about her contributions to Harihar's life, family and career. She took the credit for everything that he had been doing since their wedding some thirty-five years ago—she claimed, he owed her his living and breathing.

I was feeling sick, nauseated. I wished the evening to end there. Manas could see that. He finally got up, wishing me good night. Others too had to leave along.

Till late night I thought about this complex human behavior; to be precise, about this objectionable supremacy of a woman. It was surely a kind of male-harassment to me. The gender theorist inside me was concerned. The humanist in me was thinking, weighing the characters of Harihar and Savita from Masculinity Studies standpoint. To me, it looked like poor Harihar was under a panoptic surveillance. Savita was inspecting him from all directions. I felt he was getting breathless with her attention, but he talked nicely about her love, dedication for him just to save his face before us elites. Maybe he didn't want us to judge him or Savita.

Poor thing. He earned my sympathies that night. Next morning, I called Manas showing my inability to go to Agra with them as I had got some urgent work in the university. I also told him what I felt about Dr.Harihar. He didn't take much interest in their matter; rather he was upset that his poetic evening with me was spoiled because of the couple. It could have been an evening of reading good literature, listening to good music, and a peaceful dinner with me and Sonu, had those stupids not been there.

He had a point. Even I would have preferred that.

***

Time flew.

I almost forgot Harihar-Savita. Manas and Shubhra called me sometimes, but we made it a point not to discuss the couple. It was, we decided, none of our business. Because Harihar had apparently no objection to whatever was happening with him—though I had serious doubts about it. Anyway, Manas asked me to forget them.

So be it!

Yes, after five months of their visit to Delhi, I happened to visit Utkal University, Bhubaneswar, to deliver a lecture. Dr.Harihar was eager to meet me; but I had no time,being the high-flyer. So I informed him over whatsapp that I won't be able to meet him.

I mostly have morning-evening-round-trips. Padmashree poet Jayanta Mahapatra was in Bhubaneswar that day, and his car was scheduled to drop me in the airport in the evening. I always have never ending chats with Jayanta Sir, and I was elated spending a couple of hours with him in the long drive. And lo! Harihar was waiting for us in the Bhubaneswar airport! He had gathered this information from someone in the university, that Jayanta Sir would accompany me to the airport. I wasn't pleased to see him there; anyway both Jayanta Sir and I exchanged formal pleasantries with him, maybe for a few seconds only, before I proceeded to the check in counter. Harihar requested us that he wanted to click our photographs, and Jayanta Sir agreed. So he quickly handed over his mobile to some passerby and got clicked with us, with a grin. I left Bhubaneswar after touching the feet of Jayanta Sir and a casual 'namaste' to Harihar. After a couple of days, I found Harihar had tagged me on Facebook, posted that picture with a long tag-line, "Wonderful time spent with Padmashree Jayanta Mahapatra and the unparalleled poet par excellence, Nandini Sahu, in Bhubaneswar. Had long dialogues with the poets on contemporary Indian literature, and possible future collaborations with both poets."

I rather felt pity than contempt and laughed it off. All I remembered was, we spent maximum one minute with him in Bhubaneswar airport, that to, he was an uninvited presence.

Harihar sent me courtesy messages on festivals, functions, special occasions, to which I responded with a wordless 'namaste' emoji. Technology sometimes makes life simpler.

After eight more months or so, once Harihar called me with a request to book a room for him in our guest house. He had some work in North-East Delhi. I told him, we are in extreme South Delhi, so he'll have to travel so much to reach his meeting venue. He said, it was ok, there were no rooms available elsewhere.

The moment he reached our guest house, he called me. In fact he wanted to meet us the same morning. Anyway, I was busy; also I was trying to avoid him. That day, at 5pm when I reached home, he was already seated comfortably, settled, in our living room. Sonu had offered him tea. He came to our place without an appointment, uninvited, and said he was getting bored in the guest house. I said, "Dr.Harihar, people who get bored in their own company seem to be in danger."Maybe I wanted him to talk about his distressed life, or maybe I despised him. He still had my sympathies. Of course, I did not respect him for being so meek and mild a man.

He took his sweet time, sipping his tea, savoring the snacks we offered. This time he looked relaxed, unlike last time when he was anxious even about a cup of tea or a *rasogolla*.

Poor thing.

He was relaxed till Savita called him after an hour (apparently, she called him every one hour!). I guessed, he lied to her about the network, and disconnected the phone. Perhaps put that on flight mode after talking to her for a minute.

"Sir, please call her from my phone. I too can wish her my regards."

"No no Madam!! Let it be. I'll anyway call her after an hour."

He talked restlessly, stridently for an hour about his work, his university; poor Sonu had to sit with him nodding his head all the time, as I utilized the time in cooking dinner, and pretending to be listening to his blabbering. I was, clearly, impolite. And I wanted him to leave. It was a wastage of time for me to have such meaningless talk.

He called his wife sharp at 7pm and told her that he was in the guest house, waiting for dinner, and then put the phone again on flight mode.

I understood. He didn't want his wife to know that he was sitting with us. Precisely, with me. A *single woman*.

Sonu asked, "but uncle, you are at our place!! Why did you lie?"

It was awkward.

Then I lied to him in order to throw him out of my house. "Sir, you may have to please excuse us. Sonu has a lot of homework, and we'll have to study now."

"No mama! There is no homework today!"

I looked so stupid.

Harihar said, shamelessly, "Madam, can I have dinner before leaving? I didn't have a proper lunch in the guest house."

We had a silent, quick, early dinner. Then I offered to drop him back in the guest house in my car, though he had no mood to leave at 7.30pm.

He reluctantly said goodbye to Sonu and sat in my car, of course without forgetting to praise an independent, super-successful woman, driving a car all by herself. How disgusting was that!

Now that I was alone with him in the car, I had no reason to suppress my infuriation for an enslaved, spineless man. He owed me an explanation for lying to Savita that he was eating dinner in the guest house.

"Dr.Harihar, I do not teach any kind of lie and deception to my son; so what you did at my place was seriously objectionable. I do not know much about you or your family or the values that you people follow. You were introduced to me by common friends. I wanted to respect you, but unfortunately, I could not. I cannot. How can you allow a person to dominate, control you to such an extent? How can you lie to her in front of me, sitting at my place? You have humiliated us and our hospitality. I don't know for what all should I reprimand you, neither do I know if at all I should talk to you! You are so laid-back! You don't have the courage to tell Mrs.Savita that you are having dinner with a respectable family! And last time your behaviour was such shameful in front of all of us!! How can a man tolerate if a woman steals the entire credit of his life and career?? Have you no dignity? No shame? Are you not suffocated? How do you live such a life??"

I was gasping angrily. I stopped the car in front of the guest house and got down. He too got down and stood at a distance.

He said, quietly, considerately, "Madam, I thought you are an extremely intelligent person, and you can see the subtext behind this text. Behind this story of 'subjugation'. But to me, now you sound like Gandhari. To be born blind is not a crime, but to turn a blind eye? How can you not see the hidden depths of this story?"

Ahh…one more drama.

"Excuse me? I am still not getting what nonsense you are trying to explain. Come to the point." I was rude.

"Ok, let me come to the point."

He scratched his head, searching for words, and then said, "My wife Savita is an empty-headed foolish woman; an erudite woman like you may not understand the mindset of such people. She is class three pass(or fail.. haha), she cannot even sign in English. She puts her thumb impression on papers I ask her to. She is from a lavish, extravagant family where she had seen women being dominated by men. She got married to me when she was 18 and I was 25. Her parents offered me a fortune for dowry, and see the bonuses I have! A mansion and couple of nice cars. She can never understand what unproductive stuff she is engaged with. She has no time to think of anything except me and my needs. She cooks, cleans, takes care of all my wishes— I get great food, clean bed, clean tables to work, fresh towels, clean book shelves, healthy tea, health care, in fact everything for a comfortable living. In return, I ignore her foolish talks, her self-styled *supremacy*. She feels emancipated, empowered by 'dominating' me. Can you believe--she signed her entire property in my name—I mean put her thumb impression—without an inkling of what she was doing. I told her that she had to sign the documents to secure her property."

I was amazed. My mouth agape, eyes wide open. What a revelation!!

"And Madam, which qualified person in my friend

circle will believe that a class-three-fail woman, who looks like a dumb fool, who opens her mouth only to reveal her imprudence, her foolishness, has actually shaped my great academic career? Rather, some laugh at her foolishness, and some, like you, give me their sympathies!! Actually, it's a win-win situation for me."

I sat in my car without a goodbye or a good night. Reached home absent-minded, with a void in my cognizance, rethinking, swotting 'masculinity'.

Echoing in a Lullaby

There are many stories about love. But there are some stories of love, not precisely love-stories, where one can see a common human being turning uncommon with the touch of love.

Love and lullaby – aren't they virtually the parallel terms? Teacher and adoration—aren't they synonymous?

I lived in the United States for past ten years. The place where I live in India with my daughter since past two years, was supposedly a jungle a few years back. Muddy, dark, back waters leading where nobody knew, near Gopalpur-on-sea, a village turning into a small town. Working in the university in the nearest township Berhampur, Odisha, I drive ten kilometers every day, and drop my daughter Neera on the way in her public school. I have decided to live here, because I always wanted to live life looking at the blue. Now this place is slowly turning into a port, and engineers from the state as well as the national capital throng this area every day. It's becoming a city of flowers. My daughter has learnt to sing William Black and Shelley in place of "*Ahe dayamaya visva bihari*"; and her Miss has replaced her grandmother. The teacher Miss Shruti Palo who prefers to be called as Miss Paul, speaks Odia kindly, like Katrina Kaif speaks Hindi, tells her stories. She has introduced her to *Rath Yatra* as the 'Car Festival'. She takes them on excursions sometimes and shows Lord Jagannath, *Kainchamali*, the wooden horse, the jute bags, Pipili canopies, and tells them, "See children! Have a look at our ancient culture." Neera reads out her paragraph writing in the evening to me on the topic 'Our Villages'-- where the villages are shown as places out of this world, where strange creatures lived, and life was weird. Where people and cows walked on the narrow lanes together, people ate rice thrice a day, women wore nothing but saris, children had hardly any homework or classwork except listening to stories, sometimes mugging up the multiplication tables in a singsong manner. This summer vacation I took Neera to my village, because she had to prepare a project for her social studies on 'Our Rural Odisha'. We went to the place where my widowed father lives with his widow mother, some 200 kilometer away from Berhampur.

My grandmother is eighty eight years old, but still strong in her mind, if not her body. She told Neera stories of her childhood and her village. Neera thought it was some ghost story, a fantasy. Great-grandmother, *Budhimaa*, was a liar.

How could a metro girl have believed that in the past, life was beautiful like poetry?

Life was like poetry when we were kids. Early morning the scavenger woman brooming the roads. Mowing of calves to suck the left-over milk from mother cow's breast after the milkman had collected his day's milk. We would get up with the metallic sound of fuel coal dropped into tin containers for measuring. One *dabba*, a tin container, was 50 paise, supplying kitchen fuel for a week. Mother carefully watching, lest the coal-*wallah* might cheat. But did anyone cheat anyone? *Pata mausi* scrubbing utensils with ashes near the well. There was an eternal fight between *Pata mausi* and *Phula-budhi*, the old woman supplying flowers for our daily puja, since *Pata mausi* got fresh flowers for people for less money than the old woman. *Sudama bhaina* bathing his buffalo near the well that reminds Neera of her Mom's car washer. Mother sprinkling cow dung water in the backyard, father sipping tea while listening to All India Radio. "*Aakasha-vani. News bulletin by Gouranga Charana Rath.*" Madana going to the temple with stolen flowers, chanting mantras all the while; *Oshibou* scolding someone, perhaps her daughter-in-law. Our neighbor's name was Chairman Digal. Villagers fancied giving peculiar names to their children. Proper names were truly connotative in the sense that whatever was precious – for example kerosene – was a prospective name. Whatever was a respectable position or job, was also a prospective proper name. That is how, many villagers ended up giving weird names to their kids, like Chairman Nayak, Kerosene Pradhan, Amitabh Bachchan Digal,President Nayak, Darmendra Nayak or Hema Malini Pradhan.

It would be still dusk. I and Raju bhaiya, my brother, would brush our teeth sitting beside the well and drowse. Chairman Digal's mother coming to the well to fetch water would nag. Grandmother would us get hot water to mix with a bucket of fresh cold water from the well to bathe, then braid my long hair into two folded banana plaits with red ribbons of floral patterns. My two aunts were at home, all the time doing embroidery on hanky or window screens, waiting to be married off. I and Raju going to Hatapada UP School, to class one and two, respectively. The school looked like a warehouse from a distance.

There were teachers like Padhy Sir, who oiled his hair so much that he had acne all over his forehead. There was Sabita *didi* (in our schools, teachers were addressed as *didi* even if they were sixty years old!), who was young and beautiful, whose saris I used to touch and feel sitting on the front row while she would be writing on the black board. There was Sahu Sir, our Maths teacher, whose Draconian law scared us to death. Deduct whatever less marks you have gotten from one hundred, and get ready to be whipped that many times by him.

And then, there was *Budhi didi*, the class teacher, in fact the only teacher for all subjects, for class-I. My favorite teacher.

I still didn't know what her actual name was all those years. She was fondly called as *Budhi didi* by all, may be because she was the oldest among all the teachers.

We would reach the school at 7 am and there were prayers. *"Aahe dayamaya visva bihari, ghena dayabahi moro guhari"*. Some naughty boys would replace the second line by *"tuma bariade saga kiyari, tume kete khumti khunti khaucha, aame magile tike na daucha."*,(which meant, you have spinach all over your backyard, which you don't care to share with us) and I would giggle. Sahu Sir, the Maths teacher, would stare at me, and I would squeeze into the lap of *Budhi didi*.

Then the roll calls. Class-I was never a class room, it was a verandah, like open theater, with a black board and a chair in the centre. *Budhi didi* would be sitting on that for a while, then get down and sit with us on the floor, wiping our nose, picking lice from our head, telling us stories, singing songs, teaching us the alphabets by writing on our note books, making faces to tease us, feeding us if we were hungry, giving us wild berries which were forbidden at home; and even singing a lullaby to put us to sleep on her lap if we were sleepy. She was with us in the same floor from 7 am to 1 pm, sharing life with us.

Budhi didi was the most beautiful woman I had ever seen. Why she had only one sari, off white or it had grown grey by overuse, I couldn't understand. My mother and grandmother had so many saris, father used to get new saris for them at least thrice a year. My father was the village Sarpanch, and we were well-to-do. I wanted to gift some of our saris to *Budhi didi*. Even I asked her once, that if I could get her a few saris from home, and she said no, *one should never steal. One should never tell a lie. Wash your hands before and after eating. Touch the feet of your parents. Don't be jealous of anyone. Do good and be good.* Whatever she told was like the Veda for me. She truly represented the simplicity of a villager. She was more than a mother to us children.

During roll calls, she would mark all of us present, even without looking. Because we were never absent in her class.

Her face was angelic, with disengaged features – a flat nose, wrinkles, uneven teeth and bright eyes -- she was very beautiful in my eyes. She had a motherly fragrance, the smell of love. Her bosom was soft. She was the best teacher, she taught us numbers, alphabets, music, just everything, all subjects. We never did projects, we had no holiday homework, no study tours, no unit tests, no semesters, but our learning was long term and brain-based. Whatever she had taught us, is still printed in my mind, saved permanently in my hard disk.

She was not only teaching us, she was preparing us for life. We learnt piousness, generosity, honesty, truthfulness and empathy from her. We learnt the alphabets of love from her.

During winter mornings, the headmaster Mr. Valentine Pradhan, one more person with a connotative proper name, asked us to come down and sit in the sun, because the verandah for class-I was too cold. On one such occasion, I left my school bag open and went to relieve myself in the fields as we had no washrooms in our school, to the utter surprise of Neera. In the meantime, *Budhi didi* was busy with some correction work and other children were playing. A cow entered the ground where our bags were kept and ate away my Maths book, almost half of it!

"Oh God! Today Maa will beat me. What shall I do now?" I went on crying.

She lifted me onto her lap with her left hand. I was reed thin, was hardly a few kilos when I was in class I. (And my Neera is fifty kilos when she is in class V. After all she is child of luxury--a pizza, burger, French fries' kid!)

She patted my head and wiped my face. "Don't cry mama", she addressed us as *mama* out of love, "I shall copy the entire book for you from my book, ok?"

She actually did that, overnight. Was she alone at home? Had she no other work at home? My mother and grandmother were busy all the time cooking, making *wadi*, pickles or cleaning the house. In the school she didn't have a moment's break, with sixty naughty children in her class, making her crazy.

After many years, when I was young , I went to see her in her house during my annual vacation, she told me for the first time that she was *Aparna*, not only *Budhi didi*, and she got married when she was fifteen years old, had two children; then one day her husband got converted to another religion and went to England with the kids, leaving her behind, for he had found a beautiful woman whose brothers sponsored his foreign trip and a job abroad. She was a loner. She tried to see her children in us, give a meaning to her life by taking care of us selflessly. She had heard that her children were married and settled in London, she had grand children now.

But I had never seen tears in her eyes. Always a smile, motherly comfort, heavenly patience, womanly self-confidence. That made her the most lovable, most beautiful woman.

Budhi didi used to reach Hatapada U.P. School, our school, very early in the morning. At least half an hour before other teachers. Because she took care of the mid-day meal for the poor children. The government had a scheme of mid-day meal made of *daliya* for the children below poverty line. *Budhi didi* used to cook it with utmost care, because she thought that the cooks supplied by the government were very careless, they never cared about hygiene and taste of the food. By the time we would reach the school, the aroma of freshly cooked *daliya upma* would be in the air. I would start salivating and wait for the tiffin break at 9 am and discreetly go and sit in the row of the BPL children to gulp *daliya*. I never wanted to eat the *paranthas* and cauliflower curry that my grandmother packed for me and Raju in two separate boxes. I used to give it away to some other child. *Budhi didi* always noticed this.

"Don't do this mama. Your parents will not like this. This food is not for you."

"Why *Budhi didi*? This is so yummy."

"You find this yummy? Only boiled *daliya* with salt?"

Now whenever I cook *daliya* for Neera with milk, sugar and dry fruits, I don't get that aroma of the *daliya* of *Budhi didi's* cooking. But it makes me nostalgic, for sure.

Class-I was over, and I had to study in the same school for another four years, with other teachers. But my weakness for *Budhi didi* was never less. I would spend sometime before our classes began,then the entire lunch break, again the *chutti* time with her. Chatting with her, touching her, leaning on her shoulder, running away when she would try to pat my back for some mischief I did.

Time is a universal phenomenon, as certain and unstoppable as death. Undaunted by the sun's truant ways, it ticks away mercilessly, merging day into night and vice-versa, with unwavering precision.

Time balances, levels all—that's a separate matter. Time is a great leveler—that is immaterial for *Budhi didi* kind of people.

This year I reached our village with Neera, which can hardly be called a village anymore. Neera got busy with my father and grandmother, taking details about village life from them for her Social Studies project. She was literally pampered by them.

I wanted to see *Budhi didi* . My father told she is in a very bad shape. I rushed to her hut, and discovered that she was lying on her bed, talking to herself.

"Ninu, you came *mama?* I knew you would come."

Hardly and she begun, then a short, stocky and dark old man entered the room with a woman, pretty older than me. But she had a striking similarity with me! She was her daughter and he, the father of the daughter, *Budhu didi's* husband, who had left her years back.

Did she love me so much because I resembled her daughter? But no, she loved every child! Panic-striken, *Budhi didi* looked here and there, seeking something she couldn't find. An empty water jug and an upturned tumbler were kept on the table, and they hadn't bothered even to fill that.

I suddenly felt low. My excitement to give her the good news that I am going back to the States on a fellowship for three years, with Neera, vanished. I had decided to spend the whole of June in the village, to give Neera an understanding of rural India, and to give myself some good time with my father, grandmother and *Budhi didi.* Our tickets were booked for the first week of July.

Why have these people come after all these years? When did they come? Why is she looking so bewildered? She caught hold of both my hands and whispered something. Then sobbed. Her sighs and sobs filled the backyard and darkened my face. She leaned on my chest like I used to on hers when I was in class-I. Then wiped her tears herself and told, "Ninu, this is my husband and my daughter. See, how much she looks like you! But no! She is not like you. She has never loved this old woman."

She continued, "After retirement the headmaster wanted me to be the children's hostel superintendent. There is a small hostel in Hatapada U.P. School now. But I denied. I wanted to live and die in this house, where I had come as a bride years back. Now these people are asking me to vacate this house because they want to sell this property off and go back. They need money. I was dying to contact you *mama*! I knew that you would come and take me to Gopalpur. At least I can spend the last few days of my life peacefully. They are asking me to shift to the old age home today itself. Their papers are ready."

She was speaking restlessly. It was not good for the heart of an old person. I asked her husband and daughter to leave that room. She put her head on my lap peacefully and tried to sleep. As if it were her last sleep, the very last one. I had got *daliya* for her from home. I fed her a few spoons before putting her to sleep. Liquid food spilled out from her mouth.

I was perhaps humming a lullaby to her, bewildered, echoing the lullaby of my childhood, that she used to sing for us. Noiselessly she opened her eyes for a few moments and stared at me, as if I were her erudite preacher.

The Shadow of a Shadow

Ragini was lying on her belly in her room, room no 12 of Mahendra Tanaya Ladies' Hostel, in the Berhampur University campus in Odisha, year--1995, and reading a poem by Sappho. It was a poem about the errant sexual behavior of a lesbian, her emotions described in fragments:

"Even in Hades I am with you
Andromeda…. Gongyla….My desire feeds
On your beauty, Gongyla. Each time I see your gown
I am made weak and happy …You of all women whom
I almost desire, come to me again…

You lay in wait behind a laurel tree…You
A woman wanderer like me… I barely
Heard you, my darling…. You came
In your trim garments…..And suddenly
Beauty of your garments!

Hermes came to me in a dream. I said
My master, I am altogether lost…
And my many riches do not console me
I care only…….to die….. and to watch the dewy lotus
Along the banks of Acheron, river of hell…..

I have no embroidered head-band for you, Kleis
And no idea where to find one
While Myrsilos rules in Mytilene…..The bright
Ribbon reminds me of those days when our
Enemies were in exile……o Kleis……"

Ragini couldn't help smiling to herself thinking of Sappho's desire for all her girl friends, Andromeda, Gongyla, Athis, Kleis. So many? She had read somewhere that Sappho of Lesbos was a poet, writing liberally about her sexual desire for her female friends and her poetry was subjected to tremendous violence in the Christian West. She was a victim of the state mandated management of *compulsory heterosexuality*. Still her work survived and was oft quoted until in 1000 AD the church destroyed all her poems and quotes. In 1073, her poems were publicly burnt in Rome and Constantinople by the orders of Pope Gregory VIII. Still some Egyptian papyrus preserves her poems in the form of quotation!!

Ragini was amazed. A woman has to suffer so much of suppression, mutilation, censorship and disparagement, only because whatever she thought or freely wrote was thought 'unnatural' by a group of people? But in the norms of Indian civil conduct it is quite 'natural' when a woman's soft emotions are crushed on the nuptial bed and she has to undergo marital rape throughout her life! Still she can be called a respectable married woman, feeding her limbs to a man whom she might not love, and drying his underwear proudly, lifelong, like the national flag.

The implications of the word 'unnatural' seemed to her quite unnatural.

She was reminded of her elder sister who was married to Rajib *bhai* at a very young age. She bore three children for him by the time she was twenty, yet his lust was never satisfied. He would shout at her at the drop of a hat, humiliate her for not being as qualified as him, call her names, but she had to be with him in the 'natural' circle of her 'happy' married life, without a choice. She had never seen him speaking to her softly, touching or patting her shoulder any time, even when she was in labor pain. He had never got a single rose for her even on her birthday. Since their father passed away leaving two young girls and a boy behind with an ailing widow, her mother, it was decided that her sister Shalini, who was in +2 first year Arts by then, should be married off to Rajib *bhai*, a Deputy General Manager in a multinational company. Their mother had got some amount from her dead husband's office which was not enough for the higher education of three children. Shalini's marriage ceremony was simple, but the dowry was not so. A Wagon-R car, refrigerator, T.V., and whatever else is required for a household, their mother arranged. After that Ragini was sent to a hostel since she got a scholarship. Since then, she has always been on fellowships, staying in hostels, now doing her Masters in the university, staying in a single room which she voluntarily shares with her friend Suni, Sunita Malhotra, from Chandigarh.

Ragini couldn't divert her mind form the thought of her sister Shalini, how she went to her in-law's house, scared, crying all the while, when she was just sixteen. After fifteen days she came home with a *mangalsutra* around her throat, bruises on her neck and nape, lips and eyes swollen. She had been to a honeymoon which Rajib bhai's friends had sponsored, in Delhi, Shimla, Kulu and Manali. Their mother was so happy to see that at least one of her daughters was *settled* in life. She couldn't see, or perhaps she didn't want to see, her stony dead eyes, chopped wings and blue-black bruises.

Ragini had to get up with a start with the loud ringing of the bell for lunch or breakfast, whatever you can call it, at 10 am. Oh, she was late. Today the first period was to be taken by Prof. Mohapatra, her favorite teacher. He taught them theory – post-colonialism, post-modernism, ecocriticism, feminism, narratology and new criticism. She rushed to the bathroom. There was no water supply. Water supply was from 8.00 to 9.00am, one hour, and you have to queue up to get your turn. Or, perhaps store two buckets of water so that when the rush was over, you could bathe peacefully. Thank god, Suni was her roommate. She had collected two buckets of water for Ragini after she bathed in the morning. Suni knew, Ragini would study from six to ten in the morning, and she would never like to be disturbed for trivial things like water. So Suni had willingly taken that on herself, to help her almost every day.

"Thanks Suni-di, it's very sweet of you."

"Ok, ok, now bathe quickly and come to the dining hall. Today there is egg curry. I have asked *Bhagban bhaina* to keep two eggs for you."

Ragini couldn't have thought about her hostel life without Suni. They were two extremes – Ragini was a good student, serious about her future, because she never wanted a life like her sister Shalini. Or, it's better to say that the life that had been imposed on Shalini. She had a secret desire that someday she would become an IAS officer; earn so much that it won't be impossible to for her to rescue her sister from that snare. She needs a lot of money and empowerment for that; she has been focused in her career.

Suni was different. She had no such aim in life. She was the single child of rich parents, her Papa always on business trips outside India and Mummy was busy with her kitty parties. The daughter was left to the *ayah*; thus she preferred to share her life with her hostel mates rather than with servants.

That was how she was here, doing certificate, degree, diploma courses one after the other, aimlessly, just to be facilitated to stay in the university, particularly in the hostel, far away from home. During the first two years, she had a single room of her own, which used to be always locked. Because she never wanted to stay alone. She had befriended the senior girls and used to chit chat with them, help everyone with money and personal care. She had enough spare time with her. Whenever someone was ill, someone was upset, heartbroken, disturbed, had to go for shopping, had some relative in her room, Suni was there. She was so good-natured that within no time she became everybody's favorite. She had long hair, great skin, a charming smile, she was a real beauty, and Ragini was very fascinated to see her in the dining room or T.V. room every day. She envied her, how much time she had! When did she prepare her notes? When did she study?

The fact was, she never prepared notes, never studied and never wanted to be 'something' in life. She was just living in the present. During the summer vacations when everyone was excited, shopping for their family members before going home, Suni had nobody to buy things for. Because she couldn't find suitable designer saris for Mummy or suits for Papa from places like Annapurna Market in Berhampur where her friends preferred to shop.

After all they had to buy fashionable yet inexpensive stuff. And there was no point going to a mall alone and buying things for Mummy which she may not like and give away to her servants. She wanted to breathe fresh air, live like her friends, be happy with small things in life. But she got only big things, big hurts;and she was supposed to fulfill the big hopes of her parents.

Like, on her last birthday--when her friends had arranged a tea-*samosa* party in the common room, she got a call from her Mummy.

"Darling, we are in the town today, for my speech in the Women's Welfare Association of Odisha tomorrow. Why not come with me, I can buy some birthday present for you, and have dinner with you".

"No Mummy, thanks. Actually my friends have organized a small get-together in the common room."

"Oh come on! Forget that. I am reaching in ten minutes, now get ready".

In the evening Suni came back to the hostel with a diamond ring, five designer suits, sandals, perfumes, and vacuum in her eyes.

Mummy sent her to the mall and then to the hostel with the driver with an order of what things to buy for her only daughter, because she met the local M.L.A.'s wife in the restaurant.

During long holidays, the hostel was closed, and the rooms were temporarily given away to the sportspersons coming for different championships from other states. So the hostellers had to vacate their rooms in a short notice, lock their cup-boards and suitcases. Suni would always leave the hostel on the last date, and come back on the re-opening day itself. Because there was nothing much to do at home. She never liked to join Mummy's parties where the gossip was about the recent fashion trends or the personal lives celebrities or about saris and the diamond jewelry those socialite ladies were wearing. She was fish out of water in Mummy's parties.

Some evenings when Papa was home, he would enquire a thing or two about her university and retire to his bed room. Mummy and Papa were like two parallel train lines, never to meet. But still they were together. She had never seen them talking, going out together, forget about ever holding hands or having any physical contact.

Was it *natural*?

Can two people share their lives for convenience? Papa had so many female friends; Mummy had many male friends, who would drop her home, drunk, at the wee hours of the morning. Papa had no objection.

Was it *natural*?

They believed in giving space to each other in their marriage. This concept of 'space' was beyond her comprehension. She felt trapped at home, and hostel was her rescue.

That was when she met Ragini. They had seen each other as two strangers, exchanged smiles in the dining room, but had never spoken to each other. Ragini was in the first year and Suni in the second year. Suni spent her spare time wandering through the market place. Making the rounds of shops had become her habit; she got a pleasure out of it. Hockey, chess, table-tennis and cricket were played at the university campus in the evenings. She never went to the university tournaments. She didn't even bother with the daily newspapers, although many of the girls in the hostel including Ragini were regular visitors of the central library for newspapers and journals. But the game she liked even more than cricket was to select a shopper from the crowd in front of her and follow her. Roaming through the supermarket was her favorite pastime hands down. She herself stocked everything in her room; it was more like a household. She restocked on salt, lentils, rice, coriander and chilies, even dry shrimps in her room, which she had seen in the servants' quarters at her place, and which she relished.

That day Suni was roaming in the basement and afterwards took the escalator to the main part of the store, to the cosmetics and soft toys section, where creams and rouge were displayed like magazines and lipsticks and artificial hair sets shimmered like wedding *dupattas* pinned behind the protective glass. The mannequins were inviting to the clothes section on the other side. Though Suni had never bought anything other them an Olay Total Effect, she liked walking through the cramped lanes of the mall, which was familiar to her in a way the rest of the town was not. She rushed her hands inside her coat pocket and found an election campaigning card with rich aroma and smiled to herself. Girls in the ladies hostel were least bothered about the qualities of a prospective candidate for the posts of President, Vice-President or General Secretary in the Students' Union annual elections. They would smell and check the quality of the perfumes they sprayed on their cards and decide whom to vote. They would accept a bunch of cards from each candidate with all politeness, as if they were actually going to campaign for them inside the hostel; and then push the cards into each corner of their suitcases and cup-boards so that the aroma would stay with their clothes for some time.

Whose card is this? Devendra Bishoy's? Suni smelled it and put it back in her pocket.

Then she spotted a girl from her hostel, Ragini, in

the super market. The hostel gates would close at 6 pm, so Ragini had to pick the 5.30 road-train, which comprised two buses attached by a thick iron chain, and the first bus would drag the second one, like a mother dragging her naughty child home in the evening to study; this created a funny sight. Ragini was in hurry, picking one thing from here and one thing there, lest she might miss the road-train. She saw a lovely snow-white teddy bear, and checked with the price tag. No, it was beyond her budget. She was paying the bills at the counter when she heard the horn of the university bus. Suni wanted to help her with her bags, but was hesitating. She might think what was she doing in the market if she had nothing to buy? At that moment, Ragini, while trying to hold her handbag and the shopping poly bags in the left hand and pay with the other hand, dropped all her bags. Suni had to join her.

"You let it be. I'll pick your things. You pay the bills and let's rush to the road-train".

"Oh thanks a ton!"

But they were late. That day the bus left sharp on time, unlike some other days, and they missed the bus. Ragini was very worried, as any first year student would.

"Not to worry, we can hire an auto. I am your senior, so it's my responsibility now," volunteered Suni.

"I am Ragini. You are?"

"Sunita, can call me Suni."

"Yeah, I have seen you in the T.V room and the dining hall. You are in the second year, right?"

"Right. Yes, here's a chocolate for you. I always wanted to give you one. Because I have heard that you were the university topper last year."

"Oh yeah, thanks again. Even I always wanted to speak to you. Everyone says you are so nice and helpful."

They had a nice chat. They spent 40 minutes in the auto talking about the university, their classes, departments, teachers, the road train and its antics, all fun.

The next day, they again met in the canteen and Ragini noticed that Suni was alone. Why was she always alone? She invited her to join her friends.

Ragini discovered that Suni was an introvert when it came to sharing her feelings with people. She seemed docile, feminine, quiet and lost in herself. That mysterious silence in her sad eyes got Ragini attracted towards Suni. They started keeping a trey for each other in the dining hall, whoever came first. They started sending a word for each other through the ward-boy if there was a good movie in Doordarshan on Sunday evenings. Suni gave Ragini a bottle of pickles which she had taken from the supermarket, because she saw that most of the days during the part-I university examination, Ragini would take her dinner to her room to eat after late night studies. But next morning the tray would be kept outside her room, the food only nibbled, may be because of the tasteless curries.

There was one thing common between them. Both of them were lovers of nature.

As soon as Ragini came from the department, she would toss a few morsels of food down her throat and hop away like a bird to join Suni in the garden. Suni had created a small kitchen garden beside her room where she had grown tomato, spinach and green chilly. Every weekend she used to cancel their meals in the mess and cook for both of them. She loved cooking. Suni would be busy with her gardening and Ragini followed her around and watched. During such hours Ragini's hands and feet constantly itched for some achievement in the garden. But she was good at nothing except studies. Suni would pluck tender tomatoes and chilies and tuck them away in her *dupatta*. Ragini walked behind her, ineptly plucking leaves and grass which she thrust into Suni's *dupatta*. Sometimes she would happen to touch a worm or a caterpillar; she would scream in horror and hold on to Suni and wipe her hands on her stomach. Suni remained untroubled, as if it was Ragini's wall, not her stomach.

Ragini again became the topper in the part-I, M.A. examination, and Suni passed out after the completion of her second year. The day she was given her degree, she filled the application form for another M.A. course, so that she won't have to leave the Mahendra Tanaya Ladies' Hostel. "Oh Suni-di, I was upset thinking that you will have to leave this place and go home. It's good that you are going to continue your stay here. See, I have no best friends except you."

"But you know, I have to vacate my room and share the common room with the M.Phil, Ph.D girls,"

"Why, you can shift to my room. Being the topper, I am given a bigger single room this year. You can stay with me."

Ragini's life became smooth with Suni's presence in her room. No more queuing up to bathe in the morning, no more worries, like "what shall I wear today?" She always forgot to press her clothes when there was power supply. Most of the times they had to manage with a generator which didn't support an electric iron box. So she had to wear her crushed cottons to the department. She was allergic to synthetics, she was a pure cotton person, and cotton needs ironing.

Now Suni would get up at 6 am, with the bell of Ragini's alarm clock, but had nothing to do throughout the mornings after watering the plants, bathing, storing water for Ragini, an elaborate *puja* and making two cups of coffee for both of them. So she would devote some mornings to arranging the wardrobes of herself and Ragini, some mornings for assembling Ragini's study table, book shelves, notes, Xerox copies, pens, table lamp. Sometimes she would take out Ragini's cotton dresses and sit down for pressing them with her iron box.

"Suni-di, please don't do that. Let it be. I'll do that in the afternoon after I come from the department."

"When? When there is a power cut? You better concentrate in your Elizabethan World Picture or whatever you are reading. I can do this."

"Why don't you, too, sit down with me and prepare notes on your Home Science papers?"

"No... please don't ask me to prepare notes. Moreover, what shall I do with a first class? I just need to pass. When you become an IAS officer, keep me as your Private Secretary, ok? You are such messy! Just look at your suitcase!"

She was right. Ragini's workload was so much. Apart from the P.G. part II course, she was also preparing for the UGC NET examination in English as well for the Civil Service examination. You never know. You have to keep all the options open.

She learnt from Suni, what it is called to share and care. Coming from a family where her widow mother was harsh on her children, and a sister married off too early and brother, a spoiled brat, she had no strong family ties. She felt Suni was her mother, sister, friend and her family. During the morning hours when Ragini studied, Suni made it a point to finish her work in the room in an hour and go to the roof top with her wool and needles. She was knitting a sweater for Ragini; she had only one sweater. Suni would never disturb her while she was studying; rather she would lock their door from outside so that her classmates could not disturb her. Raji, Anamika, Sagarika, Mona, Damayanti, Parul, they were staying in the same row. Since Ragini was the topper, they had a kind of wariness, and they would come to Ragini and Suni's room in some pretext, to ask for a book or some notes, to clear a doubt, and then waste her time with silly talk about boys in the department or about the boys' hostels.

One evening Surabhi came to Ragini's room to ask for some Glucon-C, which Suni used to store to give Ragini when she came tired from her classes. When Ragini opened the door with a book in her hand, all the girls in the row came to her room.

"Ay Ragini, don't you get bored reading all the time? You don't have a boyfriend either! Only mug up your books all the time. What a girl!"

"No *yaar*, I was just reading something. Come!"

"Give me your Glucon-C. I am feeling weak."

"Why, is your boyfriend troubling you too much?" said Sarita and all started laughing loudly.

Reshma, the girl in the next row, had a cousin staying in the boys' hostel. So she had most information about the boys,thus she was very much in demand.

"Reshma, what's news? You are not sharing with us!" Rakhi asked her.

"Hey, you know, my cousin was telling there are the photographs of Hollywood and Bollywood heroines in two pieces in their bathrooms. All those boys go there and kiss those photos, they do all bull-shit in front of the girls' photos, you know? They even do *'that'* for each other," she said with a giggle.

"Please don't discuss all that here. Suni-di will kill me," told Ragini; and Suni was already there on the door.

"You girls don't have any study hours? At least think of the university topper. She has to study!"

The crowd dispersed.

"What is this Suni-di? I could have told them politely."

"No Ragini, you don't know such girls. They disturb you during your study hours, and then they will study throughout the night. And why should she borrow Glucon-C from you every day? Can't she buy? But she can buy new *kurtas* every month, hmm?"

"No Suni-di. Her boyfriend gifts all that stuff."

"Ragini! Please don't tell me about boyfriends!" Then Suni got very upset.

"Why? Why do you hate boys so much?"

Suni hesitated. "Do you have some time? I can tell you tonight after dinner. The mess bell is on."

That night Ragini could know that Suni was a girl with a disturbed past. Beneath her serene temperament like the Pacific, there was a hidden storm.

Suni's Papa was one of the top class industrialists of the state. He was a successful businessman, and to be successful in business he had to make many compromises. One of those was, he had promised the local M.L.A. to marry off his daughter Sunita with his wayward son Samant, without her consent, even without consulting her. The boy was a rogue. He had somehow passed M.A. from some private university, and those days he was waiting to join politics in the next general elections. He had heard about Suni's charm from his family and friends, and was waiting for her during last summer vacation.

Suni went home in mid-May, again to join her classes on 1st July. Pretty long vacation, and she was thinking to kill time by growing a kitchen garden at home too. So the next morning she was instructing the peons to get plants, manure and seeds and clean that area. At that point, a rough, shabby looking man in his late thirties entered their gate with full authority, parked the car inside and got down.

"Salaam *sahib!*" the peons told.

Who was he? Suni had never seen him! And why was he coming forward to Suni with open arms?

"Hi sweety! You made me wait so much!" and he almost pulled her to his chest in front of the peons and the servants. All looked down. Suni was still in her night suit, looking fresh and tender.

She got hyper, lost control and pushed the man as hard as she could.

"Who the hell are you? And how dare you behave like this?"

"Oh, your father hasn't told you that I am your fiancé? What is this? Call that man, hey you!" He shouted at a servant.

Suni's father entered the scene.

"Ragini *beta*, he is Mr. Samant, the only son of our M.L.A. *sahib*. I have given him the word that you and Samant are going to tie the knot next year. If both of you agree, we can have the engagement done during your summer vacations. Also, both of you will get some time to spend together. Why don't you take her out today Samant *beta*?"

"Oh, sure uncle! She is such a beauty!"

"Papa! I need to talk to you, now!" and she rushed to her bed room.

"Samant, please be seated. I would be back in a minute. Actually I couldn't tell her about you. She came home only last night."

Samant waited, restlessly.

"Papa, please don't do this to me. I want to study for

some more years, am in no mood to marry now. I am not prepared. And this man is repulsive! I cannot marry him Papa!"

"What? How can you be so arrogant? He is the M.L.A.'s son, and your father's future as an industrialist depends on him to a great extent. See Suni, I didn't ask you to give me your decision. You have to marry Samant, whether you like it or not. And once you marry, you would start liking him."

"No Papa, I'll die if you force me. Please Papa!"

"Nothing doing. Just shut your mouth. He may hear it."

Samant overheard everything. Repulsive? Ok. He would make her jolly well understand what a repulsive man is like.

Next few days Samant tried to lure her into a relationship. But Suni was adamant. She had no desire to marry. And if at all she has to marry, the boy would be of her choice. She is also the daughter of a stubborn father-- so, *nothing doing*.

But destiny had something else in her store for Suni.

One night, the world turned upside down. There was an unlikely rain. Rain, more rain. The bird's eye view of the landscape gave the picture of the Jurassic age. The crystal clear water-world was flanked by forest black-waters. The landscape got dotted with skyscraper ghettos and massive pylon. It became a different world altogether with wild beasts around. Samant lifted Suni under the nose her father to an unknown farmhouse.

Under the fading glow of the skyline, water divided beneath the bridge. Colonies of red ants encroached the unclaimed lands, the deciduous trees elongated that night, created an unlikely rain in Suni's whole being. Her mind and body caught fire in the rain.

The next morning she came back to the hostel; but not a soul was there except the warden *didi* and her children in one room. Rest other rooms were allotted to the football tournament girls from Punjab Technical University. Suni lied to the warden that she had to come back early because her parents went to the U.S. for a month, and she wanted to come back for her studies. Warden *didi* liked Suni because she was a polite and nice girl. She allowed her to stay with her family for that month till the university reopened.

Suni hated men, all men, after that night.

"My god! Suni-di!! Oh my god! Oh my god! How can you bear so much pain in your heart and still smile? How can you be normal after all that happened? I will kill that bastard. How could your parents do that to you? Why didn't you inform the police? Oh my god! I am so disturbed! Such upset!" Ragini started sobbing.

"Don't cry Ragini dear! Informing the police was of no use. His father is the M.L.A., and my Papa supports his party. Anyway, the fortunate thing is that Samant found me frigid, cold,repulsive and unsuitable to be his wife. So he denied marrying me; Mummy called up the next week to scold me that I didn't cooperate with him."

Was it *natural*? Pre-marital sex is allowed for a man with any number of women, just to test who would be most suitable to keep him happy every night! If a woman adopts the same method?

Ragini's immature brain was failing to define what was natural and what was not. She was sobbing, was most restless that night.

"You know Suni-di, my elder sister is married to Rajib *bhai*, with whom she has three kids, has also a painful story. Why men are like this?"

Ragini told her Shalini didi's story at length. That

night they spent the whole night talking, wiping tears and comforting each other. Unlike other days when they used to sleep separately, one on the bed and the other on the floor, that night they slept on the same bed.

The shadows of the neem tree near their window were softly reflected on the bed, cold breeze blowing; like white foam, the moonlight was falling on the bed in patches. The night had calmed down after the perturbing storm of Suni's story. Ragini slowly put her head on her arm and stroked Suni's long, silken hair. The sides of her temples were wet with tears, she wiped that with her fingers.

"Oh Ragini! This is love! This is heaven my dear! This is pure love, true love, which you have given me, and I have given you. I love you so much my dear! I would not regret if I die after getting such pure love in my life." She went on whispering into her ears, and drew her close. She kissed her forehead softly, then touched her cheeks, chin, neck, nape, back, slowly she touched her everywhere, drew her so close that they were inhaling each other's breath. Ragini was breathless.

Suni took the initiative. She kissed Ragini's mouth, first softly, then she went on sucking her lips, for a long time, while her hands caressed her naval and her budding breasts. And she didn't know when her hands delved deep, deeper, deepest, into Ragini's being. Like two rivers, flowing into each other and merging in the sea, they merged through the body to the soul. Like soul mates.

Both of them felt at the moment-- that was so *natural*! Like leaves coming to a tree, like flowers blooming in spring or migrating birds reaching their destination every winter, without fail.

Life was good, after all. This was not forbidden love, no.

Next morning Ragini was somewhat feeling guilty. But Suni showed no such sign. It was like every other day. Bathing, storing water, cooking for both of them as the mess was closed for the day; in fact Suni was very particular that Ragini should by no means feel disturbed.

'You sleep for an hour now. I am going upstairs. I shall open the door at 10 am, you have your breakfast, then study, ok?" She kissed her cheek and went out. Ragini felt uneasy. How can she behave so normal after all that? Was she mad? Ragini was confused.

But Suni was not. As if she always knew it. Like Sappho, she knew that she would get her consolation, comfort and stay in a woman, never a man. She was made like that. She loved all softer emotions in life, which she could expect only from a woman, not a man. Precisely, from Ragini.

Ragini was her alter-ego. She was smart, slim, intelligent, outspoken, determined, ambitious, dedicated, childlike, immature, stylish, dependent on her, and at the same time an independent, modern, twenty-first century woman with a nonchalant attitude. Which Suni always wanted to be. But she was never made like that. She could never be that devil-may-care type.

So what? Ragini's success was no less her success! Ragini's achievements were no less than her own! Life went on. Ragini and Suni, both were comfortable now. They cared, shared, loved.

One day the seniors in the hostel ordered some DVDs in the T.V. room to have fun after Ganesh Puja. One of the movies they watched was Dipa Mehta's *Fire.*

All the girls giggled. Oh shit! Oh god! What's going on? What are these two women doing? Is that possible? They have a serious problem.

Ragini prompted, "why not? Can't you see what kinds of men they have in their lives? How can a woman love a man from whom she doesn't get care, respect, comfort or emotional love? Is love all about having sex with a man? You all are so educated. How can't you realize that love is a very soft emotion, which a woman can share only with a person who needs her emotionally, not just physically? Physical closeness is another way of showing one's care and concern for the person whom one loves, be it a man,a woman or even nature. What is so unnatural about it? Being a 'homo' or a 'hetero' is not the setback in one's character. There is a problem with us if we are pervert, indecent, dishonest, violent, cheat or evil. But how can someone's different sexual preference be a problem to us? Why are we dramatizing our reaction to someone's alternative sexuality? If one is sincere and honest, what is the problem? Times are changing, so why not change our mindsets? The thought of homosexuality creeps you out? Fine. Who is asking you to be one yourself? But how does that give you the right to be hyper-critical or mock someone who is a lesbian or a gay? At least stop judging people for feelings they have no control over! Nature has made them so, after all."

What???

All the girls exchanged a meaningful glance with a suppressed smile.

After that day, whenever the gossip mongers would see Suni and Ragini together, there would be some whisper and then some giggle.

But who cares? Where there are bigger things to care, one doesn't get time to care about petty things like what people are gossiping about.

Ragini's part II examination was on, and she had to

study very hard. Suni had to take extra care that she was not disturbed by anyone.

"Suni-di, thank you so much, if I am doing well in my studies, the credit goes to you."

"Hm......keep your flattery to yourself. I am sure you want an excuse to go out with your friends for a party. Ok, go, but come back by 6.00 pm and sit down to study."

What is a mother like? Is she like Suni-di?

"What would you do alone? Why don't you come along?"

"Oh no, you all are a big group-eight boys and seven girls. G-seven, that's what you call yourselves, no? I can't stand those boys."

"What's wrong with them? They are so respectful towards you." Ragini insisted, but Suni never went out with them.

"Hey Ragini! What's the problem of that roommate of yours? She is weird *yaar*!" Reshma would say.

"Come on, she asked you that day to study during the study hours, so you are against her. But you might know that she is the darling of everyone in the hostel, including the Warden."

"Oh...but she is your darling, for sure. We wonder, would you love your husband someday as much as you love her?"

"You guys have no other topic than boyfriends, husbands? That's why Suni-di scolds me when I come out with you. She is right."

All those girls thought she had airs. Attitude.

Has true-love ever been well accepted, anyway?

Ragini's second year exams got over, and she came out with flying colours, as expected. By that time Suni had completed the first year of her double M.A. course. All first year girls of the hostel decided to throw a farewell party for the out-going M.A. students in Sonepur, a beautiful beach a few kilometers away from the university.

It was great fun. Throughout the day Ragini and her friends along with the junior girls jumped in the beach, got wet and wild, danced, sang, had sea food in the restaurant. Suni was watching from a distance. She never liked such wild fun. Even if she was junior now by capacity, but she was elder to all of them, and she liked to maintain that. She sat with the Warden and helped the cook, Bhagban bhaina, instead. And thought tomorrow she would fry some dry fish for Ragini. She loves dry shrimps.

Not that Suni was a morose and serious girl all the time. She also knew that Ragini was fun-loving, so she had to remain happy. On the way to Sonepur, the girls got down at four o'clock in the morning to freshen up near a village. Suni took them to a clean place, and asked them to relieve themselves when it was near dark. The girls were happy that before the day break at least they would be fresh. After the job was over, they went to a bore- well nearby and bathed or semi-bathed and changed into fresh clothes. While coming back to the bus, they discovered that the clean place where they had relieved themselves was actually someone's large backyard, smeared with cow dung water the previous evening, may be for some function.

"Run! Fast!"

They ran and ran up to the bus and once inside it they were laughing all the while till they reached the picnic spit, to the surprise of the Warden and other staff of the hostel.

Suni knew that Ragini was a sea-food person. While roaming in Sonepur, she discovered good crabs somewhere. Then she asked Bhagwan Bhaina if he would allow her to cook in the hostel mess the next day, just for an hour. He agreed, but it had to be done at 6 am, when nobody would be around. Suni bought two kilos of crab, alive, and hid them in a bucket and kept it in a corner inside the bus. Before lunch, some girls came to the bus to collect snacks from their bags, and yelled. All the crabs had come out of the bucket and were roaming inside the bus, like dinosaurs, creating a weird scene. The cooks and others rushed to discover that scene, but Bhagwan *Bhaina* never disclosed who had kept them there. Suni was smiling to herself, Ragini could see.

"Suni-di, you did it for me, right? God! Imagine! You want to cook crab in the hostel for me? Let's ask the warden to remove Bhagwan *Bhaina*, and you be our new cook, ok?" she whispered.

Suni pressed her palm, to keep quiet.

After lunch the girls requested the warden that they would like to spend that night in the beach and stay in some lodge at their own expense and then go back to the hostel the next morning. So the warden also had to book a room for herself and her kids to be with the girls.

They got two dormitory kinds of halls, where there were twenty beds in each hall, and they were sixty girls. Still, the girls agreed that they can share the beds, adjust, but stay back in Sonepur that night and enjoy the night sky in sea beach.

In the night, the sea was in her wild, wilder, wildest best. The silent, white, gloomy monsoon village light and the whimpering dusk did their bit to sway the girls even more. The unending wind intoxicated the sky; the earth bloomed in the embrace of the sea. Suni was whispering alone, "oh sea! Twist my life, release me from my mind's clasp... let this moment be still, unmoving. What shall I do after Ragini, my little love, leaves this place next week? Embrace my soul, yearning. You are like the fertile creation, green and fresh like the mustard fields, wet and overflowing like a river, like shimmering rhythm. You come and grow in my restive soul, drown me in your blue eyes, mix my breath with your stormy breath. You are the music of creativity; let me bloom in your embrace. I have nowhere to go, not to the house of Mummy and Papa, and I can't follow Ragini anymore. She has her career, her future. Oh sea...you are my only rescue now...."

Slowly she got up from her place and started walking towards the wild waves. She had almost lost consciousness. The girls were busy dancing around the camp-fire in the beach...

"Aap jeise koi meri zindegi me aaye-- toh baat ban jaye... han...han...baat ban jaye!"

"Sunita, what are you doing? Oh someone help! Help!" The Warden shouted. Ragini and her friends got startled. What happened? It was dark everywhere except the light of the fire and a crescent moon.

The fishermen, three of them, jumped into water and dragged Suni's drowning, unconscious body from water.

The night was quiet, silent like death, in the dormitory. Everyone was upset, whispering in a suppressed voice, scolding the kill-joy.

"She has always been like this. Weird! A big show off!"

"She has attention problem, you see!"

"Don't know how our poor Ragini tolerates such a creeper."

It was 2 pm now. Everyone went to sleep in the dormitory after twelve o'clock, and the lights were off. Suni was given food and some sedative; Ragini gave her a piece of her mind, and asked her to sleep beside her. She was extremely worried. God! What if something would have happened? Now who is going to look after this girl after she leaves the hostel? She has her Civil Services Prelims next month, and then the UGC NET exam. She has to go home and prepare. They have to vacate their rooms tomorrow and shift to the common room till they get the hostel and university clearance. The girls were in a mixed mood, looking forward to the future. Someone was going to join some job and someone going to marry. Their public life starts from the coming week. Student career is over, so are all these irresponsible, funny, happy days. They were apprehensive, yet happy in a way. Exchanging addresses, phone numbers, e-mails, inviting each other for their marriages in near future.

Life was going to take a new shape.

Ragini had to qualify either the civil services or the research fellowship examinations. Otherwise Maa would be after her life to marry, like Shalini, and settle down. No, she was not going to marry. She couldn't think of sharing her life with someone like Rajib *bhai* or that useless Samant .

Ragini tried her best to put Suni to sleep by patting on her head. She was on sedatives, so she must sleep. But Suni was not getting sleep, she was shivering all over. Ragini comforted her, put Suni's head on her chest and caressed her hair, her eye-brows, and whispered, "Sleep...sleep... now sleep..."

At 3 am., Reshma woke up by listening to some strange sound from the bed beside hers, where Ragini and Suni were asleep. It was a scary echoing sound, as if a wild beast was gorging on some raw flesh and licking, relishing it. It was a sound she had never ever heard, never ever imagined in the weirdest of her dreams.

She got up with a start and imagined, perhaps some

sea creature had entered the dormitory, coming from the sea waves, and was creating this noise, eating flesh. Perhaps the crabs had come back from the sea where they were thrown out of the bus in the morning. "Raji, Rita, get up and switch on the lights.... Please!" she whispered.

The lights were on. All lights from all directions.

Two girls, so close to each other, breathing through the nude bodies of each other, delving and drinking deep into each other!

Soul to soul.

Heart to heart.

Body to body.

Living only in that moment. As if rest other moments didn't exist. Not breathing when not together.

So much comfort!

Such warmth!

Such togetherness! Such closeness!

That was the last time when they lived. After that, limpness oozed out of their eyes, they never sobbed, cried,laughed or smiled. There was no wetness in the soil, no shower of light in the mornings. Only there was a rotten, musty, stinking wretched feeling as if they were in a bottomless pit.

Ragini left the hostel the next morning, so did Suni.

They were asked to leave, in fact.

Such moral degradation! Such violation of the laws of nature! Other girls may get misguided. Unpardonable! Most unnatural!!

Their parents were informed telephonically by the warden. Mummy and Papa were furious. Ragini's Maa couldn't understand a word of it—lesbianism !!What is that?

Both the girls were packed off; all clearances were

given to them in an hour. No one spoke to them; they didn't speak to each other either.

A silent good-bye. The last good-bye. May be, next birth, if there is any.

Suni gave her a gift, which she was planning to give her the next week, with a proper farewell.

Ragini, sitting in the train, opened the packet in tearful eyes. It was the same snow white teddy bear that she had seen in the supermarket last year, but couldn't buy it. The day she had met Suni for the first time.

Suni was not articulate like Ragini. She had only written on the teddy, "It's me....!"

Outside, there was a storm. Was the train moving very fast? The storm grew giddy, playing with Ragini's unkempt hair, yet there was a cemetery like silence inside.

She was quietly watching the shadow of the train on one side of it. And her own shadow.

The shadow of a shadow.

Her life's stress was caught up in the mind-web of her own. She just remembered two lines by her favorite poet,

"Ecstasy is rare in this living,
Rare is it in the heart's beating..."

■

That Elusive Orgasm

An elusive orgasm, that was indefinable, subtle, intangible, indescribable, fulfilling, soul-searching. She wanted to experience that every single time she had those rare intimacies with her husband. But she was far from getting that—always. Because two creepy hands, a stringent body and some distant fishy odors crawled into her cataleptic and subconscious mind during those moments.

Can one even blame her for thinking about those while having sex with her husband? I suppose one cannot, actually.

Jhumpa Chatterjee was a chubby cute little girl, all of sixteen, when Mai(her mother) got into the wheel chair due to paralysis of her lower limbs. Babai(Jhumpa's father) was in his late thirties, and he had to bear the grunt of serving an ailing wife and looking after a teenage daughter in the small town, Sonagachi, a few kilometers away from Kolkata.

Sonagachi was a place close to nature, because it was essentially a forest, with tall trees around. It was so untouched by city life that even the roads here were dirt tracks, instead of proper paved ones. The area was inhabited by jackals, spotted deer, elephant, foxes, and many kinds of colourful birds, including parrots, kingfishers, ducks and woodpeckers. This was also the largest red-light area in Asia.

In Bengali, *Sona Gachi* means 'Tree of Gold'. According to some folklore, during the early days of Calcutta, the area was the run of a notorious dacoit named Sanaullah, who lived with his mother. On his death, the grief-stricken woman heard a voice coming from their hut, saying, 'Mother, don't cry. I have become a Gazi', and thus the legend of Sona Gazi came into existence. The mother constructed a mosque in remembrance of her son, although it fell into poor condition within no time. Then Sona Gazi was transformed into Sonagachi.

The documentary *Born into Brothels:Calcutta's Red Light Kids* won the Oscar for best documentary award in 2005. It illustrated the lives of children born to prostitutes in Sonagachi. *Born into Brothels* talked beyond the well-known prostitute-clogged streets and about the homes of the children who lived in the foulest place. A ten-year-old boy Avijit's natural stimulating compositions through the lens got him an invitation to the World Press Photo Foundation in Amsterdam, and he was from Sonagachi.

But Jhumpa was far from all those things happening around her, being dedicated to her preparations for the NEET for Medical Science. All she wanted was--to become a doctor. When did Mai's partial physical paralysis become a metaphorical paralysis for Jhumpa's life, even Jhumpa couldn't realize. Everything happened so fast, so erratic.

At that point of time, Jhumpa was good friends with Grace and me. Jhumpa and me were from Hindu/Brahmin families and Grace was a steadfast Christian. We used to go to school together, play and study together, and my late father and Grace's father were school teachers in Sonagachi.

One day Jhumpa stopped coming to school, and bizarrely, she got completely cut off from us. Her Babai and Mai didn't even allow us to meet her. There was no Internet, no Whatsapp or Facebook when we were kids. Grace was smarter than me, any given day, thus she tried to get in touch with Jhumpa by hook or crook. To my dismay, my father got a transfer from that town and I had to leave that school, consequently, Grace, Jhumpa and everyone else.

For the first few months, I wrote letters to Grace, asking after Jhumpa. But there was no news of her, ever. And no news was no good news!

We grew up. With time, my childhood friends became distant memories, though Jhumpa remained a persistent ache in the secret chamber of my heart. I left India with a fellowship, did my PhD in America and came back to join as a Professor in an Indian university in the capital. In 2020, I visited Kerala to meet Grace, my childhood best buddy, after having met her once again on Facebook. Grace had left Sonagachi after I left and she had settled down in Kochi. Our happiness knew no bounds. Finding Grace was like reviving some lost paragon, a hidden treasure. We met like wild streams in a rain forest.

That summer vacation was so full of excitement, enthusiasm, love, togetherness, happiness and then, sudden heartbreak!

On the very first day of our meeting, I asked Grace if she knew the whereabouts of Jhumpa. Grace avoided the question and took me to show her huge farmhouse where she did organic farming. Her two sons got along well with my son, and we became too busy handling the three naughty boys while we had so much to catch up after years of separation.

After a week, one early morning I heard Grace talking over phone in a suppressed voice. She was whispering, "Jhumpa, have you lost your mind? Once again you are going to that hell! If you do it, this time I am not going to protect you, especially when Ninny is here after years. The poor girl has been asking after you and I am avoiding. She can't handle this, you know she is hypersensitive."

Next moment, I was face to face with Grace, with legitimate questions about Jhumpa and her whereabouts. Grace, of course, couldn't avoid those any further.

***

In 2005 after I left Sonagachi, Grace became lonelier than ever as Jhumpa too had stopped coming to the school. She had joined some correspondence course to complete her education from home. Grace's father sent her to a hostel in Kerala to do her college and university education, and she too fell out of touch with Jhumpa. But in 2008 when she went to Sonagachi to spend the summer vacation with her parents, she got to know that Jhumpa's parents had been to their village for a month or two to perform the death rituals of their parents or in-laws. Jhumpa was alone with the maid, who was strictly instructed not to let her go out. That is when Grace discreetly got into her house with her cousins, Remchaso, Alwin and Thomas, all of whom were officers in the local church and were doing very well. To her utter disappointment, she found Jhumpa in a rundown, ramshackle state. She looked like a full grown-up woman, eyes lost in thoughts, nothing like a girl of eighteen or nineteen. Her demeanour disturbed Grace. She bribed the maid handsomely and took Jhumpa out of her house-arrest.

Jhumpa wasn't comfortable in the streets, after almost three years she had come out. Grace and her brothers made her comfortable, offered her nice delicacies in a restaurant, did some shopping with her, and then took her to the church for a prayer. Jhumpa was happy; she was astonished to see the freedom of people there. She couldn't understand the freedom of speech, being a caged bird. There was this Confession Box in a corner where everyone was talking their heart out, with probably no one listening to the conversation between the person and the God that s/he believed. After everyone had finished their prayers and confession, after the Carols and the chants had calmed Jhumpa, she agreed to go to the Confession Box and have a chat with her personal God, if there was any.

Grace confessed to me that she had inconspicuously fitted a recorder there with the help of her brothers. And then the moment of epiphany for us, with what Jhumpa spoke there. It was like a bombshell, it was devastating like a lightning bolt.

Jhumpa spoke, rather she keened her heart out in the Confession Box, "Oh Lord of this beautiful, tranquil place, I want to share my story with you here. I am confused, I don't see a road ahead of this tunnel. When I was in class XI, Mai was in the wheel chair and my Babai had to work whole day. My parents were the ardent devotees of some ferocious looking Goddess, whose temple was in the basement of our house. Babai performed pujas there for hours every day. They did *Kumari Puja* and *Kumari Sadhna*. Babai and Mai told me, I was the offering/ *prasada* of the Goddess and I was a sacred girl. That is why they stopped my going to the school, and that night Babai did an exclusive puja for me when Mai was chanting the *mantra*. Once I was offered as *prasada* to the Goddess, Babai took me to the bathroom to cleanse me of the worldly sins. He gave me a bath in his own hands, like never before. It was uneasy in the beginning, but he explained that he was the devotee/*sahdak* of the Goddess and I was the *prasada*, so I need not feel shy and should allow him to do it, by just closing my eyes in surrender to the Goddess.I did as Babai instructed, guided. Mai was asleep in her room. Babai bathed me, touched my breasts and genitals tenderly, and then he vigorously rushed into me when I bled so much. It pained me, it was very hurtful. I cried, Babai consoled me, put me in his arms and put me to sleep after the act. Since that night, every night he follows the ritual of bathing me, his *prasada*, and repeats everything. And I don't mind it anymore. I like whatever he does to my body; in fact these days I don't get a sleep unless Babai does it and puts me to sleep. But what I don't like in here is—Babai and Mai don't allow me to talk to anyone, not even the maid. I am not allowed to go out; I miss my friends, I miss my school. I am no longer preparing for the medical entrance. All those dreams I had are actually forgotten. Today I am relieved after confessing before you, whoever you are. Grace told me that if we confess before you, our worries come to an end. Oh tranquil god, please tell me, am I going to have a secluded, secret, clandestine existence for rest of my life? Shall I never experience freedom like Grace and others out there?"

Jhumpa came out with tears in her eyes; Grace, Remchaso, Alwin and Thomas were burning with anger to hear this incest story of disgrace and shame. It was apparent that the unending consensual incest had set an increasingly ugly chain of events in motion in the life of an innocent girl. The worst part was, she didn't consider this as unusual, obnoxious, objectionable. She was too tender a girl when she was introduced to this underground world of aenigmas.

Grace, Remchaso, Alwin and Thomas met the church authorities and devised a plan to salvage the ill-fated girl. Luck was in their side as Jhumpa's parents were in their village for two months. Grace counselled Jhumpa day and night about normal man-woman relationship as well as father-daughter relationship. Jhumpa realized that she was being trapped into a bottomless pit and only Grace could take her out of it. Jhumpa dreamt of becoming a nurse, if not a doctor. She cooperated, and within a month she was baptized to Christian faith. Her visa was applied as an independent adult with special recommendation of the church that she was keen on going to the US along with three other staff nurses from the church to serve underprivileged children in America, and it was granted. She flew three days before her parents returned.

Babai was mad at the maid and of course he threatened Grace to file a complaint. Grace was ready with the audio recording, on the basis of which the man would have lost his job on the charge of promiscuity with his daughter and prolonged child abuse. His wife asked him to keep quiet for sometime as she didn't want to lose her caregiver.

Jhumpa apparently had a good life in America. She did her Bachelor of Science in Nursing there and dedicated her days to social service.

Anyway, her nights were difficult. She thought about the serpentine creeping of two male hands on her body, bathing her, interleaving her contours with restless respite.

She met Abraham, her colleague, who seemed to be attracted to her. He befriended her, told about his orphanage in Kerala, India, where he got education and support as to come to the US. He was nice and kind to her; he had some idea about her turbulent past, though he didn't know exactly what was that. He believed that time is the greatest healer, and it must have healed Jhumpa by now, given the kind and serene persona that she had.

In due course, he proposed her and they got married.

Grace was very happy with the turn of events in Jhumpa's life. She was relieved that she could rescue a girl and facilitated her to lead a good life. She called Jhumpa's Babai and shared this news; he was very angry and sounded helpless. He cursed Grace over phone, Grace smiled triumphant.

But things were not as simple.

Initially Abraham thought that Jhumpa was shy and was an introvert. Thus he waited patiently for the consummation of their marriage. But Jhumpa locked her room every night after dinner, touched herself passionately, whispering something, muttering to herself. Her body was not prepared to accept the touch of any other male. Her body had its own chemistry. Abraham couldn't understand this. But he knew that Jhumpa didn't like physical closeness with him. His only desire was to give her an orgasm, a massive, fulfilling one, that is. He cuddled her, did the foreplay with care and love, tried to take her to that trance where the woman desires her man—but everything failed.

Not that, Jhumpa complained when Abraham failed and gave up. She caressed his head for a few minutes, put him to a restless sleep, and remained awake herself. During those nights, Abraham noticed that Jhumpa looked at the ceiling nightlong, and when she fell asleep, two dry tear drops would be lingering on her cheeks or eyelids.She was insomniac, nonchalant, monotonous.

When Abraham complained over phone, Grace asked him to wait patiently, though she never narrated the long history of Jhumpa, having a full-fledged, compulsive, obsessive sexual relationship with her father. She couldn't gather her courage to narrate this to a husband who dearly loved his wife.

Abraham tried to ask Jhumpa the reason behind her

aversion to him. Jhumpa only cried; she could never tell him the reason, because she too loved him. He was her friend and companion, but her body couldn't accept his touch. There were a couple of times when Jhumpa quietly lied down beside Abraham, eyes tightly closed, when he had sex with her cold body. Abraham hated this—it was like necrophilia. And then, he completely stopped going near her. They just lived in one house like two guests, who had nothing to do with each other. He stopped asking her questions. Some nights, even he stopped coming home.

Jhumpa felt lost, once again. Her existential, empirical questions about life troubled her. She wanted a break and called Grace if she could come to her place, spend a few days with her. Grace asked her to work on her marriage instead and spend quality time with Abraham. Then Jhumpa threatened her, "If you are not willing to keep me for a few days with you, I would rather go to Babai's place and resolve with him."

That was when I caught Grace reprimanding her over phone early morning.

I was petrified, shocked with this unwarranted story of my long-lost friend. I probed into our past and thought about the unfair, raw deal life had done with her. Was her Babai a paedophile? A narcissist? Womanizer? Sick man? Did his wife's inability to have an intimate relationship give him the freedom to abuse his girl child and ruin her life? Was her Mai so selfish that in order to shield her future with her 'provider' and caretaker, she became a party to the vicious plan of her husband and sacrificed her own daughter's life? I somehow blamed myself for leaving Sonagachi when Jhumpa needed her friends. I told Grace, "Let us save this girl, Grace! We cannot sulk now, especially when she is in grief. She needs us."

Next morning, Jhumpa was with us in Kerala. At first, she didn't talk much, we just had casual exchanges. Grace told her that I knew it all. Jhumpa wasn't very comfortable with this. I tried to make her easy and diverted the topic to tourism, politics, food, fabrics, shopping, friends, anything in general. I invited her to spend a few days with me in Delhi. Our children played with her. Jhumpa tried to cooperate, but her eyes were always lost in the horizon. When we went out on long drives, Grace and I sat in the front and Jhumpa sat on the back seat with children. I looked at her discreetly in the rear-view mirror, she tried to smile, but her eyes were numb and she had a poker face when she was absentminded. Anyway, she did cooperate when we cheered her up. She called Abraham without fail, twice a day. She checked mails and did her office work dispassionately.

One night, Jhumpa shocked us by sleeping nude, very casually, on the couch. Grace reprimanded her. "Don't you think it is disgraceful, Jhumpa?"

"Come on Grace, what is there in the body! It's just a concealment for the soul. And I am soul-dead since my childhood. I have been sleeping like this since my sixteenth year, and I don't find anything wrong with this. Why do we have such inhibitions about the body?"

Grace, anyway, threw a blanket over her fair, curvy, nude body and we went to the children's room to sleep.

We didn't judge her. She was a survivor; and we were glad that she had started talking.

After a couple of days, we received a call from Jhumpa's Babai, telling her, since she was in India, she must visit her Mai, who was, apparently, counting her last breaths.

Babai always knew the whereabouts of Jhumpa.

Despite our protests, Jhumpa went to Sonagachi. Mai was in a bad shape, Babai looked fine, in his fifties.

Babai didn't exchange a word with Jhumpa; they had met after a decade or more. He had no complaints; he was calm. He was busy looking after his sinking wife, taking care of Jhumpa's food and comfortable stay. Jhumpa's room in the first floor was neatly done even after her long absence.

She felt the unmistakable presence of someone in her room even when she was alone there.

Was it the calm before the storm!! Jhumpa wondered.

When Grace called her during lunch, we overheard her father's voice, asking her to take a second helping of the fish curry and not eat like an American. Her mother was perhaps asking her to eat what her Babai offered. The thought of what might be happening there sent us shivers down our spines.

"Grace, we must call her frequently tonight and ask her to come back tomorrow itself. It was such a bad idea to allow her to go there in the first place."

Grace agreed to my idea.

I asked Grace, what exactly was the problem between Abraham and Jhumpa, now that Babai was not in her life and the couple loved, at least liked, each other. Grace told me, "Jhumpa had never had an orgasm with Abraham, maybe because the childhood sexual abuse was still traumatic for her."

I suspected that simplistic approach, because Abraham seemed to be a very matured person, with lot of patience, not to coerce or frighten Jhumpa.

I doubted something else, very complex, encrusted and layered that I got a hint of, specifically from the salamander appearance of Jhumpa last few days.

"But tell me Grace, why should an orgasm be so elusive for a healthy female when she has the sexual act with a healthy male!" I tried to sound clinical.

"Foreplay, cunnilingus and all such things are very seminal to achieve an orgasm, but it's not that simple. Because for most women, an orgasm is a matter of the heart and mind rather than the body. Perhaps Jhumpa's mind is not able to concentrate when she is with Abraham."

"There you go Grace! Do you think her mind and heart are still there with her Babai? Was her childhood abuse a guilt-ridden pleasure for her? I am just thinking aloud Grace."

"What nonsense! Too much reading has made you so complex Ninny! You like to problematize everything!"

I kept quiet, kept thinking.

As decided, we started calling Jhumpa every fifteen minutes form 7 pm. Whatsapp video calls.

Jhumpa knew the purpose, and she was agreeable with us. From 7pm to 9pm she was with her Mai downstairs, and then she went to her room. We talked casually, inquired about her mother's health, but everyone was tight-lipped about her father. She wanted to sleep at 10 pm, and we three were talking about her return tickets for the US, and a short trip to Shillong with children before the vacations for all of us would end.

Jhumpa was startled by a suppressed, surreptitious knock at her door at 10.10pm. We had anticipated it.

We almost knew it.

"Jhumpa!!! Just shout at him that if he continues to knock your door, you'll call the neighbours from the balcony. You'll call the police. Don't just open the door, and keep the video call on. Got my point?" Grace yelled at the peak of her voice.

I was shaken, bewildered, scared, my BP went low, mouth was dry, and I was crying. I couldn't talk.

"Jhumpa, you have to survive the night. You have to withstand. Be strong, ok? You are a true devotee of our Lord, and a faithful wife to your husband. You are a chaste, upright, virtuous woman. Don't forget that." Grace kept on talking aloud.

Jhumpa's face looked different, she didn't respond to Grace.

We looked on. My tears rolled. I was trembling. Grace was terribly mad at her.

Jhumpa whispered, "No Babai, please, please go! Don't do this to me!"

"Open the door Jhumpa, my love. I am here, for you. I'll take care of you, I'll soothe, pacify, mollify, comfort your sad body. You are my *prasada*, how can you forget that? You were born only for a *devotee* like me. I won't hurt you. I will put you to sleep. You look so tired, you haven't slept since ages."

Jhumpa looked pale. Dazed. Benumbed. Emotionless. Motionless. Weary.

Before going towards the door, she disconnected our call and switched off her phone.

That night, Jhumpa slept peacefully. We knew it. Next morning, I had a lump in my throat.

The Juvenile Love Letter

It's my life-time regret that I could never read my juvenile love letter, delivered to me on my fifteenth year, which was as thick as at least my Ph.D thesis--the meaning of which I understood after I actually submitted my Ph.D thesis years later.

Life had got over me, by then.

Did I hate that letter? Did I loathe the touch and feel of that letter? Honestly, no.

What was there in the letter that I faced that with such bewilderment, looked around like a mirror, and in evanescence it even surpassed the bubbles that figure on water?

This story may sound somewhat ornate, a make-believe one, or almost a lie. But it's true, like the rain drops or the moonlit nights.

At that time my world was just a child's play. I was never torn between faith and infidelity, the existence of that letter never mesmerized me; yet I was caught, trapped in fancy's snare.

Ever since Samal Sir handed over that book to me, (yes, actually I thought that it was a book!) the meaning of all other books and brooks were laid bare. Since then, the cuckoo has stopped singing songs of love and happiness in spring. All other birds have been bearing with storms, rains, heat and cold patiently in the seasons of pain, waiting for spring when the cuckoo will sing them the songs of love and happiness again.

But since then, the earth has seen only five seasons, sans the spring season.

Thirteen is always my number, be it good or bad. I saw him, I mean Samal sir, when I was thirteen, in class IX in our girl's high school. Our batch was the smartest batch, as the teachers would say. We were happy-go-lucky kind of girls, always doing *masti*; of course in studies, and in extra-curriculars, we were the best, making our teachers proud whenever there was an inter-school competition. I had a special privilege in the school, first, for being the literary champion of the school, second, for being the daughter of one of the teachers.

I was in section-A, but most of my friends were in section-B. My best buddy Saloni was also there in section-B. Anyway, at that point, we were not best friends, we were only formal friends, even though we used to be best friends during our lower and upper primary classes. When we were in the primary school, we were deeply attached. The moment we reached the school, we would go behind the bush and exchange our frocks for the day. How I loved her sweat-smelling frocks, which were much better than mine in texture and quality! She was from a rich family, her father could afford good frocks for her. Mine were always those cotton frocks made of floral-patterned, bold coloured clothes, with no embroidery, no frills and no lace. My mother used to buy an entire rim of cloth from Sahoo Vanijya Pratisthan on a wholesale rate, and frocks were stitched for us sisters in similar pattern with the same clothes. If any cloth was left over, it could very well serve the purpose of being a blouse for Maa or hankies for Baba. We never liked it. Anyway, nobody laughed at us as most families followed the same. Saloni loved my frocks. We would wipe our noses and sweat in each other's frocks throughout the day, and during the last period, again go behind the bush and change, wear our own frocks before going home. Things changed once we came to the high school. Our sections were different, so was the friend circle. Initially we both shed tears, but later on her *makara* (a way of addressing the best friend) and other friends convinced her that I was arrogant since I stood first; and since my Maa was a teacher in the high school, hence I had every reason to be proud.

Anyway, years later, during our graduation, again Saloni and I became best friends, friends for life.

Back to high school, I was a cool kid, completely tomboyish, *bindass*. I lived life with a careless care in the sense that I was casual about everything else except academics. I could never tolerate if anyone got even half a mark more than me. I was certainly not jealous, but my revenge was in getting at least ten marks more than that person in the next examination. Ours was almost a joint family, always relatives or friends of my parents coming home at the wrong time. Sometimes even Baba would forget which girl was in which class, perhaps due to over-population; and of course he had a busy schedule being the only man in the household.

In class IX, a new girl came to our school from Bhubaneswar. Sonalika Das. The only daughter of the Branch Manager of State Bank of India. She was fashionable, she spoke with an accent, and became the darling of the school within no time. Even my childhood friend Saloni left no stone unturned to be in her good books.

Before that, my friends in section-A, like Nirmalaa,

Gita, Saraswati, Tripti and everyone else used to pamper me. I helped them with studies, and in return I was bribed with pickles, sweets, berries and delicacies from their homes. Since Sonalika came, she became the only attraction, everybody tried their best to please her, be her close friend. Nirmalaa went to the extent of crying to draw her attention, and got bag full of berries, chocolates and pickles for her. Suddenly I became secondary for them, even though Sonalika herself had respect for me . Because she was told about my accomplishments by her parents and the principal of the school.

The worst thing had to happen. She managed to get one percent more than me in the half-yearly examination since she had opted for Sanskrit as an optional subject which is a mark-fetching subject. I went under depression for a week , shut myself in the small room in my terrace, and went on crying. Maa was not upset about it since both I and Sonalika were selected to appear in the forthcoming National Talent Search examination to be conducted after four months, covering the syllabi of both IX and X classes. Maa knew that I was self-motivated; after crying for a few days, I would come forward and study. During such moments, she rather told my sisters and father not to interfere with the stubborn girl. I never liked anyone nagging with me or being questioned. Exactly that's what happened. I didn't take a moment's rest till I got two percents more than Sonalika in the next examination. Anyway, she left our school because her father got a transfer to Cuttack. Till today I keep searching for her on the Facebook, not to take any revenge, of course. Just to see how she is placed in life now, the girl who defeated me at one point in life, even though momentarily. Last year when

Saloni's sister Mama told me over phone that Sonalika has been a housewife, perhaps I was secretly pleased. Human nature, after all.

Back in the school, the National Talent Search (NTS) examination in class IX was going to cover the syllabus of even class X ! My parents, as a policy, never sent us out for private tuitions, because they were teachers. That is a separate issue that they never ever helped us with studies at home. I was worried, how to cover so much within such less time, and which chapters were important since there was no guidance. I was good at literature and social sciences, but science was my trigger. We didn't have a trained science teacher in the school; Sonalika, Saloni and every one else was dependant on the private tutors. Thus, my condition was hopeless.

At that emergency situation, Samal Sir joined our school, as our new science teacher. A fresh M.Sc graduate from the University, he was sent to us. Poor thing, a young male teacher in a school of all girls and most female teachers, including the principal. You can imagine his condition.

Samal Sir's first class with us ended up in a disaster. He wanted us to introduce ourselves, telling our names and hobbies. Everyone wanted to give her best bio-data seeing a good looking, new male teacher, just to rag him. When my turn came I told, "I am Nandini, my hobbies are elocution, debate, reading books and cooking".

"Sir, she is our Hindi teacher's daughter."

"Sir, she is our class monitor and literary champion."

He tried to calm us down, but in vain.

Then Saraswati giggled and asked, "Sir, what are your hobbies?"

"I ....I ....don't know. Not sure. Now let's start with chapter -5 today. Open your Science books."

"Sir, what's the hurry? Please talk to us for sometime *na*!"

"See, I may complain the principal if you all do not cooperate. Science syllabus is vast, please concentrate!"

At that point, the bell rang, and all the girls burst into a laughter, as loud as possible. He instantly left the class, leaving the attendance register on the table due to nervousness. He was sweating; his fair cheeks had become crimson, eyes protruding from under his powerful glasses. I felt pity for him. "Girls, you should have behaved! Now, what was that? Do you behave like this with other teachers?"

"Oh, seems like you liked him a lot?" teased Tripti.

"No....I liked him. Spare him for me, ok?", snapped Saraswati.

Saraswati was the eldest girl among us. Her womanly features, blooming breasts, seductive smile, long hair and sensuous walk made her eye-catching, which I understood years after we left school. At that time, looking at myself, I would only think sometimes, how can a girl be like her, she is actually a woman! Some girls told, 'she is an aunty'.

Next one and a half years, till we completed class X and left the school to join the local college, Sarswati tried her best to draw Samal Sir's attention. She would wear blood red suits and lift her *dupatta* up to her neck during school picnics and roam around, ogling him. She would stare at him with moist eyes in the class while he was teaching. Would drop a pen or pencil and lean down to pick it so that he can look at her. She would sing love songs for him during *antaksharis* on occasions like *Ganesh Chaturthi* or *Sripanchami*. One day, she even dared to go to his bachelors' mess in the pretext of some doubt in studies, which, that poor gentleman had to clear standing on the verandah beside her while all the passers by glanced meaningfully. Because he didn't like to call a girl inside a bachelors' mess.

This was the talk of the class most of the time – that Saraswati was head-over-heels in love with Samal Sir. I anyway rubbished it. "We are here to study, to get a first class, and make our parents and teachers proud. Not to fall in love with teachers, right?"

"Don't be a Mahatma Gandhi. We all know that these days Samal Sir is going to your house every evening. Your Maa is a teacher, so it's easy for you, no?"

They were right. It was not much difficult for me to have him in my house, because he had respect for a senior teacher like my Maa, who invited him to our place.

In fact, it was not Maa's idea, it was Baba's and my eldest sister's idea that since I didn't go for a tuition, and I had to cover the syllabus for the NTS examination, the new Science teacher from our school can be requested to come for an hour in the evening to our house and clear my doubts till the examination was over. Later on, he can be paid in kind if not cash.

Sir agreed.

The science-teaching-sessions from five to six in the evenings started.

Four to six in the evening was the play time for all, but I had to sacrifice an hour for the home tuitions. Samal Sir was a very good teacher. His concepts were clear, so was his diction. His only problem was he was nervous. He had never had the guts to have eye-contact with me at home, sitting on the same table with me, even though in the class he would always spot me the moment he entered and would smile. He was quite formal with us, both at home and in the school. He spent his spare time in the staff common room reading some bulky books. One day I asked him, "Sir, what do you read during the break time in the school? Are you always with a story book!"

"No, I don't understand stories, or literature for that matter. I am preparing for the Bank P.O. examination and other competitive examinations."

"But you have to leave teaching for that! You are our best teacher. How shall we study without you?"

"But by the time I qualify in some competitive examination, you would have completed your X Board exam. You would be in the college and get much better teachers. Then you will forget me."

"No Sir….no teacher would be as good as you. I shall never forget you. You are the best."

"You mean it Nandini?"

That was the first time he directly looked into my eyes during our private classes. That was when my eldest sister entered the room with two cups of coffee for them. She was older than him, was doing her M.Phil in the University at that time. She had come for the summer vacation. We were scared of *didi* , maybe because she was the eldest. And there is something in her personality that is awe-inspiring and she is seriously, definitely authoritative.

"What's up? Studies over?"

"*Namaskar didi.* When did you come?"

"I came yesterday. So, how is your student doing? How many days left for the examination?"

"One more month. Her progress is remarkable. She is thorough with all the chapters by now."

"Oh! Then why are you teaching her more? She need not be spoon-fed."

"No, we are revising. She has to compete with the best students of every school."

"That's fine. But don't make her over-dependant on

you. We had never had tuitions, and we did well in our studies."

He kept quiet, sipping coffee. I was uneasy, *why is she talking to Sir like this? He is most respectable.*

"By the way, your name is Samarendra Samal, right?"

"Yes, *didi.*"

In the evening I heard her asking Maa, "Is this Samal a Brahmin?"

"No, Samal is not a Brahmin surname. Why?"

"No, just like that."

There was only a week left for the examination. My workload was more. Studying for the regular classes, doing class work, home work and also preparing for the NTS examination. Samal Sir was a great help. He used to prepare charts for me from each chapter during his break time and bring those for me in the evening. I was eagerly looking forward for the evenings for the charts, notes, classes, and for him (?!). He had become a habit, even though he hardly ever spoke to me,not even a word, after an hour of study. He would abruptly get up and leave the room before I could thank him for the day. He was a thorough gentleman. He was good, if ever anybody was. In the clay-like mind of a fourteen years old girl, his sincerity, clean fingers, gentle smell, shining teeth, spectacles, sharp nose, curly hair, slim, tall and fit personality, everything had an impact, even if I didn't comprehend that then.

Because I was no dreamer at that point. A very practical and ambitious student, my only aim being to be the topper.

That day before leaving he told me, "By this time next Sunday, you will have no more tuition with me."

"Why Sir?"

"Forgot? Your exam is on Sunday morning, after

that you don't need tuitions anymore; you'll study on your own, madam has told."

My heart sank in.

Perhaps my eyes were moist.

I started doing *tip-top tip-top* with my tip-top-ball-pen restlessly, thinking something which I don't remember now.

Suddenly he stopped me by gripping my thumb, took the pen away, put it gently on the table and still holding my thumb, he said, "Don't do this, don't be restless. At this time you need to be patient. You have to qualify and get this scholarship, for my sake, for our sake."

Our sake?

I snatched my thumb after a few seconds, and suddenly felt my mouth was dry. I felt queasiness. A bottomless feeling. I didn't know what it was. Told, "Yes Sir, I am trying my best."

He got up to go. Had one last glance at me, intently, and left.

I guess, since that day he started his adventure -- of writing a nearly five hundred pages love letter!

My evening classes were over. NTS examination was over. Within a few months we were promoted to class X. A new Science teacher joined that year who took over our Science classes. She was a senior and good teacher again, and Samal Sir was forgotten by most of us. Of course Saraswati didn't.

Saraswati was trying her best to go and meet him in the staff room or the corridor in some or other pretext, and to her utter disappointment, he was always the same old expressionless, stony, ruthless man.

And I didn't. I, never, can.

But I never spoke to him, except on a few more occasions. Like, there was a Science Exhibition in the district headquarters and I was selected from our school to represent. I prepared a project on the seven colours of the rainbow, called *Varnachakra*. The day I went to the district headquarters, which was two hours by bus, he accompanied me. The school sent him as he was a competent and responsible science teacher. Two other juniors were with us, Saibali Pal and Tanushree Mishra. We three sat on one larger seat and he sat on the other side, where my face was reflected directly to him on the rear-view mirror. To his advantage, it was not visible to the other two girls. All I could feel was, two moist eyes were intently, painfully, sagaciously looking into my eyes through the mirror, and this time I was quiet, expressionless. On the way back, he ensured that we three girls reach home safely, never volunteered to drop me home alone after the other girls had left. On the other hand, he told the juniors, "let's drop the senior girl first, then you two can go together since you are neighbors."

Every day we had a prayer class before the day began, where the girls of different classes would queue up separately, and one senior could sing a solo *bhajan,* line by line, and others would follow her. My turn was on every Monday. I was almost an acceptable singer, if not good. Every Monday I found him waiting much before time in the prayer class while he skipped it on other days of the week. I had told him sometime that white was my favorite colour. Now all his shirts were white, off-white or shades of white. Of course, that suited his clean personality and innocent countenance.

He made friendship with a teacher of my father's school who was our distant relative, a cousin. But I am sure that he never told him anything about me out of fear.

Now I can realize how dismayed he must be feeling, and how restless. But it was not reflected on his calm, peaceful eyes, like the *Buddha*'s. It seemed as if his gaze was always fixed on the distant horizon, looking through things, not looking at them.

Such a strange man he was.

Today I am writing his story confidently, because I am sure that he must be a Branch Manager in some bank by now, who must be least interested to read literature, forget about a short story. He might have even forgotten that I wanted to be a Professor of English.

After the test examination of class X , we were given preparatory holidays. Most of us stopped going to the school in order to study at home. I am sure he must not be feeling like going to a school where I was not there. I was the centre of his world; I had inadvertently sowed the seeds of the moon in his heart. I was his only wish, without uttering a single word. His words might be in some other form, fully drenched, fully wet, deeply drowned, wrapped in illusions or completely nude, but never articulate. I was his gorgeously decorated goddess, wild enthusiasm, burning incense. For him it was enough to light a lamp in front, be the candle and the light-worm himself. He was running aimlessly in a solo-faced tunnel, with the knowledge that he would have to run back all the way as there was no opening in the other side of it. Still he loved running in complete darkness, alone. Now I wonder, quite often, what made him fall in love with a girl like me, with no looks, no sense, no understanding of love, wheatish-skinned, ignoring Saraswati, a complete woman, with body language of a classical beauty and hair like Shakuntala's.

The reason can be any or many.

I knew that he hailed from a family of all boys; even

his mother was dead. He had only his father and brothers. He must have been very studious, given his standards and academic career. He joined a girls' school at a young age as a teacher, and the girls started leg-puling, harassing him. Perhaps he saw respect for him in my eyes, and admiration. I made him comfortable and feel at ease with me during those few months of private classes. I was the first girl he spoke to, ever, and instantly he fell in love with me. He must have discovered a similarity between him and me, which I realize now. We both were fun-loving, studious, both were eager to learn and had a scientific bent of mind, were foodie people and lovers of music. But there was a binary opposition too. I was talkative, extrovert, he was quiet, introvert ; and he didn't know how to express himself. That is why, perhaps, he was a science teacher and I am a teacher of literature . Opposite poles attract, which he realized the year he met me, and I realized now, after two decades, after I learnt all the lessons of life. Love is the last chapter for me; unfortunately, it was the first chapter for him. I climbed many mountains, steeped on every slope; thought love was a desert, hence best avoided.

Finally, I got swayed by the river. Love never came to me, the wild stream.

That year was a glorious year for me; I came out with flying colours in the Board exam. I was in the news papers, my family was proud, excited, my friends were happy, and all of us got busy with preparations for the +2 admissions. I faintly remember, my parents sent Samal Sir a packet of sweets and a suit piece, since he never accepted any money for teaching me all those months.

My cousin told me that Samal Sir went to the temple for the first time in his life, that day, for a thanks-giving.

I had +2 admissions in a fortnight. My classes started after another fortnight. I enjoyed my classes, made new friends, and a few of my old friends were also with me.

The college was three kilometers away from our house, and I had to go by walk since I never learnt cycling. Days passed by. My memory about the school days slowly became faint. I had new pastures now, new wings to fly.

But undoubtedly, there was something at the back of my mind, a concealed sensitivity, conceived, but never nourished. A seed, never watered, which never ever bloomed into a sapling. That feeling cannot exactly be called guilt-consciousness, since I was guilty of nothing.

So was he, I am sure.

Every morning, my classes started at ten, so I had to start from home at nine. One of my friends showed me a short cut route, a by-lane, to reach the college in just fifteen minutes, rather than crossing the main market .

After taking that route, my journey to college became easier. Start at 9.45 and reach at 10, sharp. Because I had to cook in the mornings at home.

Some days I felt that while going to the college some one was watching me from a distance. Two invisible eyes! An imaginary face! Was it real? Was someone walking behind me? Or it was just an illusion?

The first month was fun-filled. Students got to know each other, got introduced to the syllabi, to the college teachers. College teachers were different from the school teachers. The personal care and involvement was pretty much less. We had a good English teacher, Professor Hota, whose classes were engaging. I never missed his classes.

After the first five months in +2 first year, we started missing classes, sitting in the canteen or coming home whenever we felt like. The secret road was most convenient since the teachers or classmates couldn't see me. We had one Odia teacher, a lady teacher, whose classes I used to attend sometimes with my friends even if I had not opted for Odia, just to give company to my friends in leg-pulling the teacher. She used to powder her sagging cheeks very carefully, and her oily curls were arranged over her head with such care that even a bucket of water could not displace them. The Board exam was scheduled for the second year, so it was ok if we were not very serious in the first year.

Came July, came the rainy season, and we had no other choice but to wear skirts to the college. Because if the *salwars* got wet, it was difficult to stay like that from ten to four in the classroom.

That day everything seemed to have come to a stand still, all movements suspended due to heavy rain from 12.00 noon to 5.00 pm, continuously. The college was situated near small hillocks, mango grooves around. Nature was kind and bountiful. Mountain rains can be dangerous, so was it that day. Water crept into the ground floor classrooms, and Odia madam had to suspend her class willy-nilly, raising her eye-brows so much that her temple had the curls like rain water. The water in the fields was glassily still, the air had a suspended movement, trapping 80 students in a gallery in a sluggishness that made even the simple act of breathing into an effort.

I remembered that there was a function at home that day; we had some relatives out there, and I was asked by Maa to come back early. I was getting worried, even though I was enjoying the rainy day. Then it was discovered that the flood was coming through the college gate, sealing us in and everything else out; anyway, we were more jubilant. We were sure that no classes could be held now and at least a week had fallen like manna from the heavens, along with the incessant rain that preceded the floods. Thunderous clouds, more and more chaotic wind, lightning, all got together to design a brute beauty around.

Nasreen, a friend, had brought the amazing lunch box of *paranthas* and kebabs. But she hardly got to eat them. We all opened our lunch boxes and had a picnic, indoors.

It was five in the evening; the rain subsided. We just jumped into the water clog and started homeward.

I walked as fast as possible. Was someone following us?

I was with three other friends, who had to depart after one or two modes and I took my short cut route to reach home early.

Now I was sure that someone was following me. I didn't dare to look back as it was near dark and the lane was free of a single soul except me due to the rainy weather. I felt the footsteps were too close now, and I had to look back.

There he was, as I had always expected. My sixth sense had been telling me that the invisible eyes following me everywhere were *his*.

"Samal Sir! You?"

"Yes. How have you been?"

"I am good. What are you doing here at this time?"

"I shifted to a rented house in this lane after you left the school."

"Oh!'

"And I see you every day, twice, crossing this lane."

I kept quite, slowly walking.

"That makes my day. In fact, my life."

I still managed to keep quiet, unresponsive.

"Take this umbrella. You can give it back tomorrow."

"No Sir, I don't need it. I am already wet. I can reach home in ten minutes, anyway."

"Why? Why you don't need it? Why you don't need anything from me? Why don't you understand that everyone needs something, someone? Why are you becoming a goddess? Why not a normal human being? A normal girl, who can understand, read the feelings of the other person? What wrong have I done to you? Am I so bad?" He was shaking.

"No, Sir, you are not at all bad. Who says? What happened?"

I was nervous.

"Since one and a half years, I have been struggling with myself. I tried to hate you, a girl for whom my feelings have no meaning. For whom all that matters is her career. But I failed. Terribly failed. This very virtue of yours that disgusts me has trapped me into a snare. I would die without you!"

What was he telling?

What was the snare? And why was he talking of death? I had expected that he might have qualified some competitive examination by now and must have left the school.

I must control myself, since he was uncontrollable. I didn't want to hurt him.

"Sir, have you not qualified the Bank P.O. examination as yet?"

"Yes, I have. And they have given me a date. The last date of joining is sometime coming week. But I am not going to go. I am not leaving this place."

"But it had always been your dream!"

"Oh god! Again you are talking of dreams? Now I have a greater dream my dear! I wish I could have told about it to you earlier. You are my dream."

"Sir, it's getting dark. I need to go now. And please

don't try to speak to me in future. My family will not like it."

"Please, listen to me. Before taking any such decision, please read it once. Then decide if we should meet in future or not."

He handed over a polybag which had something like a book inside, as big as my Ph.D thesis, and then he disappeared into the dark. Before leaving, he told, "I shall wait to know your reaction at 10.00 am tomorrow morning here. It's the question of my life and death."

What book has he given me? And how can he expect that I can decide about his life and death by reading a book?

I rushed it into my bag hurriedly and went home. The function was postponed as it was a rainy day and most of the guests couldn't reach. Maa was cooking, my elder sister and aunts helping her in the kitchen. Younger sisters were playing outside with paper boats.

I took a cup of tea and went upstairs with my college bag. I was eager to read the contents of the book.The book, which someone who had influenced my life, character and personality, had given me after so many months.

I discreetly opened the polybag. But they were loose sheets, at least five hundreds, neatly arranged with dates on each one, the last date being today's date, I mean the date of that day.

What are these? Letters? Love letters? So many? Addressed to whom? Me? Was it some kind of an archive? A novel? Written by a person who never read even a story? A man of sciences, who was far away from any kind of narrative writing? What was there?

I was sweating. My lips were dry, just like that day two years back when he held my thumb and asked me not to be restless.

I took out the last sheet and started reading

"My dearest one! See what a destiny I have got! I love you since two years now, write letters to you every day, store them in a folder, but I hardly do have the courage to go in front of you and hand them over.

And see your destiny! You are the loveliest soul god has created, you are my most loved one. Be sure, no one will ever love you the way I do, no one will care for your well being the way I do. But you hardly realize that.

There you are sitting on the high platform, seeing the ferry lights crossing, criss-crossing the big river. Here I am, the wild bird, sitting on the deck of the ship, living many lives in this life. My voice is like the sea waves, my dreams are like descending rain clouds...."

Oh! I could read no more. No more! I turned the page and looked at the last few lines, ".... Redeem me. Heal me or kill me. I cannot bear the burden, the weight of these undelivered letters, unspoken words anymore. My life is lit with the fire of a single flame, lit from your pious hands. You don't know dear how grateful I am to you. Innocently, unknowingly, you have taught me the greatest lesson of life when I was teaching you your bookish lessons. You taught me a syllable that orders the world, constructs history and builds civilization. It's 'love'! You taught me love, you made me a real man. Oh! How dearly I love you...."

Stop it! I must not read this anymore. It will turn my world upside down. It will swallow my earth like a wild sea swallows the islands.

I rushed downstairs. Went to the kitchen and called my eldest sister. She could guess that something was wrong. I took her to the bed room and handed over the packet.

"Didi, Samal Sir has given it to me."

"What is this? Letters? God! Are you still in touch with

that man? I had expected it. Are you also writing letters to him? How long has it been going? Did you read those?" She had a thousand questions. I left the room quietly, with tearful eyes. I was utterly disturbed.

Maa and didi were very angry, annoyed; they were grumbling.

"She is just a child. Had she read these rubbish stuffs? Had she been misguided? Trapped? It's good that she showed the letters to me. She just reached home and handed over the letters to me. Hope she hasn't read them in the college. Thank god!"

The next morning I was asked to stay at home at least for a week, and collect class notes from my friends later. In the evening he was summoned to our house. Baba was sent to the market, we sisters were asked to stay in the bed room and not come out. He reached at 6 pm, without fail. Perhaps the letters were thrown on his face. Perhaps, he was rebuked. *How can you try to misguide a child? How dare you? We can file a case of adultery against you. We can hand you over to the police. How dare you? How dare you??*

All I could hear, or overhear, was his calm footsteps, going out of our house. All I could see or peep, was (that was the last time I saw him, ever) Sir holding the same packet of letters, close to his chest, face--down, eyes--swollen, going out of our house. He left the town, quitting teachership, the next day.

After more than twenty years, today all I can think is – I am not sure what was wrong or what was right. Who was wrong and who was not. I am not going to judge. Only that, I missed reading a masterpiece, perhaps more potent than someone's heartbeats, more life giving than breathing and more honest and truer than the creation.

Those few lines that I happened to read remained in

my memory in the form of the silence of the fallen dew. The roots of those silent letters have been piercing my earth, sucking the rivers flowing at the middle of the night, till today.

The Quarantined

E very night Joyita used to ponder before sleeping, *what makes this woman laugh, moan, shout, celebrate, party--even during the quarantine-- when the whole world is becoming a lazaretto*!

Corona virus was the only buzz word, no one talked about anything else, there was a general atmosphere of the 'Great Depression'; people were waiting for an end to this uncertainty and for a normal life again.

This laughing-woman Sheela, in her mid-thirties, was the immediate neighbor of Joyita; she was the daughter-in-law of Kamala and wife of Adarsh.

Not that Joyita had any such problems in her own life which made her intrude in others' lives. She was in a relationship with Jayant, Adarsh's elder brother and Kamala's elder son, sober, lean, good looking man. Sharing life with Jayant, talking to him over phone, meeting him for a couple of hours a day, missing him when he was living next door but couldn't meet as Kamala was a controlling, dominating mother—Joyita was fine with all of that. The son needed to give an explanation to Mom to meet even the neighbors, and the worst part was, Jayant thought, that was perfectly alright. He did not agree that it was an abusive mother-son relationship. In a way, Jayant was always quarantined in the house-arrest of Mom, maybe since his birth.

Now he took occasional escapades with Joyita, which were rather adventurous.

Before the outbreak of Corona, before the curfew and a total lockdown, Jayant and Joyita used to go out on the weekends, enjoying their clandestine meetings, laughing at their own lies to Jayant's Mom. Those were beautiful days, meeting like teenaged couples, eating out, shopping, watching movies hand-in-hand, kissing in the darkness of the theatre, feeding the first bite of each meal to the other, holding hands in the market and on the roads. They were always rushing to the theatres halfway through the movies, but Joyita never complained though Jayant took hours to get ready. Back home, Jayant would make some plea before Kamala, some urgency of meeting the neighbor Joyita Ma'am who had great potential of entrepreneurship, through whom, Kamala believed, her son can achieve some benefits. So she allowed him to meet Joyita for a couple of hours any day. Jayant and Joyita made the best use of those hours. Jayant would visit Joyita's place with his laptop in the name of serious business. Joyita waited for him with some delicacies that she cooked for him, wearing her soft silky attires that he loved. She looked forward to these meetings with dreams in her eyes. Joyita had official and academic work for long hours, she didn't prefer to go out with friends on the weekdays, though there were invitations galore. She enjoyed these couple of hours with Jayant on the working day evenings, and their romantic dates on the weekends. He was her world.

All this was before the quarantine.

Joyita was living in Mumbai as Jayant's neighbor, she was originally from West Bengal. Living alone suited her, given the kind of career she had. She was self-sufficient, independent, with a decent salary and a good support system at her workplace. She needed Jayant for her emotional fulfilment, she loved him because he made her a complete woman and because he was a good man. Jayant was like a kid, he was always ready to surrender to her, eat her food with gratitude, appreciating even a small thing she did for him, thanking for whatever small gifts she bought for him, ordering surprise gifts for his fashionable lady, listening to her never ending chats, and making love to her passionately. They completed each other.

Joyita heard him talking sometimes about Adarsh and Sheela, his younger brother and sister-in-law, who had been trying to have a baby since five years, but to no avail. Kamala wanted a baby boy at home. Sheela needed an engagement. So a baby was a must. Sheela was working as a daily wage worker in some company in Andheri-Goregaon area; she travelled from Borivali to Andheri by local trains. For that she needed to leave home early morning, and come back at 7.30 in the evening. Beyond office hours she had to do household chores, clean utensils and clothes of the entire family as Kamala did not believe in hiring maids when a daughter-in-law was readily available at home.

Joyita thought, Sheela had a mysterious life. Her bed room was adjacent to hers with a thin wall dividing the two. Willy-nilly, Joyita had to bear with the conversations and activities of the couple, Adarsh-Sheela. Adarsh was a short, dark, hunchbacked, bald man; he looked simple. Sheela was a little more than four feet, flat chested, had pimple marks on her fair rounded face, she had long unkempt hair. She was always dressed up, was never without heavy make-up. Perhaps she persuaded Adarsh for overt sex every night, her moans and beseeching created that impression.

They watched porn movies noisily till late nights; Joyita imagined that they tried hard to have a good sex life, and conceivably they failed.

There was a kind of frustration, anger and aggression in Sheela's personality. No one noticed or admired a short, flat woman; apart from that, a daily wage job, household chores in the morning-evening and busy weekends made her hostile to everyone, everything.

Her only source of joy was Jayant, her elder brother-in-law, *Jeth-ji;* she took great care of him, she took deep breaths staring at him while serving him food and tea. Joyita caught her red handed several times, on birthdays, get-togethers, or on the stairs, rooftop.

Every time Joyita and Jayant came back from weekend outings, Jayant got down in the nearby market to come home after sometime so that Kamala couldn't know his whereabouts. Joyita would drive back, park the car, go to her apartment on the second floor. Sheela would invariably rush to the door, stare at Joyita, look back to see if Jayant was also there, and then got disappointed not to find him. She waited at the door till Jayant came home, both Kamala and Sheela waited in the hall for Jayant. Joyita found it creepy. The entire family, except Jayant and his uncle, *Chacha-ji,* was creepy, weird. There was no individual liberty, they didn't understand concepts like human rights, freedom of opinion, free-thinking, living life on one's own terms. Joyita tried to explain these things to Jayant during their private hours, but failed. Jayant believed, if someone is feeding you, she has the right over your life, your freedom. He wasn't ready to believe that a mother had no rights to be the destiny-maker of her children.

Jayant never got married, he preferred meeting Joyita covertly. Kamala and other elderly family members doubted his manhood behind his decision of bachelorship. Joyita couldn't control her laughter. "Stupids! They should ask me!!" For her, this was perfectly alright -- meeting him, loving him, taking care of him silently. Marriage was not on her cards. Had the life condition of Jayant been different, she might have at least thought about it. But marriage with Jayant had its side effects, implications, complications. Kamala and her family would become a part of the story along with Jayant. She had no such aims to complicate her life. Being Jayant's partner, lover, friend,confidante was enough for her.

Though sometimes Joyita had apprehensions, self-doubts. "Are we just two convenient people for each other? Is it a relationship of convenience? The day Kamala discovered our relationship, she will house-arrest you. You can't fight with her to meet me." Jayant got upset and that night he wrote her a mail, "Dearest, if there is a choice between my family and you, I'll only choose you over them." That assured Joyita for sometime, though she problematized the word 'choice'. Again, she pitied poor Kamala, '*poor woman, her lifetime achievement award Jayant promises to choose someone else over her!! This is what happens if a mother is possessive.*' Anyway, she had no intentions of taking away Jayant from his mother.

But somehow Joyita was not able to handle Sheela's advances to Jayant since they were living under the same roof. Sheela never left an opportunity to complain Kamala about Joyita, her arrogance, her leftist ideology, etc. She convinced Kamala that Joyita Madam is a highly connected and powerful person. "Now she is fine with our family, but the day she gets upset with us, she will ensure that all of us are behind the bars Mummy!" Kamala was foolish in comparison to Sheela; she trusted her daughter-in-law. Then she stopped Jayant from meeting Joyita for a few days. They had fights over phone on the idiocy of his mother. During such fights, and even otherwise, Jayant had this ridiculous habit of not checking his mobile for days, avoiding all phone calls, hibernating and sulking.

Joyita got restless without any message, but she didn't have the provision of knocking the neighbors' door bell. She had promised Jayant that she'll never enter his parents' house, as desired by him. Joyita had plans of buying a house in Godrej Hills, Khadakpada or Ammu Nagar in Thane West, where one room will be kept for Jayant to come and stay whenever he wanted. Jayant was excited about the dream home.

But Jayant disliked Joyita's overreaction to small things, Joyita disliked Jayant's lack of punctuality, self-esteem and disrespect for appointments, commitments. All their arguments were based on these. Anyway, after every fight, Jayant had to struggle to convince his Mom that only Joyita can help him with his career, and he must meet her. Greed prevailed over sense for Kamala kind of opportunists, and she once again allowed her son to meet the *padoshan*, Joyita Madam. Joyita had a serious problem with the word 'allow'. How and why should someone 'allow' or 'disallow' another individual to pursue a career? Or even to meet anyone of their choice! Elders should facilitate, support, encourage youngsters, but 'allow'?

Joyita sulked when Jayant came to meet her after seven days, rebuked him to go home and sleep on Mom's lap. Jayant wasn't angry, he understood that Joyita was missing him. He said sorry, pleaded guilty, wiped her rolling tears, running nose, and held her close. She tried to let herself loose, he pulled her back in his arms, kissed her nape that got numb with his touch, caressed her hair, shoulder, back, neck, lips, eyes and kissed her all over. He whispered sweet nothings in her ears, and she melted, like every time. His tender love worked on Joyita, his simplicity amazed her.

His relationships at home were complex, nothing like his simple, honest bonding with Joyita. In fact, all relationships were complex in his family. Sheela hated Kamala for her dominating nature, though they pretended to be nice to each other. Once Sheela gathered the courage to ring the door of Joyita Madam. Joyita was surprised; anyway she was cordial with her, offered her some juice, and asked how she could help her. Sheela said, "Ma'am, can you offer me a job in your office? My workplace is very far, and I get tired traveling so much."

"What is your qualification Sheela?"

"I have completed Graduation."

"Subject?"

"Simple Graduate, BA General, no Honours."

Joyita was at a fix; her office was a high profile place, even support staffs were Graduates. But she somehow kept the conversation polite.

"I would suggest, do your Post Graduation, and then forward me your CV. I am sure I'll be able to help you."

"But Ma'am, there is no space for me to study further in this house. My mother-in-law makes me work hard beyond my office hours. She says that maids should not clean the clothes and utensils, and I am forced to do everything."

Joyita thought it's not her purview to comment. Just said, "Still, I repeat, do your Master's Degree, I will definitely help you in getting a job."

Sheela was rather disappointed that Joyita did not offer her a job, whereas she started a lucrative business with Jayant as her partner, with Kamala's approval. Sheela was angry to think that now Jayant will have a career which should have been actually offered to her. She was upset to imagine that now Jayant will be closely associated with Joyita. She took out her frustration by brainwashing her mother-in-law against the business, against Joyita's arrogance, and things got difficult for Jayant-Joyita. They had to be more careful with the meetings. There were arguments, misunderstandings between the two due to Sheela and Kamala.

Anyway, the couple always sorted out their differences at the end of the day. Love always won, repugnance of Kamala and Joyita could do nothing much to the bonding between Jayant-Joyita.

All this was before the quarantine.

In January, people got to hear a never-before entity about human health hazards. The new coronavirus (Covid-19) spread to nearly every country in the world since it first emerged in China at the beginning of the year. Lakhs of people were infected and lakhs of deaths recorded. The source of the coronavirus was believed to be a "wet market" in Wuhan which sold both dead and live animals including fish and birds. Such markets posed a heightened risk of viruses jumping from animals to humans because hygiene standards were difficult to maintain if live animals were being kept and butchered on site. Typically, they were also densely packed allowing disease to spread from species to species, from animals to humans. The first case of coronavirus was confirmed in Mumbai in the beginning of March 2020 and by the end of the month all states of India were terribly affected. It was a war like situation, the government announced curfew in mid March, closed offices, schools, colleges, universities, malls, theatres, markets, flights, metros, buses, just everything. Only emergency services were allowed. The lockdown went for months, and watching news on the TV was eye opening as well as frustrating. New cases of Corona came everyday with deaths and more deaths. April, indeed, was the cruellest month. **Kasturba Gandhi hospital** in **Mumbai** became one of the official isolation centres in the state, which was the nearest hospital to Joyita's place. Hospitalisation of people suspected of **coronavirus** infection became a systemic issue, and Joyita saw from her balcony and heard ambulances coming to their colony more often than not, taking patients hurriedly to the hospital, relatives talking to the helpline people wearing masks, fully covered up; the patients looking hopeless and crying miserably. Going in the ambulance was like going to the war from where you never come back the same. 'Stay home, stay safe' became the password of everyone, people called it the 'new normal'. Going out of home unnecessarily invited whips from the police.

The quarantine was depressing. Relatives and friends couldn't meet each other, and people waited for a future that may never come. It was like 'Waiting for the Godot'. Sensitive people started helping the needy financially and by cooking meals for the migrant labourers. Joyita joined the support-group. Her heart was broken for the homeless, she felt restless.To make herself of some use to the society, she cooked thirty meals a day for the hungry. That kept her engaged. It was a tough time. For months, humans continued to stay at home whereas animals roamed about freely. They must be wondering, what happened!!

Joyita, the optimist, believed, this, too, will pass.

During such quarantine period, Sheela played the mischief, characteristic of her, and convinced Kamala to disallow Jayant from meeting the neighbour, or from stepping out of home, lest he may catch the Corona virus. Jayant called Joyita to inform that Mom has asked everyone to stay at home, "so let's not meet for a few days, please don't get angry...". *This not-meeting period, too, will pass.*

Joyita was upset but ok with not meeting as long as they were in touch over phone. They had casual chats, she kept him informed about the support-group, its activities. He appreciated her social commitment, but from a safe distance, as instructed by Mom. Joyita had no time to sulk, cooking for migrant labourers and attending online official meetings kept her engaged. She tried to stay positive and avoid depression.

Even during those quarantine nights, Sheela's bed room was active till wee hours. Loud music, porn movies, promiscuous laughter, wanton orgasmic moans, everything continued; basically, the quarantine period was picnic time for Sheela, oblivious of the crisis of the beautiful planet. Adarsh's voice was never loud though. Those nights, Joyita literally closed her ears with ear buds and had disturbed sleep. She complained Jayant over phone, but he sounded helpless, as ever.

One early morning, maybe at 8am, there was some commotion from the neighbourhood. Kamala was shouting at the pitch of her voice, Adarsh was arguing, the entire family was in the adjacent bedroom of Joyita, in Sheela's bedroom. Joyita called Jayant over phone to ask what was the matter. Of course the call went unanswered, so typical of Jayant! Incommunicado.

Had Kamala seized his phone? Did she see our photographs and messages!!

After a lot of apprehension, finally there was a call from Jayant at 12noon. He was speaking from the bathroom, in a suppressed voice.

"Joyita, sorry I couldn't take your calls. There is a mishap."

"What happened?"

"Sheela, my brother's wife, is missing since this morning."

"What!! I mean, where could she have possibly gone during the quarantine? Did you inform the police?"

"No no, please don't talk about the police. Mom will kill us. Sheela will come back, she must have been to some friend's place."

"But during the quarantine? Without informing anyone? Does she go to friends' places alone? Did you call all her friends?"

"Let's stop this discussion, please. I'll get back to you soon."

There was pin drop silence from the neighbourhood throughout the day. Joyita was hypersensitive. She was anxious about Sheela. *What if something wrong happened? This is Mumbai. And these people are not even informing the police!!*

Towards 9pm, there was some noise on the stairs. Joyita ran to the peephole/magic-eye of her main door. She saw that Sheela came home with Bablu, the good-looking grey-eyed *presswalla*, the washer-man, who had a shop to wash and press clothes in front of the building, whom Joyita had caught staring at their building in the past, several times, for some mysterious reason.

Sheela looked exhausted, but she had a contented smile on her face, maybe she was drunk, her clothes dishevelled, hair ruffled. She entered the house quietly, without reacting to Kamala's rebukes. Bablu informed with a grin that he found Sheela-*ji* on the beach and brought her home.

Found on the Mumbai beach? During the quarantine? She spent one whole day there??

That night Joyita heard the hullabaloo from the other side of the wall, she presumed some domestic violence too; Kamala's abuses were hurled at the daughter-in-law. But Sheela was silent, lost.

Complete silence. Complete lockdown of two weeks. No pandemonium, no disturbances, no late night movies, no giggling, no moaning of Sheela.

Life went on. Joyita and Jayant chatted regularly, though Jayant avoided talking about Sheela whenever she asked. He said, "my brother and mother are with her, we need not interfere."

After ten days or so, Jayant came to her place, Kamala 'allowed' him again as he convinced her of a lot of pending business related work. Things seemed normalized.

After a couple of days, one evening Jayant was sitting at Joyita's place, sipping tea, and Kamala called him, asked him to come home immediately.

"All ok?" Joyita was alarmed.

"Mom said Sheela is seriously unwell, so ambulance has to be called. Adarsh is panicking, I have to go."

"But you never told me that she was unwell!"

"Yes she has fever since a week. Mom has been looking after her, you don't worry."

"Do you need my help?"

"No no! Don't panic, don't go to our place."

Jayant left hurriedly, leaving his mobile on Joyita's dining table, as he did most of the times.

After an hour and a half, almost at 10pm, the

ambulance came from Kasturba Gandhi hospital, some people got down from it.They came to Jayant's place with a stretcher and took Sheela away; she was coughing, sinking, she was in pain. They took away only Sheela, no one accompanied. There was no human touch, no love no compassion; only the movements of human shapes of medical professionals, fully covered like astronauts. Maybe Kamala wanted to keep her sons safe and disowned Sheela, and no one accompanied her to the hospital. Everything was done in a hush hush mode. Every cell of Sheela's body fought to retain life, but the virus won.

Kamala knew, she always knew, being contaminated is a crime, and Sheela deserved the punishment.

Kamala thought that no one in the building was watching them, oblivious of the fact that Joyita's tearful eyes were watching everything clearly from the peephole.

Joyita felt a vomit like bile on her throat and a sudden headache. Holding her breath, she called Jayant, but the phone rang from her own dining table in the other room. Something occurred to her, she just unlocked his phone to find hundreds of unchecked WhatsApp messages. Last many days, Jayant had been only chatting with her and a medical consultant about the viral fever of Sheela, mentioning 'my relative' has fever. The medical consultant had been advising him to get her tested after a few more symptoms were seen. Jayant had written, 'I will get back to you after consulting family.' 'I'll call you in case the four symptoms you mentioned are found in the patient'.

Joyita scrolled the message box down and found a couple of messages to Jayant from Sheela, sent on the morning she went missing, two weeks ago. The messages were, as usual, unchecked. Joyita was annoyed with the same old habit of Jayant of not reading messages for days.

"Dear Jayant, I will not address you as *bhaiya*, I cannot pretend anymore. Adarsh is not fit for me, I doubt if at all he is a man, he is dysfunctional! I am wasting my youth on him, I am quarantined in this marriage. Not KOVID-19, but this lifelong quarantine will surely kill me. You are single, you are a man, and I can make you happy. Let us not waste ourselves, let's have some fun. I need you. I am going to the room of my friend who lives near the beach. She has given me her keys, she is not there now. Here is the address. I am leaving my mobile at home, don't call me, just reach there. I'll wait for you. Please do not disappoint me."

The other message was the address of an apartment near the Mumbai beach, from where Bablu, the washer man, had brought her back that night, before two weeks.

Joyita's mind went blank, water bubbles floated in front of her eyes.

■

Post-Quarantine

I am Jayant, Joy, as she addressed me sometimes.
Joyita's Jayant. Or I better say, no-more-Joyita's-Jayant.

Post quarantine, five long years post Covid-19; year 2025, January, cold, chilled, busiest city, New Delhi, I was sitting on the bench, near the iron gate of Joyita's mansion, my Joie's new home.

She liked when I addressed her 'Joie', till the year 2020, when we were together in Mumbai. I was going through her last mail on my mobile, in fact I had gone through it several times last few days.

"Joy, my friend, it's time that I leave. I do not want to continue being the 'inconvenient woman' in your life any further. I am leaving this city tomorrow morning, going to Delhi, though I had never thought that one day I'll have to leave our dream city Mumbai. Before leaving, I shall only repeat on 13th June 2020, this day, that I never ever wanted you to shift with me, leaving your old parents; after all they are your responsibility. Who else will look after them if you leave them? I only wanted to keep a space for you in my house which i called my 'home',with a room, a bed, food, comfort, love, and our business, for your engagement -- which I have done with utmost sincerity last few years. I only wanted to continue this forever. That is a separate issue that I never appreciated your mother's dominance and her interference in your personal life. But then, you mistook that for my desire to snatch you from her. Today I put it on record that that had never been my intention to separate a young son from his old ailing parents. I am a family-oriented person, I value relationships. Please stay with them, always, and take good care of them.

Of late whatever havoc we are going through, and especially what happened last couple of days, is very unhealthy for both of us. It's shameful, horrifying. After this, I don't have any reason to live in this city as your neighbour. I had always told you that one must say a proper 'goodbye' in any relationship before they say quits. Good bye Joy. Wherever I go, the comfy room will be kept for you, no one else will fill that gap; the vacuum that I am taking from this separation will never be filled. That's your share in my life. In fact, I couldn't have given you anything more than that—love, respect, comfort, care, and a *room of your own* in a place that I call home."

I read, re-read the mail, shivering, gnashing my teeth. Oh how do these Delhiites survive this cold? It's difficult for us Mumbaikars to even breathe here. How could Joie have accepted this new city five years back, when she left Mumbai broken, shattered? Even I didn't try to contact her all these years. How did she start a new life post Covid, in a new city, all by herself ? Has time healed Joie? How has she been handling our residual, unfinished story? Our incomplete business?

Yes, she always had been a strong woman, 'bold and beautiful', as everyone called her. Here she is today, the senior most IAS Officer, Cabinet Secretary to the Government of India, living in an elusive large mansion at Janpath, close to the house of the PM and other Cabinet

Ministers, with a shining Mercedes-Benz S-Class Car in front of her building and security guards in the uniform. Shall I ask the guards to allow me inside? Will they, without an appointment? Already one of them is ogling me with suspicion, a gun man that is.

To be born blind is not a crime, but to cast a blind eye? Every man is an island, surrounded by a booming noise of the turbulent ocean, trying every second not to give into the irresistible waves, to keep his head in the air, being persuasive here, mounting there. But no one will ever come to know, for him, what tribunals and misfortunes, what pain of fruitless fights lurk behind the cool and calm peripheral charm. More than the exterior dangers, it's inner anxiety and tension that man loses his battle to. I, too, lost Joie to my 'self'.

But looking at her infectious smile, so full of life, who would have thought that she was succumbing to such a long silence? A silence of five years!

Looking at the light in the last room of the bungalow, I was thinking, Joie liked waylaid rooms as her bed room, maybe she is taking rest there. Well what else will people do at 11.30pm in a cold Delhi night? Stand on the roads, stare at a building, dither, shiver, regret, crave to see Joie, at least once?!

***

In another such cold night in February 2020, in Mumbai, my brother Adarsh's wife Sheela was sent to the hospital alone, after being tested positive for Covid-19. As luck was on her side, after a prolonged suffering, she survived the disease, and was released by the hospital in mid-February. But mom didn't agree to bring her home, lest she may contaminate us, and she asked her parents to keep her with them for sometime. Thus, Sheela had to be home quarantined with her parents in their one room flat in Dharavi till mid March. Adarsh was in touch with Sheela over phone during and after her treatment, and by mid March Sheela was fit, healthy to get back to household chores. Mom called her back, there were no maids during lockdown, and it was not possible for mom to cook, clean.

Sheela had become morose and upset after her Covid-19 treatment. She clearly felt cheated, being sent to the hospital alone and then for home quarantine with her parents. We all were feeling a bit guilty, so tried to be nice with her when she came home. We tried to forget Bablu episode, in fact Adarsh had thrown him out of our lane with the help of the RWA. Sheela got back to normalcy, doing household chores, humming, laughing, and of course taking special care of me. We both pretended that she never sent me those whatsapp messages. Joie had cleared chats from my phone, I don't know why. Perhaps she didn't want anyone to see those and talk about me.

But I had made it a point by then that Joie became the talk of our house. A strange bitterness was gripping me—maybe because of some inferiority or superiority complex, I am not sure. The day Joie told me that uncle, aunt, dad and even mom requested her to employ me in her business, I felt threatened. *Employ? I was her employee?* What nonsense they were talking to her about me!!

There was some pressure on me from family to work, do something for myself rather than sitting lazy at home. Everyone was busy with office or household work, but I had nothing much to do. I used to sleep early, wake up late, take a leisurely breakfast, bathe whenever I felt like, and spend hours on whatsapp or political debates on the TV or facebook posts of every other person. Mom and Adarsh hinted a couple of times that everyone should contribute to the household expenses—I definitely didn't like that. I was the rightful heir to my parents, and no one should monitor my expenses. Grandma used to get a good amount as pension of Late Grandpa, and I being her favourite grandson, she allowed me to handle her bank accounts. That amount was good enough for my pocket money. But they shouldn't have expected me to handover my Grandma's money for provisions of the house! Plus, I was the physically weak son of the family, so I deserved that advantage of not going out to work. Uncle, aunt, dad forced mom to talk to Joie about my job. So once she took me to her house and told her, "Madam, actually Jayant's *Mousa ji* has a big business in Noida, and he wants Jayant to join him as a partner, but I don't want my *child* to work with relatives. So I was wondering if he could join your business? He is hard working and successful you see! If he likes, he will continue, if he doesn't like, he may quit after a few months. What say?" Joie said, "Yes why not? Let him work with me, I have just registered for this business in some relative's name, but Jayant ji can be the Area Manager." Joie was hiding her happy smile.

That is how we started working together, and meeting regularly. When I went to her kitchen to fetch a glass of water, mom told her, "We don't pressurize him to work, because he is a weak child, *bechara hamesha beemar rehta hei.*" Joie said, "Yeah, I understand." But I thought she respected me less, looked down upon me, thought me to be the weakling, sickling of the family. She didn't like my self-love, my hypochondriac behaviour, as she told me some other time. I didn't like that.

I found her repulsive, arrogant, self-righteous and

aggressive day by day. But I still wanted to be with her. I was possessive of her.

My first step was -- I distanced everyone in my family from her by convincing them that she did not have respect for our family, she looked down upon us; thus, whatever little courtesy they used to exchange with her, that completely stopped. My strategy worked. In the afternoons, mom and others would surround me and ask about her nature, her past, her connections, bad habits, because I was the only person going to her house during the quarantine. I pretended that I was forced to go to her house just because of the collaborative business, and I'd stop working with her the moment I found a better job, post quarantine. I had no fear of anyone crosschecking as she didn't come to our place, and my family didn't talk to her. Yes!!

This tag of 'unemployed' was at the back of my mind since my dad, aunt, uncle told her that I had not been working since past eight years. Initially when she came to our building and we became good friends, I told her that I was the Senior Executive in a company after doing MBA. And that, I had night duty; every night my office cab picked me at 10pm and dropped back at 6am. Joie got worried about my food and sleeping habits, but I told her it's ok, I have been used to it, and that, I sleep throughout the day, to meet her with a fresh mood in the evenings. Oh, how happy she was! She was happy with small things, she never looked for big achievements, though she was an achiever. But, to my utter disappointment, just one month after our friendship, my family members had told her the truth. She was a sensitive person, she didn't want to hurt me; she created this business for me, and never quoted my 'unemployed status' until I instigated her to do so, one final day. And one more nail was hit by Sheela when she went to Joie's house to ask for a job and informed her that I was a simple Graduate, I never did MBA. Joie was hurt as I had been lying to her, but she kept quiet till the end of the relationship. She had tremendous capacity of keeping secrets, internalizing hurts.

Joie was basically the tenant of my aunt who lived in the same building, on the next floor, and we were her immediate neighbours. She had her own flat in Malabar Hill in South Mumbai, which she had rented out as it was far from her office. This entire building of seven flats where we were living and Joie was a tenant, was the property of my late grandfather built some 60 years back,post independence, and now we were ten people living in grandma's property. Except Adarsh, no one in the family was working, rent amounts from the tenants was our only source of income.

My aunt had built a rapport with Joie even before we became friends, and she shared the family secrets with her—how my mom had cheated her of the property that we inherited from grandma, and ill-treated her during her youth, made her work like a maid in the household when both families were living together. Something that mom was apparently doing to Sheela now—treating her like a maid. Joie had every reason to dislike my dominating mom. By that time, Joie and I were developing a good rapport; she did not judge me on the basis of my qualification or career, she liked and trusted me. That is when she created this business for me and the business became a cause, a plea, a medium for us to meet every evening, and that is when the heartrending love story between us materialized. But within no time, the bitterness sprouted, at least from my side.

***

In April 2020, my brother Adarsh was sent to Pune on an important official tour for five days. Sheela packed his bags with enthusiasm. The day he left, mom-dad also went to a relative's place for four days for dad's physiotherapy. I called Joie to inform that; she asked, "now only you and Sheela are at home?" I said, "So what??"

"No, I mean, why does your mom always make it a point to leave you alone with Sheela?"

"Shut up Joie! You have a dirty mind." But mom actually did that, every time.

That night, Sheela cooked her best meal for me, fed me with care. While I was eating, she sat in front of me, shedding tears. She smelt strongly of garlic; mom had asked her to eat raw garlic thrice a day to get pregnant. Her pregnancy was the national issue at home.

She said, "Jayant, you didn't even see the messages I had sent you that day? Why didn't you come to my friend's room?"

"Sheela, you are Adarsh's wife, and let's not talk about that day."

"I am sorry if I upset you by going to my friend's room on the beach without your *permission*; actually, I shouldn't have. Anyway, let me tell you today that I shall always be there for you, to feed you. After all, we are family, your brother is your blood relation. You should understand the importance of family and not get into the traps of arrogant neighbors. That Joyita Madam is making you her slave, I don't like that."

Slave!!

I closed my bedroom door, saw Joie's messages, but slept without responding to her, no, *I wasn't anybody's slave.* There were missed calls from her, I did not call her back. I did not meet her till mom-dad came back; I messaged her next morning that I had fever, and Sheela was looking after me, no need to worry. Neither did I talk much to Sheela those four days. She tirelessly took care of me, and didn't do anything without my *permission*. She waited for me with a glass of water at the door whenever I came from somewhere.

I liked that.

But *'permission', 'allow'* kind of words were not there in Joie's dictionary. After all she was a free thinking woman! A Feminist! Marxist!!

Things were no more normal between me and Joie, it was becoming a strained association. Those days I did only one thing with her—fault finding. She was always at fault, for everything and anything, and I expected her to apologize if she wanted to meet me. Initially Joie took it lightly and said a sorry, *forget it yaar*, laughingly, to avoid a quarrel, and also because I was little younger than her. But as time passed, she realized that she was always expected to say a 'sorry', for no fault of hers, or for a minor issue. Just to satisfy my ego! Once she told me, "Joy, any relationship isn't healthy if one person is always at the receiving end, and always in an apologetic mode. What is there to say *sorry* between us for such silly, mundane issues? Can't we just keep things simple? Why can't we keep life beautiful?"

Sometimes Joie asked me about Sheela's health after her covid infection; I replied, "It's not your business."

I liked to hurt her.

At home, we had long discussions about Joie's living alone, without family, and we liked to believe that she was an egoist, *feminist,* so everyone had left her. Mom and Sheela were specially proud to declare, off and on, that we are a 'family', with great sharing-caring-feeling among ourselves, and Joie was a selfish-single-woman, living all by herself.

We had birthday parties and anniversary get togethers every month, and my family made it a point to celebrate with loud music, lot of *chhole-puri-alu*, and running around in the building and stairs. On such occasions, we never invited Joie, though at the end of the party mom or aunt went to her house with a piece of leftover cake, to observe her reactions to our party music, clapping, enjoying. She politely accepted and then she sent an expensive gift, without fail, through Shyamanand, her cook. My family enthusiastically accepted her gifts. Then we didn't judge her; we forgot that she was an arrogant woman, at least temporarily we forgot our disliking for Joyita Madam. Once she told me, "Joy, if possible please ask your family not to send those leftover cakes to me to remind me how lonely I am, and that, no one invites me to their parties. It's actually not so. I have good friends who invite me every evening, but I don't go as I have work; and I don't want to roam after office hours. I want to read, write, relax, or at best meet you. I don't believe in close-door parties; I have an open house, everyone is welcome here. You have seen my colleagues coming here, cooking or eating freely in my kitchen. I don't appreciate the way you people avoid me in your parties, and then send me a piece of cake. I anyway don't eat your cakes."

Those days I satisfied Sheela's ego by not meeting Joie as frequently. Joie noticed my affinity for Sheela for the first time when I bought two toy teddy bears, similar patterns, for her and Sheela, justifying, "She takes care of me, err... she cooks for me, I must thank her". Joie was surprised, but silent. She talked about it after long, when I hurt her for some other reason.

During Covid-19, each building in the colony had whatsapp groups, where people shared concerns. But we had ensured that our tenants didn't talk to each other, because we were charging different rents from each one of them. Joie was paying six thousand rupees more than other tenants, and she knew it. But she never bargained, her office was paying her HRA. Once she told me, "Joy, I know that you and me are just friends, and I feel insecure during corona times. What if something happens to me? Your mom won't allow you to meet me. I better join the colony group".

She actually did that. I hated her colleagues in the colony who gave her advice, showed concern for her during the lockdown. She was well informed about/by the colony people, even more than us though we were house owners. She learnt from them that ours was rather a much-disliked family in the colony; people called us frauds. From them, she got to know that she was charged more rent than others.

Joie was a good story teller. I particularly liked to hear the stories of her formative years, how she created a niche for herself coming from a poor family from rural Bengal to being an IAS officer, getting a lucrative position in Mumbai. But also I wanted to tell her that even my mom was a great personality like her. She had a satirical smile on her face whenever I told her about my mom's struggles and success stories, though I had to struggle to create those false stories. Her suppressed smiles were as if teasing me and telling, *what sort of struggle Joy, when a big property is handed over to your mom from her mother-in-law, and a doting husband has been mollycoddling her? And what success are you talking about? She is just a homemaker and nothing more!!And now she has you for her slave! To boost her ego!!*

Sometimes I told her how my mom was *struggling*as Sheela-Adarsh didn't have a child, and the relatives were pressurizing my mom. Joie asked, "why don't they visit a specialist? A doctor, or a fertility clinic, maybe?" I said, "Arre I am *struggling* because of them."

"Haha Joy, looks like you are taking too much of *struggle* for Sheela?"

I retorted, "Don't be mean Joie, she is *family*. And I am the only person in the family who can drive a car, so mom has assigned me to ensure that every time she goes to the fertility clinic, I should accompany her, and she shouldn't go by an auto."

Joie asked, "Is she comfortable going to the Gynecologist with you?". "Why not Joie??". "Ahh..I see Joy. Yes, it sounds ok to me. Anyway, pregnancy need not be such a big deal to have a baby. India is full of lovely children deserted in orphanages; they can always go for adoption of a child. That way, an angelic child will also get parents, and your mom will get a grandchild, and her *struggles* will be over."

Only the crazy woman Joie could have had such ideas. I said, "What rubbish!! What if some *Mussalmaan* has deserted her/his child and the orphanage gives that child to us?"

Then Joie Madame replied, "So what? Children are angels, whatever be the religion."

My typical pain with Joie was, I could neither handle her, nor keep her away. I loved her head massages, her jovial nature, her home cooked food, her love-care-simplicity, also I needed our business to survive; she had become my habit. But I didn't like her as a person anymore. See the paradox! It's complex.

Whenever we had serious arguments, I wanted to hurt her by any means. Once I took her to meet my friends, she came with me gladly, because she had a feeling that

I had been hiding her from others like a 'dirty secret'. She used to tell me about her friend Seema who was in an open relationship with her doctor boyfriend, and they went everywhere together, without hiding the love, which we couldn't do. I said, "Yes she can be in an open relationship because the doctor is not a fresh candidate, he is a widower." Joie burst into a humiliating laughter. "Are you serious Joy? What do you mean by 'fresh candidate'? The doctor is a lesser mortal or a less eligible candidate to love someone, because he is a widower? But I thought the eligibility criteria should be only love and respect for the partner." And then she added, "Hahaha yes, you are a *fresh candidate* for sure." I was annoyed, but I didn't want to spoil it as I had already promised my friends to meet them with my female friend.

We went to a restaurant in Bombay Central, my friends Sohan, Rajesh and Lucky met her. She had quick repartee, ready wit, easy manners and humility; my friends got comfortable with her. She told my friends clearly that she was a few years senior to me, and she will always be there for me. But my quick reply was, "Sachin Tendulkar's wife too is senior to him!" I tried to hide her age, though she was never bothered about it. She used to say, *one's age should be in proportionate with his/her achievements in life, otherwise one feels old and worthless at any age.*

Anyway, she had wine and very little food, my friends were teasing me all the time for being head over heels in love. Overall, we had a happy evening. But back home, a few days after that evening, we had an argument over family matters, and then I told her, "Joie, we are not compatible. Even my friends felt that— they said you look much older than me, you are a *buddhi*; and you are dominating, you shall always overshadow me. So we better break up." I remember, I had told her any number of times that we should break-up, though she thought it was my immaturity, and the next day I actually reconciled with her. That day she was very angry, and said, "I really don't care about what they said, because I am never going to meet them for a second time. What you think is important." She cried the whole night when I was sleeping blissfully after hurting her. Ahh yes! *She used to tell me, age is just a number. It's not an accomplishment to be young, one shouldn't be an ageist. What is the definition of youth?*

Today, at this point, I confess that my friends never said any such thing, they rather appreciated her, congratulated me for having such a charming and accomplished lady in my life. They thought I had an enviable life, great future because of having Joie in my life.

Joie was a full-bodied Bengali woman. Sometimes I told her that obese women were not so pretty, though I felt her curvaceous, 61 kilos, 5 feet four inches tall body, with no bulges, no love handles made her a complete woman. She explained that body shaming isn't a welcome gesture, and everyone is unique and everyone is beautiful; yes, she had this weird habit of thinking everyone beautiful. But the day I humiliated her by lying that my friends thought she was fat, she reacted. Without mincing words, she said, "I know that I am a curvy, healthy woman. Real men like voluptuous women, dogs like bones. Decide what you are." Of course, she laughed at her own sense of humour, trying to stop the matter there. Then I boasted how slim my mom, aunt and Sheela were, and told *"ahh you know...my mom is fitum-fit"*!! That infuriated her further; I always did that to her, instigated her, till she lost control. She was annoyed, and said, "I don't want to hear about those dry fish kinds of 30 kilos, flat chested, wrinkled women." I was terribly angry, I shouted my lungs out, but she didn't react. She had hit my ego; I left her house with anger. I had this pattern of punishing her -- say *bye, see you tomorrow,* run away, then avoid her for a few days with the plea of cold-cough, and of course avoid her messages, calls. She was becoming the inconvenient woman for me. She said, I needed a lot of flattery and ego boosting, else I would disappear, and that was the design of this relationship. I was so predictable for her. In fact, I was getting a sadistic pleasure in disappearing, when I knew she would suffer, call me, message, but won't ring our doorbell. Also I got a sadistic pleasure in quoting her age, pointing out that she was older than me.

Joie clearly had become the 'difficult woman' for me, I just wanted to get rid of her, but the collaborative business was something which my family didn't want me to drop; it was fetching me a decent amount, I had good money at least for my online shopping. Also, I didn't want to take the responsibility of breaking a relationship, she knew I didn't have the guts to say quits. So she took the responsibility of the last-goodbye, at the cost of her broken heart. I checked her mail two days after she had left Mumbai, I was shocked, but secretly happy that she had left. I didn't try to call her, but checked the collaborative business bank account immediately, to discover to my utter dismay that the account had been permanently closed and whatever money was there in that account, was transferred to my mom's account with a note, 'Mrs.Kamala , the entire money of this account belongs to Jayant. Please pass it on to him. Thank you.'

After a few weeks, I checked the business details on Google and discovered that the new Area Manager of my erstwhile company was her junior Mr.Sapan Kumar from Karnal, who was her committed, faithful subordinate, who had been requesting her to associate him in the business since years, but she had been avoiding him as it was only Joy-Joie's dream business. She thought this business had the potential to keep us together forever. At least that's what she used to feel, though I always knew that we were in a temporary relationship. Joie was a dreamer, she told me several times, "Joy, I want you and me to be like Amrita Pritam and Imroz,and live the rest of our lives together. I know you have commitment phobia, you don't want to marry; but it's ok. Marriage is not on my cards as well, at least at this point, till you have a career and you are prepared."

I hated to see a few lakhs credited to her salary account every month, even during the lockdown. I used to think, *wait, I too will get there Ms.Joyita!My parents weren't clever, so I was misguided. Otherwise, I am more talented than you!*

She was a free-thinking woman, and she had no issues with housewife-househusband concepts—she said, any one person has to be there at home, if that suits the household, though there are alternatives to stay-at-home; one can always work-from-home. She supported the concept of virtual offices during the quarantine, and she herself was working hard from home. When she talked to people about it, in webinars, public speeches, I felt humiliated. I don't know why, but I felt she was insulting me. When I was annoyed with her ideologies, I wanted to hurt her a bit. Once I proudly told her that even if I was a so called 'unemployed man', but pretty women were after me; I was marketable. I had the 'marriage market'; plus I secretly thought *Sheela was an additional advantage who was too willing for me.* A friend's wife whom I addressed sister-in-law, *Bhabhi*, sent me a message to send her some of my pictures with a note that her sister was willing to marry me. I promptly sent her my choicest photographs. Unfortunately, Joie caught me red handed, talking to the *Bhabhi*. She was very upset; for the first time she lost faith in me, and said, "I hope the Bhabhi knows that you are not working?"

I fumbled. I was scared of her, of her straight forwardness. Though we compromised after that fight, as ever, but the patch, the hurt remained.

Mom hated Joie, though she never dared to say that on her face as she was her son's employer. Joie avoided taking the change back from the poor vegetable vendors, gestured them from her balcony to keep the change, and they had a beaming smile. During such times, mom and Sheela bargained loudly with the vendors for each one rupee. The vendors treated mom as a poor greedy woman, because of Joie. Joie never sold her old newspapers to the *Kawadiwalla*, gave those away to them for free, while mom stood with a weighing machine with them and bargained each kilo of *kawadi*. Mom had every reason to hate Joie, the egoist. Joie's generosity made us feel poor; her large-heartedness made us feel small.

We also detested her domestic help, her office attendant, Shyamanand. When Sheela was in the hospital and then at her parents' place, mom had to cook, grumbling all the time, and I had to clean the utensils, broom the house as Adarsh had to work from home for his office. Though there was huge pay cut for him, but he still was the *kamau-putter* of the family, as the relatives talked about him. Private offices had pay cuts or terminations during the lockdown, but Joie was a central government employee, with a secure job. She relaxed on her couch after her working hours and Shyamanand did her household chores. Unwittingly I told

Joie one evening, "look at you, you are relaxing with a glass of wine, your domestic help is working for you, and we fought the whole day about cooking, cleaning, brooming, mopping." Pat came her reply, 'Ahh..your Big Boss house!' Unwittingly, she insulted me. We always complained her about Shyamanand keeping the garbage bags at the wrong places, his coming to the building during Corona times. I complained her aggressively about the smell of her garbage bags, and told, no other house in the building had such smelly *kuda*. She laughed off, "What? Are you serious? You guys even go and smell the garbage of tenants to distinguish them?? Haha."

I felt so humiliated!

She was nonchalant, actually she avoided such talks; for her those were 'small talks'. Apparently, her best friend from Kerala, Shikha, who was an ugly-dark-skinned-duckling, who, Joie claimed, was the prettiest woman, had advised her, *"ignore fools!"* So she ignored my family. Joie had a strange, mysterious relationship with Shikha, and also with her male friend from Kolkata, whom she had met just thrice in her entire lifetime, but he was her best friend. She used to seek their guidance for every small thing, and overestimated them. Her Kolkata friend Dr.Shubhodeep Sorkar had only advised her not to close the business after leaving Mumbai, rather handover the entire responsibility to Sapan Kumar from Karnal. And she of course did that!

Joie had this shameless habit of forgetting previous evening's fights and starting a new day each morning, with a good morning message. I told her sometimes, "are you crazy? You must see a Psychiatrist. You need help! Do you have three buttons in your mind? One to fight, one to love , and a third one to change your moods within no time and behave normal after a serious fight?" She said, "My dear Joy boy, it's only the third button that gets the world going and keeps relationships alive, else we all would fight and break up with everyone everyday. With this button, I forgive and forget hurts, this button is ego-free."

I thought, *what an ideology! Crazy woman.* She cooked for me almost everyday, she liked to cook some delicacies for us after her domestic help left, and fed me with utmost care.

Joie had sessions and lectures on the National TV channels most of the lockdown evenings. That evening, while cooking for us after a TV session, she was in a mood to discuss big issues like *Manu Smriti,* Rousseau's *Emile* or Maulana Ashraf Ali Thanwar's *Conduct Book* which apparently was a classic gift to Muslim brides. She said, Pundita Ramabai's *The High Caste Hindu Woman* questions Manu's laws. Tarabhai Shinde's *Istri Purush Tulna* critiques the practice of dowry, women's love for jewelry, and the acceptance of 'otherness'. Joie used to read a lot about self-expression and self-questioning— books like Virginia Woolf's *A Room of One's Own* and Simone de Bevour's *The Second Sex.* I was irritated, what all she was talking about? She said, these are Ecofeminist issues--water preservation, livestock, challenging a culture of thrift, saving, preservation, conservation, archiving, documentation, challenging the culture of waste, environment, challenging capitalism, colonialism, climate change, issues of the girl child, education and food for all, issues of acceptance of all, protection to senior citizens, subaltern issues, masculinity studies, et all.

But then, I was in no mood for her long speeches, I said, "Don't cook so much, mom has fed me enough today, *mummy ne jabardasti bahut khiladiya hei.* And we bought lot of groceries today, five liters wala expensive hand sanitizers, so much of online shopping we did! God! How much we buy, my family member only buy,buy, buy, eat, enjoy; I am really tired after so much food and online shopping."

And then, she was pissed off; she overreacted, as ever! "Your mom feeds you? And why on earth you always talk about food, shopping, groceries, hand sanitizers, when there are such important issues to discuss! Do you even think about the beautiful planet earth? About the message Corona virus is sending us? Do you guys live to eat or eat to live? Have you heard, great people discuss ideas, mediocre people discuss people and only low people discuss things?"

I was very angry, we are 'low' people?! I shouted. "You Bengali woman, so chatty! Always cooking with those strong spices, mustard oils, spreading negativity in our building. *Tum jao yaar yahan se, niklo hamare ghar se,* find another place for yourself. Get out of here! I am going, I don't want to eat here."

I always asked her to get out of 'our' house. After all, we were the landlords and she was the tenant!

That night she too did not eat, and sent me a message that she won't ever offer me any food. I was feeling bad, *'poor thing, she cooks only for me, and perhaps I shouldn't have shouted at her. Also, if she stopped feeding me, I'll end up getting plain dal-rice of mom'.* We had just one income of Adarsh, and ten members to feed, so sometimes Adarsh-Sheela used to return the grocery I ordered online. I was used to eating good food at Joie's place. Was I going to miss that forever?

No, of course not. The next day, she switched on her third button, and offered me food, as usual.

Those days when Joie and I had some argument, face to face or over phone, I recorded that for my best buddy

Rajesh Khatri. He was going through a divorce and he had convinced me that all women were mean. But my aunt had told Joie the other side of the story—that Rajesh didn't love his wife, he and his mom illtreated her, so finally she ran away with her lover. Even my aunt had told Joie that I was friends with Rajesh for his money, he was a rich man. Apparently, I was with him for wrong reasons as he paid my liquor bills, though Joie didn't buy those statements. But Joie had sympathy for Rajesh Khatri's wife. Even my mom had told her against Rajesh Khatri when Joie offered her business to me—mom was overwhelmed that day and told her that Rajesh was jealous of me. But then, I was fond of Rajesh and had saved the recordings of his wife's fights on my mobile, which he had sent me for fun. When I teased Joie that I had recorded her arguments with me, will send those to Rajesh, Joie said, "you and that Rajesh Khatri, both are Misogynists. I pity such people. Do you think you men are perfect and only his wife was at fault? You will end up missing the beauty of life minus a partner, you both will be cornered and live alone. So please proceed and send him the recordings; I don't care about him or you for that matter."

I said, "No Joie madam, you will live and die alone, if I leave you. I have my family beside me even if you leave me some day."

"I see. So you think that your parents will be alive for ever. If not, Adarsh and Sheela will offer you free food for rest of your life? Joy, if I could give you one blessing and one curse, my blessing would be, you should get a settled job for yourself, so that you don't remain dependent on these people. And the curse would be – the ten members in your big-fat-happy-family, your big drama *hum-saath-saath-hei-family*, should be ghettoized in separate towns, live lives alone, each one of you. Then you will understand the meaning of living alone." How despicable she was!

Once Rajesh Khatri sent me a message that all these rape and molestation cases against women are false, and 75% of the rape cases are fabricated, manipulated. That's the way for clever women to trap men into false accusations and legal cases.

I announced that before Joie. She was very angry. "What the hell!! That Rajesh is a fool; but I don't expect you to talk rubbish like this. India is the rape capital of the world. If you say such things in a public platform, people will throw stones at both of you. Woman harassment is fiction? Not fact?"

I lost it. I was mad at her. I said, "You feminist, egoist, Marxist woman! I hate to be here." And I left her place; of course by then I had eaten a good dinner cooked by her. Back home, I was glad that I had used so many adjectives, which were more like abuses, *gaali,* meant for her.

And I categorically believed that when a man is drunk, women should be careful while speaking to them; they would rather keep quiet or at best say 'yes' to their men rather than starting any kind of discussions at that time. But Joie had this disgusting habit of 'celebrating', 'talking' normal even when I was drunk. A couple of our serious fights were because of her ' normal discussions' when I was drunk. Next morning I realized that I was wrong, but then one need not say 'sorry' for every small thing. Women should learn to forget those bad words uttered by drunk men.

Joie used to say, *Peace is the only religion and only the sane can follow it.* And that, she was *a Renaissance woman.* I found all that fake, her *pseudo-feminism.* Once I took her to Shani Mandir, the temple for Saturn, and I poured a bottle of oil on the Shani idol. She was surprised, "Joy! Why are you throwing expensive oil on a stone? They can be used for poor people's food, right?"

She used to question me with a tone that offended me.

I tried to explain feebly, "Shani Bhagwan drinks oil".

"What??!! Why??"

I hated those nonsensical questions. We had ideological differences. She argued in favour of Romila Thappar, Arundhati Roy, Sonia Gandhi, and I called them anti-nationals, Leftists, Marxists.

She would ask me every evening, "What did you do today?" My answers were, "I did some weight lifting, did some Puja, went to buy groceries, talked to Rajesh Khatri." She never realized that I was intimidated by this question. She used to say, *'we all must contribute to the enrichment of the civilization in terms of work, creativity, productivity.'* And I thought that was bullshit. She used to say, *'an idle's mind is a devil's workshop.'* I thought she said that to me, hinted at me.

She felt, our ideological differences were affecting our intimate life as well. But I was clear about my needs – I was an avid eater of chicken and other nonvegetarian foods -- every day except Tuesday and Thursday, and I abstained form sex those two days; those two days I did elaborate *pujas*, Sheela helped me with flowers and other arrangements. Joie argued, "If you are an animal eater, you should eat animals any day; I don't think Gods are watching you more carefully on Tuesday and Thursday only; they have better business. Else, you should be kind to animals every day and become a vegan." She was a vegan. About sex, she had no specific needs; she responded to my desires whenever I had the urge. Sometimes when she had important official work, and I had the urge, she would just try to make it quick. I could know that and asked her, "Am I forcing you?" She said, "No!" I didn't bother to ask her, if she had any urge on my fasting days. I believed, women need not be vocal about physical needs. One Tuesday, she tried to test my patience and attempted to seduce me. I was fire on her; I shouted, "You can't even control yourself two days a week?" Her firm reply was, "Joy, I love you, and to get an orgasm, I don't need you, I have my own means, you are not my sex-toy. I was just checking, how ritualistic you are. Because the other day you were claiming that you are not serious about Tuesdays and Thursdays, and you said you were just joking!!" She used to catch me red-handed. She was too independent, strong-willed! And who would like to spend life with such people?

She had this disgusting urge of correcting sentences and words even in whatsapp messages—she was a victim of the OCD called Grammar Pedantry Syndrome. She happily, gigglingly admitted that while meticulously correcting everything that I wrote.

I felt she tried to distance me from everyone including mom and Sheela. Was she possessive of me? Was it her business to point out their mistakes? After all, they were my *family*!

'But at the end of the day', she delivered a speech sometimes, 'we should maintain the 'basics' of a relationship -- that is love. We must agree to disagree, and accept each other, despite all our differences'. Perhaps, this was her third-button, which I never understood. For me, life was either black or white. But she believed in all shades of grey.

Time flew like fine sand from the fists. May was over, then few days of June. Corona positive cases were multiplied by lakhs in India, Mumbai being the worst affected city. People whom we thought were inevitable in our lives, were succumbing to the disease, Corona deaths or to depression. Every day the newspapers reported of deaths, failure of the governmental policies, suicides; nothing seemed to change. Joie was still working from home; she had a couple of Skype interviews in the meantime for higher positions in Delhi, one was for the Cabinet Secretary in the Union Government.

Those days I spent more time with Sheela in her room in the plea of watching TV. We had just one TV for the entire family and Sheela made it a point to fix it in her and Adarsh's room. After Adarsh left for office and parents got busy with neighbours, or were at the rooftop, or slept in their room after lunch, I and Sheela sat on her bed and watched all TV serials by Ekta Kapoor, and discussed the stories, and had three square meals. Of course I liked to argue that Ekta Kapoor is a ridiculous woman who has ruined Indian television. That made me feel intelligent.

I met Joie once in a couple of days, leisurely; she said she was going through depression due to all those Covid deaths of near and dear ones.

Those days I had started criticizing Zoie's home cooked food, which I liked very much in the past. If she made red sauce pasta, I told, "you could have made this with white sauce, I have eaten red sauce several times" She made white sauce pasta the next week, but I preferred to remind her that red sauce was any day better. I did the same about anything she cooked, and gave her examples of the amazing cooking of my Mom, Sheela and Bua ji. She got confused about my choices, but she was never angry. She believed that my family members actually cooked great, and she had no issues with that. She confused me with this laid-back attitude – had she no competition with anyone? Strange woman indeed.

In my scheme of things, Joie was the last and least priority. Sometimes I sent her a message that we will meet at this or that hour. She was irritatingly punctual. She would die, but never cancel an appointment or be delayed by a minute. I was always delayed, and delayed by 30 minutes to two hours, unapologetically. She got restless, called me, but I didn't bother to answer. After all I had a *family*! And she had none. During her waiting-for-Joy hours, appointment-with-Joy hours, restless hours, my priorities were -- helping mom with the washing machine, drying clothes, taking out and changing our curtains, placing online orders for Sheela-Adarsh, picking-dropping family members at the metro, helping my friend Amit in the basement, switching on and off the water resources of the building, applying henna on my hair, taking long showers—in fact many things to do! So what if she cancelled an appointment with her colleagues, boss, doctor? She could always take another appointment with them, right? During those hours she waited, got angry, sent me messages, I didn't respond. I anyway met her after two hours or so. What was there to be so punctual? And Joie had this bad habit of laughing at our 'Diwali cleanings'. One month before Diwali,we were in a celebration mood and mode. Cleaning each almirah, shelf, bed and under the beds, bedsheets, curtains, clothes—just everything. I would ignore her messages and calls during Diwali cleaning— Mom, me and Sheela would be busy. She said, "One should clean their house round the year, why only on Diwali? And why do you guys follow every ritual meticulously?" Her house was always spic and span, and she was proud of that. I was angry with her when she laughed at our ritual cleaning. And she had the audacity to point out the mistakes of my family. During Covid times, she suggested that I need not visit each relative's place to handover a packet of

Diwali sweets; one can always order a gift prepaid online for relatives and friends rather than gathering crowds in the markets and roads. I was disgusted—how will a loner understand that Corona was much less important than giving sweets to relatives personally? I and Mom travelled all over Mumbai for seven days, distributing sweets among relatives. There was traffic jam like hell, but we never cared, we reached markets pushing the crowds. She didn't like that. I hated her for that.

During Covid days, sometimes I went out with Rajesh Kharti and came home at 1am or more. Mom was annoyed, but next morning she was fine. But Joie cautioned me next morning, "You never know the safety measures taken in the places you are visiting late nights; you better avoid late nights till Covid is here." I was terribly angry. I said, "You cannot miss a person according to your time and comfort, right?" She said, "When did I say that you should come home early because I *miss* you? Did I ask you to come to my place yesterday? I knew you were busy, so was I!" I somehow managed to prove that she was wrong, always wrong. Because deep down, I was annoyed, frustrated to see her continuous online meetings during office hours even during Covid days. If she could be busy with her office work, why couldn't I remain busy with friends?

During those Covid days, I attended all my relatives weddings with family(despite the strict rule of the government that not more than fifty people could attend a party). The relatives were also clever; they made separate arrangements for the eating-joints of fifty people with a few feet gaps. I went to those wedding parties despite having cold and mild fever, and Joie didn't like that one bit. Joie had a close friend named Suchismita from North-East India, and they used to go for shopping, movies sometimes. This woman had invited me to her place several times for pujas, dinner, parties; she used to cook a lot of nonvegetarian dishes for me and wait as Joie had told her that I loved those. But every time I had to cheat her at the last moment, sometimes because I had a cold and sometimes to accompany mom or Sheela to the market. Finally, Suchismita had termed me at a clinical liar, to which Joie protested, but couldn't help. Suchismita invited us once again on Dussehra, just the two of us, and this time I strongly assured her that I won't cheat, though Suchismita had anticipated it. On Diwali morning, I had a mild cold; I kept messaging my temperature etc to Joie the whole day, and declined the invitation late evening. Joie didn't protest, she just left alone for her friend's place. They enjoyed the evening; and next day when I asked if her friend was angry, she just said, Suchi knew it, so you need not bother. I didn't like two things—how can she be so cool about my absence and enjoy herself with her friend? And next, was she hinting at my attending relatives' weddings despite having cold and fever during these Covid months?

During those days, once I asked Joie to lend me fifty thousand rupees to clear my credit card, online shopping bills. She said, "But the company account is with you, and you can spend all the money there. I do not anyway take any money from there." But I wanted to save the company account money, I might need that in future. She gave me the money, but I hated thinking that she had to transfer that to my account; after all she had an upper hand now! I hated her for earning. Sometime after transferring the amount to my account, she said, "You can use the publicity strategies I have sent you to upgrade the company to the next level—if you do it, your company is sure to be financially benefitted." What the hell was that? Did she think that I simply mellowed out in the company? Did I enjoy myself without doing any work? If I did, that was none of her business; my mother was there to feed me. Why should she lend me fifty thousand rupees and then advise me to work? I was angry. I said, "Don't talk about your earnings (no, she hadn't, actually.). I spit on you and your money!" I made a gesture like spitting and abruptly ran away from her house.

Lord Krishna cut the throat of Shishupal with His Sudarshan Chakra after Shishupal committed his one hundredth mistake; He waited till then, patiently. In a way, Joie waited for me to commit my one hundred mistakes before she broke the relationship. Yes, of late I had started assassinating her character, talking about her rapport with her colleagues, whenever she sounded problematic to me, asking her, "how are your *brothers* in the office? *Dharm-bhaiyas*, right?" Or I asked, "How is your Bengali friend whom you never met, but who guides you at every step?". I wanted her to retort, but she told me calmly, with a certain eeriness in her voice, "Joy, you are a little younger than me, you are a pampered, immature brat; and I don't want to hurt you. That's why I put up with your nonsense, thinking you may change for better one day. But let me tell you, as long as I am vocal about your mistakes or am trying to correct you by arguing, crying, fighting, things are fine between us. But the day I am silent and stop reacting to your nonsense, it's all over. I know how to recede in a relationship; I can flow backward like the backwaters of Kerala. If I go away, I won't look back. Learn to fear my silence Joy."

She was good at keeping promises. She never entered our house, except that one time, on that eventful morning. She did not come to meet us the day she left Mumbai. She left quietly, sending me that mail.

That emotional, chocking voice echoed in my brain several times last few months. Yes, she never looked back after she left Mumbai.

***

But eight days before that, on 5th of June 2020, Adarsh had an official trip of ten days to Pune. After dropping him in the airport, in the evening I met Rajesh Khatri and we got drunk. Joie called me, as ever, after her office hours, to ask after my wellbeing, I said "yeah I am good, will see you tomorrow".

I vividly remember that night when Mom brought Sheela to my room, and ordered me to allow her to spend a night, rather a couple of nights in my room, saying her AC wasn't working. I hesitated. Mom left, closing the door, taking my mobile from the table. It was getting awkward, I slept in one corner of the bed, and asked Sheela to sleep on the mattress laid on the floor. She couldn't sleep; after tossing on the mattress for some time, she got up, went to her room and came back with a bottle of Paul John Single Malt Whisky and two glasses. She offered me, I said, I am already so drunk; I had a migraine, and I needed to sleep. She said, "Can I at least give you a head massage?"

I committed the gaffe of my life by responding, "yes, you can."

After all, she was *family!*

She poured a large peg and kept in front of me, and softly massaged my head. I started sipping the whisky, enjoying the massage. She poured some more, and still more, till midnight. I don't know when her nimble fingers had stopped massaging my head, and were roaming all over my body. My young body responded, though I didn't want to. There were convulsions, I was hallucinating about Joie,

Sheela shut my mouth with a kiss from her garlicky mouth. I lost control and gave in. I took her with great force, pressed my body against hers, fondling her flattened chest and hating her garlicky breaths. Within seconds, we both exploded, I was completely spent inside her. Suddenly I slept. But she couldn't. In another hour, she woke me up with deep kisses; it was obligatory for me to repeat everything, mechanically. I wasn't tired this time, the whisky did its job. Sheela had saved her energy since years, for me, and she whispered that during the act both the times.

Next morning, I woke up startled, beside her boyish, nude body.

"Where are others? Why are you here?"

"Relax Jayant, mom-dad went to the relative's house last night, they'll be back after four days."

I was feeling awful, with a lump in my throat. Throughout the day I kept the mobile switched off, it was lying on the dining table. I closed my door and slept whole day, munching whatever Sheela kept on my table. Perhaps she too slept the whole day. In the evening, at 8pm, Sheela came to my room with dinner, and some whisky again. I had it, and then she took me practically by force, I didn't resist.

It went on for three days, we had sex several times (no, we didn't make love!), till I was drained.

On the fourth day, at 9am, our doorbell rang. Sheela opened the door. Joie rushed in, breaking her promise not to enter our house. She caught me unawares. She was wearing a mask, covering her nose and mouth, and directly came to my room, sat on my bed. She had lost patience, she couldn't take these four days' silence anymore.

"What is this Joy?"

I didn't know how to react. Sheela asked her to get

out, Joie didn't pay her attention. Rather Joie was worried thinking I had fever, or maybe I was Covid-19 positive. She abruptly removed the thin sheet I had covered on my body to check my temperature, to find me lying without clothes, and Sheela's undergarments all over my bed, some inside the sheet. She was awestruck, flabbergasted, and shouted, "What the hell is this Joy? You seem to be fine, and still your mobile is switched off since four days?? What is this woman doing in your room? Where are your trousers? Whose clothes are these? Where are mom-dad and others?"

Sheela took over the charge of protecting me. "Madam, you have to get out of here right now. Mom-dad will come back today, they have gone to a relative's place. We are together—I and Jayant. Hope things are clear ?!"

Joie rushed to the sink and vomited; she had this nasty habit of vomiting her lungs and intestines out when she couldn't handle stress.

Joie came back to me and looked at me with blood in her eyes. She was panting for breath, tears rolling down. Without wiping her tears, she asked, "Joy, have you been locked with this woman in this bloody house since three days, and these goddamn clothes are hers, all over your room? Are you her gigolo, you hopeless maniac? What is this incest going on here? Was I not enough for you?? I will kill you!!"

She was practically shouting her lungs out.

I said, "Madam, I am not your *slave*. You have not *employed* me, ok? Don't you shout at Sheela, she is my *family*. You can please go."

"Oh really? I just hate you." Words were poor for her immense hatred for me at that moment.

Joie left my room in the lightning speed, casting a look at me, full of abhorrence. She looked   dreadful and violent at that point.

That was the last I saw of her.

Mom-dad came home. Mom took Sheela to the kitchen and they talked for sometime in suppressed voices. Adarsh came back from Pune. Mom told me, "If Joyita Madam wants you to work with her in her company, she has to say sorry to *me* first, because she shouted at you. Who is she? Is she feeding you? I am feeding my son." Sheela had reported it well to mom, yes.

I had no mood to meet or talk to anyone, I kept my door closed for two weeks or more; and opened it only for food or drinking water. I never saw Sheela in the hall or kitchen when I came out for water; and whenever Adarsh saw me, he avoided eye contact. I heard mon-dad talking that Joie left the building, in fact Mumbai itself, to join her new assignment in Delhi. Mom told dad, before leaving, she had transferred all the business profits and the entire amount of that account to mom, not keeping a single rupee for herself though it was her business, with a note to mom; and that she closed the account.

Joie knew how to settle accounts.

I read her mail a few days after that.

***

In July, Sheela's pregnancy was confirmed. Her garlic sessions were stopped; also, her talking to me was restricted. Mom took special care of that. In fact, I was shifted to the top floor house where a group of young boys were tenants; mom got one room on that floor cleared for me, and she sent me food and tea to that room through Asha, the maid. Yes, now we hired a maid as Sheela was pregnant.

Adarsh had accepted his wife's pregnancy. He had to. Only then I got to know that it was a premeditated action by *family* for the sake of a child, though Joie had always guessed that.

Not that I didn't remember Joie in my new life, new room, but I wasn't prepared to get back to her. Occasionally I googled her. She was a public figure, her life was transparent. I knew what all she was doing in Delhi in her new role, and I had nothing against her. I learnt to live life minus her. Rajesh Khatri met me more often than not, whereas other friends got distanced, they had lost faith in me or my future after I lost Joie's business.

Joie had become a disappeared person for me, leaving no traces at all. She had taken with her a vacuum and left memories with me. What would she have done with my slightly flowering toothbrush and my unfinished Vivel soap kept in her bathroom? What would she have done with the shorts I wore at her place? Who would have drunk the Beer I had left in her refrigerator? I had such questions lurking in my mind.

By December 2020, Corona scare was over, life had become almost normal for people. Post quarantine, people had been adjusted to the 'new normal', wearing masks, socializing only when it was highly necessary, avoiding public places or inviting guests or meeting relatives and friends. I got bored in the evenings, reminiscing those evenings that I had spent with Joie.

In early 2021, Sheela gave birth to a baby boy, everyone except Adarsh seemed happy. Mom made it a point that the baby wasn't left with me, ever. And she also made it a point that Sheela ties a *rakhi* on me next Rakshavandhan onwards.

Time flew. In 2024, when the baby boy was four years old, the relatives said, "Oh..the boy exactly looks like his *Tau Ji*, Jayant, with curly brown hair, pink lips and fair skin! Ah..how cute he looks!" Though I preferred to believe that the boy looked like the washer man, Bablu. Once I mentioned that before mom, and I had to bear with her rage for one whole week.

Adarsh stopped meeting relatives. Sheela and Adarsh were a smart couple, handling their and our lives and our ancestral property smartly. Adarsh had been spending for the household since past ten-fifteen years, and mom-dad blindly trusted his expertise with accounts; thus they signed wherever he asked, without questioning. In January this year, we got a notice from the court that out of the six houses in the building, only one was left with uncle-aunt, rest other houses were the legal property of Adarsh-Sheela.

Mom-dad were devastated. They left for our village, Podi. Mom wanted to take me along, after all I was her only proud possession!

No, I don't want to go back to village. What shall I do there? I want my Joie back. I want our business back. I read, re-read the lines from her email several times, "Wherever I go, the comfy room will be kept for you." Has she kept that *room of my own* in this mansion in Delhi? Who knows?!I stared at her house with a deep sigh.

We ten members of the family were ghettoized, in separate towns, in separate houses this time; and I was roaming on Delhi lanes. The big-fat-happy-Indian-family was no more there.

Ahh…Joie..What did I do!! Why did I do that to us??

You still are a shadow presence in my life. You have tumbled-down the symmetrical configuration of our lives.

***

Today, standing at the vintage point, I recollect Joie-Joy love story. Is it too late? The huge gate in front of her house, the two gunned security officers, the cold winter night of Delhi, everything was adding to my phantasms.

Walking slowly towards the Janpath market, I saw

a *banzaran*, bangle-seller, nomad, fully covered, protecting herself from the chill; she was holding two burgers. She offered me one, I took it nonchalantly. She was kind.

"*Oye chickney*, I noticed you staring at that bungalow throughout the day, what's the matter? Want to work there? The madam of that house is a good woman, she offers donations to our slums. I clean her gardens and walls weekly; tomorrow I can take you to her guards."

I was sleepy, she offered me a sack. There was a dull pain in the body and mind. And then she offered me a poly-packet of hard liquor, which they called *pawa* in Delhi. I slept, I have this blissful habit of sleeping tight. My mind was blank; and in the middle of the night my hands felt, the *banzaran* woman was flat chested like Sheela; and she too had garlicky breath.

■

Scarlet Fly—the Red Velvet Mite

I was just reading a post by someone on the Facebook about the scarlet fly, the red velvet mite. The gist of what the post read was like this --- *what we call Sadhaba Bohu in Odia, meaning 'Bride of the Seafarer', is the species scientifically named as Trombidium grandissimum. Alternate names for it include 'Bir Bahuti', 'Birbaboti', 'Scarlet Fly', 'Lady Fly', 'Velvet Buchi', 'Aarudra Purugu' and 'Rani Keeda' (in Hindi/Urdu). The mites are visible in large numbers early in the monsoon and so are also called 'Rain Mites'. In Gujarat, the term for velvet mite is 'Gokal Gaay' or 'Mama Ni Gaay'. Strange, but it's reportedly used as an ingredient in traditional Indian medicine (the oil from this red velvet mite is claimed as useful for treating paralysis) and due to its alleged ability to increase sexual desire, it has also been termed by some experts as 'Indian Viagra'. It folds its legs when it comes in contact with a predator. The act is to protect the legs, but also to place them in front of the main internal organs, which can be clearly observed when picked up. It will unfold its legs and start moving once it feels that it's out of danger; and it can be observed walking again after some minutes if left untouched...*

Then there was a YouTube post about the scarlet fly—a school of them—velvety-red, sheer, romantic mites roaming on a green landscape under a downcast rainy sky.

My eyes were moist. They took me to the memory lane. To home in India. From New Jersey.

She had a tendency, which got worse as she grew older, to brood. My best friend Lata, Madhvi Lata, from Jaipur, Rajasthan, India. She lay awake at nights doing it, unremitting all day long and it washed like stilted water through all her actions. She was good at what she did-- dealing with her students in the university and her research scholars, attending seminars and book launches, but still she wasn't engrossed by any of it. It was all just a skill she had, like her social manner which was fascinating and functional, but had rally nothing to do with her real life. By nature she was solitary, and most of her evenings were spent alone. She didn't feel like talking to anyone, except when there was usually something urgent she had to say to Siddharth, Sid, her friend, paying guest, who hardly ever 'paid'. Often I wasn't home from the kitty parties when she called up, but she didn't leave any message on my recording machine either, she only hung up in frustration. Occasionally my maid answered and then she would hurriedly say, "Tell her that Lata had called up", muttering somewhat in discomfiture. Sometimes, she even said nothing, but hung up like a clandestine caller.

Thinking perhaps about me and Sid, who was her only family now, she wouldn't take a nap and pace up and down, smoking many cigarettes. Diminutive pulses beat esoteric in her. All the time, all through her body and also inside her skull, and she didn't know what it was.

About me, she had always felt passionately, but not like this with these physical symptoms which made her quiver as with electrical currents pulsated through her these days. She was growing into a lonely woman. Day and night were categorically the same in her flat. Under the tremendous chandeliers, she was walking around making large mugs of lemon tea for herself, engrossed in her own thoughts as Sid was in his. In her youth she had resembled a charming jolly Bollywood actress, but now she was more like a tragic heroine, tall, steady, dressed in raw silks, her hair never dishevelled, melting eyes, she appeared always to be hearing some awful solitary music. Yet at the same time there was also something peaceful about the way she sat there sipping green tea in the late nights as though it were the middle of the afternoon.

Sid used to stay back at his friends' places some nights, just to avoid her. Forgetting that it was she who never asked him to pay the rents even though he was her P.G., and had been paying all his bills. It was she who cared for him the most of all.

"Of course there is no use quarrelling with him", she kept nagging cantankerous about him, grumbling all the while. "No use questioning him anything. Terrible even to exchange your views with him! I tried to call him; no answer! Just fool around with that foolish mobile. Someday I'll kick it to pieces!"

Day by day I felt trapped between Lata and Sid. After all I am not an 'agony aunt'! I was only her guest and friend. I was on a trip to India with my husband Chakko, who was on the Fulbright Scholarship at JNU, New Delhi, India, for a period of 10 months.I spent the first two months with him in Delhi, got terribly bored, then spent two more months with my old parents in Odisha. How to spend five more months in India? Chakko had been busy, as usual, forgetting everything else, when it's his career. I complained. He suggested why can't I spend my time with my childhood friend Madhvi Lata, a professor in Rajasthan University, separated from her husband since years.

Thus, I ended up being her guest for five long months.

She received me with super excitement. Cooked all those Indian delicacies for me which I had kind of forgotten living in New Jersey for two decades. We shopped, went to Govindji Temple , Jantar Mantar , Hawa Mahal--the palace of winds, Moti Doongari and Lakshmi Narayan Temple , Jagat Shiromani Temple,Jaigarh Fort , Nahargarh Fort, Jal Mahal , Amber Palace and Fort complex , Swarghashuli/ Isar Lat , Ram Niwas Bagh , Albert Hall , Dolls Museum , Sisodia Rani Garden , Vidyadhar Garden , Gaitore , Birla Planetarium and Chokhi Dhani. Rajasthan kept our spirits buoyant, colourful. We giggled and shopped like little girls.

First few days, everything seemed to be normal. Just like any other single woman, Lata was a bit over-possessive about Sid, sometimes even over protective for a man who was more than thirty. She was even possessive about me! The way she had been years back.

I and Lata were neighbours, friends. Studying in the same class, she was better than me in studies. But I was far from being jealous, we had that kind of bonding. Rather it was a great relief to me that she used to write my assignments, do my class work as well as homework, write essays and debates for me, comb my unruly hair, feed me like a kid whenever I was lazy, switching on the alarm clock on my bedside table before going home so that the next morning I could go to school on time, arguing with anyone who tried to embarrass me for not being good at studies. Once she even dared to argue with my mother who would keep me busy helping her in the kitchen during the study hours.

"*Maasi,* how can Mrinalini study if she cooks every

evening? Why don't you finish cooking before watching your T.V. serials? Every day she goes to the school without doing her homework and does it during the prayer class."

My mother was furious. Lata was denied access to our house for a few weeks.

Lata had decided that she was going to 'bring justice to the world'! Once she discovered that my mother was giving more pocket money to my brother than me and my sister. In fact my mother had the habit of pampering my brother. Even when I would ask her some money to buy my Laboratory Manual, she asked me a hundred questions, but it was not so in case of the monthly cricket bats and gadgets for my brother. Lata dared to object to it, in full public view.

My mother hated her, and we too were obliged to do so. It was safe to dislike her. And most desirable.

My parents were happy in a make-belief world of their own—believing the best that would suit their moods by the wilful suspension of disbelief. They had never been practical, were always busy talking about their favourite characters from the T.V. serials as if they were their family members. I mean the issues of the characters of T.V. serials were definitely taken more seriously than ours.

I would have been left alone, but for Lata. Her clock revolved around me. She seemed to have not been attached to her siblings as much as to me. I was kind of her world, apart from her studies. A world which was simple, pure and joyous.

Lata had been ambitious since her school days, unlike me. She wanted to be a professor in the Oxford University when she would grow up. She had a loving and caring disposition.

I used to tell her, "I don't want to be 'something' in life like you, Lata ! I would just marry a rich man, cook, dress up, clean my house, have two kids—one boy and one girl—and be a housewife." That's precisely what I am doing now in the States, with pride and conviction. Every marriage anniversary I receive one more diamond necklace from Chakko. My collection is fabulous now, and so is my life!

Lata used to call me a 'scarlet fly' when we were kids—she thought I was innocent, beautiful, romantic, vulnerable and velvety. She would shower me with her love and care, like a parent would do to his/her child.

In the twelfth board examination, we both had opted for Science. Lata passed with good percentage, and I failed twice. My parents and relatives had almost given up. But Lata didn't.

"This time you fill your form with Arts. I will prepare notes for you and make sure that you learn every answer thoroughly."

She actually did that. After her study hours, she would sit with me for two hours or more and prepare notes on History, Political Science, Education and Logic—all in English. Understanding anything in English was a tough task for me. So I arranged help books on all those subjects from the market in the vernacular medium, and read; but I didn't dare to discourage her to prepare notes for me. One day before my examination, she discovered my help books. She was completely under a shock!

"Why didn't you tell me ? I have been wasting my time all these days!"

"Would you listen to anybody? You are so stubborn. Anyway, don't make a scene now."

She kept quiet, of course after crying for an hour.

Once when we were in the college, there was a state level essay competition for students of first year. Lata was already in her final year since she was my senior by now. One had to write an essay of five thousand words and send that to the organizers by post. Lata did that in my name and I got the first prize! Everyone was happy and congratulated me. Only I didn't find any excitement in that. After a few weeks, she asked me to give her the photocopy of the essay which she had given me to keep carefully, so that it could be developed into an article and sent to a journal for publication. But I had kept that somewhere and forgotten. After all that was just an essay! Lata was upset. Then she cried and cried. But she never ever hated me for anything that I did. Not even for taking her for granted.

When I was writing my M.A. final year examination, she was doing her Ph.D. I didn't want to study anymore, but for her. My father was also adamant that at least I should be a Post-Graduate before getting married. That day I jotted down all those difficult formulae on small pieces of paper and took those to the examination hall hidden under the sleeves of my dress. Prof.Das caught hold of me within no time and warned me. But I had decided to take the help of the chits. When he discovered me cheating in the examination for a second time, he snatched my copy, warned me that I would be debarred for five years and asked me to get out.

I rushed to Lata.I had no other choice.

She was Prof.Das's favourite student, was a Junior Research Fellow in the department. She pleaded with him to allow me to write the other papers. He scolded her for a good thirty minutes-- that being a role model for the juniors in the department, how could she support an unethical practice like this? She had to bear with that, I was allowed to write the other papers and somehow I managed to pass.

Lata kept quiet about it forever. Well, it was her duty,

her responsibility, to protect my honour. After all she was my friend!

Both of us had arranged marriages after a few years. She joined a university as a teacher, I came to the States with Chakko. We had completely different lives now. I got busy with my household and almost forgot her. But she couldn't. She still was there where I had left her.

Anyway, her next 'target' of pamper was her paying guest, Sid.

Lata had compromised with her abusive husband for many years before the final separation. She had never loved him; and now it was as if all the love she hadn't had for the husband was showered on Sid. Sid looked somewhat like Lata's father, with the same fair complexion and sharp features. She sulked that she could not do enough for this 'boy'; she wanted him to have everything in the world, but the boy valued nothing. The more she tried to do for him, the gruffer he became; and even sometimes seemed to hate her. But that only prompted the lady on to love him more and she spent more time thinking up what else she could possibly do to make him happy. Like she used to do with me years back. She wanted to receive that much-hyped 'moral support' first from me, then perhaps from her husband, and now from Sid.

Lata was an intelligent woman herself, and she was confident that Sid must be the same. All those books she had read out to him must have made him brilliant! She was sure, by now, knowledge was built into his bone marrow.

This was the time when I met her again in Jaipur during Chakko's Fulbright Fellowship in JNU.

Lata was like a emerita circus animal etherised on her leather couch now. But it was also true that she could look bottomless into others and see what was going on there. It was an instinct. She had a skill, a gift, something almost inessential to her own disposition which she herself acknowledged to be that of a mammoth egotist. Popularity, adulation, name and fame bored her now. Sid was like her test-tube, to experiment all her love-and-care bouts on him. She was, anyway, wonderful with children. And for the cause of women, of course.

"Phaolene, Katrina and what not! Why did women come to monopolize storm names?"—she never liked if women were associated with any kind of violence.

During those days in Jaipur, any number of times she would rush off to hug and kiss me or even to Sid, pamper us with her care. I was used to such display of affection from her. But I felt, of course she should have stopped throwing such tantrums of love at me or Sid.

She sometimes talked and talked with the fear of losing our company. During some of the parties at home, Sid would tease at her at the pitch of his voice, "Won't you give us the delicate pleasure of your delightful company Ma'm?" His friends would interchange looks of glee. "You have the most repulsive voice,did you know that?" He would complain later. "You always speak as if you are lecturing an audience. I suppose you do it so often that it's impossible for you to speak like an ordinary human being anymore. It's not your classroom, Professor!"

Lata would come forward with a smile, to show off that it was just a joke, and it never hurt her.

"There she is! Now we are going to have a very creative session for free. After all her life is as perfect as a text book!"

I felt somewhat awkward, but what could I have done? I was helpless. Like her family members, I too found it safe to blame her for whatever her predicament was today. *She could have adjusted with her husband and led a normal life like us! After all a husband is a husband! So what if he knocked her sometimes out of rage? He might be in a bad mood. Look at us; we also have made compromises, even though our husbands didn't hit us! And she talks of marital rapes, domestic violence and all that stuff!! How can a husband rape? Sex is his right. What else a husband is for, after all? I didn't pursue a career like Lata, so what? I have everything today. Look at her sister. She too wanted to be a fashion designer. But now she is doing well as a housewife. And look at Lata today—a loner, sharing her house, her space and everything with a paying guest who never pays,who can only exploit her and nothing else.*

Constrained to this shell of her home, these days Lata cultured some quiet and private pleasures. She liked, most of all, to organize things in decorum. To line things up in rows. Jars on shelves at a pageant, filling up peach holes at the crooks. When by some accident somebody scattered her rows, she was never irritated, for it gave her a fortuitous occasion to rearrange them. Whatever transportable variety she found, she systematized into neat lines, according to their size, shape or tinges of colour.

Next, her deep-cleaning.

She would clean, dust, broom everything—the floors, beds, chandeliers, almirahs, shelves, even the bathrooms. After Sid or I would come out after bathing, she would quietly go inside with a wiper to wipe the accumulated water and clean the floor, mirrors, soaps , just everything. Her pots and wash basins had to shine. She had written with her neat hands on a drawing sheet, *"I understand how much you love me from the way you leave the bathroom behind."* That caption was pasted on the bathroom wall, like a gospel from the Holy Bible.

Gosh! Love and the bathroom!

These two are the last things one can think of associating!

And she had this atrocious habit of sticking to things of her choice. She had at least twenty pairs of sandals and slippers, matching with all her outfits, but she preferred to wear her grey slippers all the time—she wore it for at least twenty years, and used to say, "I would die in these slippers!" Rest other sandals and slippers were generously given away to her maids, but not this one. Never. She liked wearing a dark maroon bathrobe and these ill-defined slippers that we had already come to loathe.

That year I had to spend my 55th birthday at her place. She was anxious to have the fifty-five candles lit -- the birthday party had to be conducted along its proper fortifications, with discipline and decorum, and she felt herself to be the only one there responsible enough to do so. She felt about everything like that—that she was the most organised, disciplined person!

I and Sid were lighting the candles on the cake. We had carried it into her room and kept it on a round marble table there so that she could enjoy watching us. But she wasn't enjoying it, she looked at us with a sceptical eye as we lit the candles. And as if that weren't bad enough, she wrote a big 55 in icing in the centre of the cake.

"There is completely no need to shout someone's age over the rooftop." Sid grumbled. "Ma'am, you better go and take some time to dress up. After all it's your best friend's birthday!"

Lata took that very seriously.

After all her make-up and dress-up, the end result was anyway remarkable, and she sat ordained like a mannequin, gleaming with all her jewellery hung about her persona and her eyelids painted to match her raw silk.

She had an amazing similitude to the Victorian painting hanging on the wall above her, with its skinny outlines and eyes visibly blue.

I looked on!

There was something in that house that made all of us go through with our duty with perfection. It may have been the rigidity of her routine that held us all up as in a steely agenda. Even our tête-à-tête had a certainty--as when we remarked on the filling of vegetables, the butter chicken and the crab gravy that she cooked with perfection.

She smiled at the moon. The moon had a small bite taken from its western brim, analogous to the logo on the Apple laptop that she used to do her office work from home last few days.

Lata had mood swings; or perhaps she was unwell; she won't speak for days now. During all of her youth she was captivated by words and felt miserable by numbers. Now she missed – without knowing what she missed – words.

Sid hated illness. And sick women were painful than anything else. Now, Lata was sick. She had this migraine, which was really disgusting for Sid.

During those days, Chakko's fellowship got over and I came back to New Jersey. Initially, I called her once a week, then a month and then after every six months and then, never. I didn't even read her long e-mails where she used to write about her loneliness, lack of 'moral and emotional support' and all sorts of things. I am sure I could have read her letters. But the computer was in the study, and I preferred to sit in the living room. My Home Theatre was in the living room. I had a mail ID, but I was lazy to check mails; Chakko used to check my mails and get print outs if I asked for any important mails very specifically. Also, I was keeping a little busy. We were constructing a new house in New Jersey.The interior designer kept me engaged most of those days.

Lata was forgotten. Sent to oblivion, for convenience.

Two more years passed by, perhaps my mail box was filled with Lata's unread mails by now. Once I happened to meet Lata's sister in a wedding and her topic came off. I was feeling a little bad for Lata's loneliness and all that. But her sister retorted, "See Mrinalini, everyone has got problems in life. Didn't I marry into a different culture and adjust so well? Have I been fighting with my husband for my career? And tell me, how can a husband 'rape'? And if your husband shouts at you once in a while, is that domestic violence? I mean, seriously!! She should have sorted it out with him. If she had any problems with her husband, she should have gone to the court of law for help, rather than coming to us. What can we do? How can we help? Lata has the habit of making things miserable for herself. Why doesn't she leave that boy, Sid or whatever, on his own? Now it should be up to him if he wants to be with her or not even if she has supported him all her life. Who was asking her to be a Mother India? Now she has been mailing us for 'moral support', which only she understands better."

Perhaps she was right! Perhaps not. Anyway, it was convenient to think that she was right and Lata was wrong. As ever.

After a few days I got a call from a hospital from Jaipur, India,to go and see an ailing friend of mine, in whose mobile the only number that was saved by name and address was mine.

This time Chakko insisted that I should go. "Who knows, you may never get a chance to see her anymore! Her doctor says, it's Alzheimer's. Also, she has been complaining of Tinnitus."

And Lata insisted that she should be shifted back to her home from the private ward of the hospital. "I don't want to die in a hospital."

***

Her dress misaligned for the first time, earrings mismatched, her coat flying uncluttered; her office-bag bulging with key-rings without keys, unused vitamin tablets, unfinished books and spare glasses, all lying scattered. I was told, she had been obsessive, firing maid after maid for not looking after her bathrooms well; but now the flat lay vacant for months at a time. The lights were dull, but that wasn't abnormal, because she didn't like bright lights when she felt low.

Lata looked solitary, meek, mild, full of love, like the scarlet fly, the red and velvet mite. She was sleeping tranquil on her couch, wrapped in her cosy scarlet signature mink blanket that she loved, just like she loved her grey slippers. Perhaps she was humming a tune, some old song of her favourite Lata Mangeshkar.

When I reached – it was already bit late in the night – I didn't like it that she was still wide-awake to receive me. Maybe she was again in a mood to trap me with her emotions! I answered her fumbling questions monosyllabically, or sometimes not at all. I just shot a penetrating glance at her, which was completely needless. Because her face needed no probing, each emotion she had, was revealed there, transparent.

■

Octopus

'Octopuses have three hearts; a systemic heart that circulates blood around the body and two bronchial hearts that pump it through each of the two gills. Octopus blood contains the copper-rich protein hemocyanin to transport oxygen.'

What a thing to say about her! My Octopus. She too had three hearts—one to love me, the second one to love me more, and the third one to love me even more.

Her name was Neelotpala. I called her Neelu.

I had a faint smile on my lips though I was teary when I read this about the Octopus. And I remembered her saying, "Varun, who says that men don't cry? They of course do! In fact, they should cry sometimes." Then she quickly added, "Not always though! Else you too will become a Drama Queen like me! Hehe."

She didn't have any of the etiquettes, mannerisms that someone from a dating app should have. Apparently, she never logged into a dating site before she came across me. She had been a single mother for the past nineteen years, busy parenting and making a worthwhile career for herself. She was dedicated to whatever she did. By the time her son was nineteen, she was already in her forties, though she was far from looking her age. Her behavioural pattern was childlike and had the heart of a child — transparent, liquid. She was liquid like an Octopus. That metaphor suited her well. So did that character representation.

She was the Director of a Post Graduate Department and a celebrity writer. Her public life was flooded with people, but her private life was as lonesome as she was. She was a private person. A time came when her son, who was her best buddy, and her close friends pestered her to find a partner before she died old and lonesome.

Neelu went to many meetings and conferences; people were awe-inspired with the super stylish Director Madame in her high heels, speaking with an accent that she used selectively. And as much as the disciplinarian Boss that she was, she was kind and compassionate by the same token. On such occasions, many a man tried to personally associate themselves to her; but she had built a cocoon around her. Her defence mechanism was a hard shell of blunt behaviour, economy of words and stern looks. But inside, she was molten like the Octopus. Who knew that better than me?

Last year during the Covid lockdown, her son Monu and best friend Esha downloaded a dating app on her mobile phone without her consent that gave her access to chatting with prospective partners. At first, she was quite annoyed and straightaway deleted the app from her phone.

That day, Esha gave her a piece of her mind and explained, it's no good, no fun, no great sacrifice to only work and work and die single. She said, "Look at me! My husband and I got a divorce last year, I gave myself one year to cry and brood. Now I came out of it, got registered on this site and talked with at least fifty people and then I met five, finally I zeroed upon one. Today I have a partner with whom I am going steady. We meet over the weekends; we both have busy careers. We talk, roam, watch movies, and have great sex."

"Sex!!??"

"Why, what is wrong with that? Of course, I did not jump into bed with all the fifty men I chatted with. I took one month to meet this doctor who I am dating, and now we are emotionally, physically and socially compatible."

"I see."

"Don't just see, do something, you silly woman! Else very soon you will be a crazy, grumpy, shitting, pitying, fretting, crying, brooding, ailing old woman. Your son will not be able to start his life happily unless he sees you happy. He will never become a man, he will just remain your son. Serving you will be his only business. Do you want that? Come on, please move on. Give it a try."

Neelu thought about it the whole night. Esha had a point. What was the harm in talking to some people? *I have nothing to lose. How will they harm me over the phone? And I am of course not going to meet any one of them. Let me just talk to some gentlemen.*

That was that.

The next day, the dating app was reloaded in her phone. The moment she logged into it with her charming photograph and without much of a description of herself, many people waved at her, sent her pleasantries. Esha responded to them, while Neelu was shuddering with apprehension and nervousness.

After an hour, swiping the mobile screen left, looking at the well-groomed, up-to-the-minute men's photographs on the site, Neelu saw my photograph. Mine was the only photograph that caught her attention, and she swiped right and wrote, "hi!"

Within no time, I responded, "hello beautiful lady! May I know your name please? It says, your name is 'N'."

It took her a while to confide in me how judgemental she was in the beginning. My audacious appearance, witty sparkling eyes, charming smile, gentle mien made me stand out, she said.

I asked her where did she live.

To my utter amazement, she wrote her name, designation and address in the chatbox.

I was bewildered. What a profile! Why would she sign herself up on a dating site!!

Maybe Esha hadn't guided her about dating app manners, or maybe Neelu was naïve, vulnerable. I felt pity for her, and couldn't help myself from telling her that in these kinds of sites, people need not reveal their identity.

She didn't get it. Then, after giving some thought, she wrote, there is no harm in knowing more people at this age. After all, we are not teenagers. We are mature people who know how to maintain their decorum.

She sincerely believed that. And her sincerity bewildered me.

I still couldn't cut through the virtuousness of her intentions. Was she trying to meet me immediately? Why was she giving me her address? Was she imprudent? An imposter? But a second look at her profile picture reversed my apprehensions, she looked sincere, honest, unassuming and decidedly competent.

Yes, *no harm.*

I was informally formal in my response; in fact, I cracked a joke to make her feel at ease. That worked. The uptight academic sent a laughing emoji. Gradually, we chatted about her work, her life, her past, her family; it was all about her, nothing about me. I discreetly circumvented whenever she asked me a question about my life. After all, she was a stranger. Unlike her, I knew dating app manners.

With a polite good night, we used to depart, after chatting for an hour every evening. There was never ever any intimate chat, I didn't want to ruin her innocence or spoil her trust in me. The gentle lady was too genteel.

After a few days, once she told me with great enthusiasm that men on dating apps were great!

"Men? Who all are you talking about?"

"Arre! Look at you!"

"I am a man, not men. Hehe."

By the way, Esha had told her that when you were dating one man, you should concentrate, focus, and you must not divert your attention to another man. That is not ethical. She followed Esha's advice to letter and spirit and confessed to me that I was her only 'great man'. She had decided that she was already dating me, without meeting me even once!

Gosh! That put me in a spot! I immediately wanted to run away from her, in fact, block her. I even tried. But by then I had Googled her, I had many of her writings and photographs on my computer—she had become the object of my interest, passion, dreams (?).

I couldn't bring myself to block her. So I decided to continue to be accessible to her, of course within my limits. That evening I told her that my real name was Varun, not Ram, which I had used in the dating app. Ram was a pseudonym to conceal my identity. She was quiet for awhile, she sounded hurt. I felt guilty. That was when I told her that I got into this app to handle my loneliness, but I wasn't divorced,though I was living separately, and my seventeen-year-old daughter Nisha was the thread between me and my wife. I made it a point to tell her that me and my wife used separate bedrooms. I used a pseudonym on the app to avoid complications in the life of Nisha.

She just said, *hmm*.

With time, we became relaxed in each other's company, or rather inevitable for each other. I made her laugh with my wit. She too had a crooked sense of humour. She had a friend in Chennai who sent her intelligent jokes that she shared with me. Every morning I woke up to her jokes, anecdotes. The binary between me and her was, she was mostly politically correct with her words, even when she was in one of her humorous moods, and here I was, always putting my foot in my mouth, telling her most unwarranted stuff, and regretting later. For example, once I told her that I am not able to call her as frequently as I would have wished because my 'cohabitates' were alert, they might get wind that something was going on in my life. I used that term for my daughter and also for her mother who was living with us at that point of time because my daughter's exams were ongoing. Neelu was amused, "Cohabitates Varun? Like three people living in a zoo? Where everyone is watching everyone in a panoptical style? Are they your owners? You cannot even close your door and make a phone call? Wow!"

I said, "Baby, don't be silly. Let's talk about ourselves."

"Varun, now I already know that you have 'cohabitates' living with you, how can I un-know that? Haha."

I regretted having said that to the witty, sharp woman.

I remember the dark humour Neelu used sometimes; she had this subtle sense of satire that was also a kind of humour. "Varun, you are an e-commerce person, so are you thinking about the 'profit and loss' of meeting me? Like, the 'profit' part is — if you meet me once a week or fortnight, there will be some physical closeness and then you'll feel confident about your sexuality, which lately has not been of any use to your ex-wife. And the 'loss' is the loss of your so-called 'equilibrium' at home. Haha." I just said, "shut up *jaan!*"

She had this typical habit of switching off her mobile at ten and studying till late at night. If she lacked anything in her life, that was 'time'. But she willingly gave it to me, whenever I asked for her attention.

I had a great deal of respect for her. Within a month of our meeting, I opened up, I became candid with her. I found her unmatched. My days seemed meaningless when we did not talk. The days we talked, I felt a strange contentment. She was my happiness quotient. She understood my moods in a way that nobody did. She took care of my emotions, she waited patiently when I was busy with my meetings, selection of candidates for my company. She never complained, and never claimed that she had a busier schedule than mine. She was always there for me. She had mastered the art of patience which was the strength of her character.

"Neelu, I am laughing now", I said once during an intense conversation.

"Why?'

"Of all the people in the world, I met you! A poet who could melt me just with words. And then, I fell for you."

"It was a celestial schema, Varun. Because I deserve you!"

She wore poetry. She knew word juggling; she had mastered the art of words too, she was the word wizard. She said, "Language is our behaviour." That day I said I wanted to merge with her, and she said, "You be the ocean, I'll be the rivulet."

There was a stinging pain of joy to see her merging with me, bit by bit. She thought, I was 'heatbreakingly breathtakingly handsome'. I chuckled every time she said that. "Ahh…one will never die if he falls in love with a writer Neelu!"

Neelu was an incorrigible romantic, she was *all for love*. She had decided, love is the panacea for human maladies, love is the answer to humanoid pursuits.

Neelu had written a book titled *'Vaidehi'*, which is the other name for the character Sita from the Ramayan. She teased me, "See Varun! Your pseudonym was Ram which was why Sita Mata was impressed with you!"

Then she added immediately, "But don't think that I am falling in love with you, hehe."

Followed by a few laughing emojis. And giggles from both sides.

She always sent that particular, repetitive message to me, whenever she talked about something flirtatious. Ahh yes, she had this delightful sense of decent, witty flirting. Attired dalliance.

Those were the days of my utter contentment, intense delight. The lady was pure heaven.

We shared movies and music. We would watch a particular movie together, from 25 Kilometre distance in the same city, and discuss the dynamics. We always thought and said the same things at the same time; she claimed that I not just completed her sentences, but even her thoughts. I was her 'Stream of Consciousness', her 'Objective Correlative'. There was some sort of soul connection between us. I felt a vacuum if she was not on my mobile screen for long. She was becoming my extreme passion, foremost engagement, my only source of pure bliss. I was the Halley's Comet in her life, she was my Earth.

We were compatible in parenting as well. Whatever I did for Nisha, I shared with her, and she too responded in kind. I was her friend, philosopher and guide. She enthusiastically gave me that status. I felt flattered, but she intended no flattery. She seemed to have convinced herself that I was the world's most gifted man.

I downloaded some software and painted beautiful pictures of her, which she thought were real. She liked even the WhatsApp GIFs I sent her, to make her laugh. Once she asked me to meet her, I assured her that someday I would visit her with white flowers, and she was excited like a girl. She waited for that day. After days, I asked her, when were we going to actually meet? She jokingly said, "On my deathbed? Or funeral?" I spent the evening reprimanding her, and she laughed all the while. "*Buddha* uncle, I am very young, don't you know? I am not dying so soon. If at all I die, I will follow you, becoming a *Bhootni*, a ghost." She knew how to camouflage her pain and wear a smile.

But then, sometimes she was becoming a burden on my conscience, which, I was not able to carry. Her honesty, simplicity, transparency, uncomplicatedness were killing me; her lonesomeness was killing her. We both were tormenting each other, wordlessly. I was craving to meet her, but something stopped me. I did not want to hurt her by giving her hopes of companionship. She was craving to meet me, but she had tremendous patience. She knew how to wait, without complaint. She said, "Varun, I can wait for you till the end of the world. You cannot fathom my patience."

I was wondering, what was stopping a single, beautiful, successful woman like Neelu from meeting other men of her match? Why was she so focused on me? What was there in me that was so compelling for her? She knew the answer. I could never know, she never told me what she saw in me, but she always said, I was her ultimate man. She said she was a sapiosexual, so much so that she considered intelligence the most important trait in a partner. Once she proudly claimed that about herself, and then I told her that scientists consider sapiosexuality as less of sexual orientation and more of an identity. I was taken aback when she didn't consider that as offensive. Sometimes Neelu was simplistically naïve, believing in easy binaries.

And then of course she added, "But don't think that I am falling in love with you, ok?" That jag was enough to make us both laugh. That invariably worked. We always laughed in each other's company, we were overjoyed, she was my lifeblood those days.

Once I read one of her old stories on the Internet where she had written about her long-distance relationship with someone named Jaydeep. I was petrified, was she trying to see Jaydeep in me? I asked her openly; she was dismayed. "I am not trying to replace you with anyone, and Jaydeep is irreplaceable".

"I am sorry."

"Varun, you hurt me to no extent. You should know that I recede very well in relationships if I feel that I am not doing any good to the other person. I am like the backwaters of Kerala, to retrocede as much as I proceed. Two more hurts from Varun, and Neelu disappears from his life, ok?" She added.

She had this strange connection with Kerala, by the way.

It was alarming. I was irritated. I too made it a point that I was the last person to take any kind of threats.

"Threats? How can I threaten someone as important to me as living and breathing Varun? I am only giving you space."

She sounded emotional. We both were upset, but only to get back to each other the next morning with all sincerity, earnestness.

There was a distinctive genuineness, solemnity between us that worked. Any day, that worked. The only woman I was 'dating' in the virtual world, was my only reality those days.

I had my private business, so my timing was flexible. But she had a nine to six job; I waited for her to reach home and message me after bathing. "Bathed, *pujaed, teaing.*" Ahh…that was pure ecstasy. Pure joy. I was rejuvenated. I learnt to live life again.

Neelu asked me to watch a documentary on the OTT platform. She was an amusing character, her choice of movies was inimitable.

She said it was an incredibly beautiful and touching documentary, based upon a legend. Neelu was a hopeless, die-hard romantic—she discovered love and trust in anything and everything. The movie had made her cry. The author allied with a female Octopus and became experimental with her way of life and all her rituals for almost a year, free diving in the cold waters. It was painful to watch how the Octopus strained to protect herself from the sharks. That night, I too watched the movie. I felt, one of the most amazing things about a human being in the movie was the ability to connect with nature. The story showed me a new-fangled world of possibilities. The man found a novel meaning and direction for his life by learning the lessons of humanity and trust from an animal. A man who was detached from the people around him learnt the lessons of life from the Octopus.

One day the Octopus met a male Octopus and mated. The life cycle of an Octopus is such that most of her body is used by her eggs to sustain and then hatch. Her life is literally sacrificed to further the lifespan of the young. Over a week or so it lay quietly in her den, hatching the eggs and her life slowly dissipating out of her. Once she is gone, her body is consumed by scavengers from the sea, and ultimately a Pajama shark comes and takes her body away. That was when I called to tell her that I was teary-eyed, and she said, "Varun, who says that men don't cry?"

The underlying allegory of the movie was, how the measure of trust in a relationship can impact one's life in any form, from anyone for that matter. And the other lesson was that one's belief that someone else has got his back covered can disappear from your life any given day—so learn to preserve it as long as it exists, however short-lived it may be.

I felt an instant connection between the man-Octopus and Varun-Neelu relationships. The man was under the impression that he was experimenting with the Octopus. But in reality, the Octopus premeditated his life. Like Neelu measured *my life in coffee spoons.*

My life had been carefully measured by '*my Octopus teacher'*, Neelu.

Early this year, Neelu bought some property, and she was looking for furnishings, fittings and fixtures in the new house. She had no idea about real estate, being a University teacher and a writer. That is why I offered that I shall do the research on her behalf and send her the best possible quotations on almirahs and bookshelves. I sent her many, she understood nothing. Her mind was preoccupied with research, teaching, creative writing and, of course, love. Love for Varun was becoming her occupation, preoccupation, obsession.

The silly girlie (I liked to think of her as a girl, her

demeanour was such!) talked to me endlessly for 51 days and wrote 51 soul-searching, heartrending, tear-jerking, poignant, simple yet complex poems, and one day she came up with a surprise for me, a complete book of poems, dedicated to me, her Muse. I was overwhelmed; never in my life had I imagined that a poet, a woman, would ever write a book in my name, for me. I had forgotten that I too am a human being, with emotions, needs, desires. She taught me the higher values of humanity; yes, she was the 'humanity side' of my character, as she used to say. She ignited me with the ideas of human rights to the true sense of the term. But alas! I couldn't learn those lessons from her, because I had been a very stubborn pupil, I learnt in her humanity classes what I wanted to learn—precisely, things that were convenient to me. I never listened to her open-mindedly. But she had this weird sort of blind faith in me – I was the ultimate source of all arts and sciences for her.

Neelu was in one of her dark moods and modes one evening when I called her. She was angry with herself for being worldly imprudent. For being impractical. She was crying, actually shedding tears, that she was not able to understand the graphs, diagrams, designs, quotations and the documents that the Builder and the company people had sent her. She was penetratingly trying to comprehend those when I called up.

I consoled her, I promised that I would be there to help her with those. "Don't worry Neelu, we will do it together, ok?"

She came to the point, without mincing words.

To.The.Point.

"In what capacity are you going to help me Varun?"

"Calm down Neelu." I consoled, "Just as a friend."

"But I never considered you just as a friend. You were always more than that."

She was flooded with tears, all boundaries broken. Her voice choked, she was inconsolable, desolate.

She was sulking, she did that so well. We talked, nay, rather I talked and talked. She sobbed and sobbed. Her bottled-up emotions were melting. I was helpless at the other end of the phone. It was getting despondent.

That is when I happened to say, "See, I am not a free man; my marriage still lingers, though I am not living with my wife or ex-wife. Did I ever commit anything to you Neelu? Did I promise anything? Why are you crying? I cannot give you anything. I have nothing to offer you."

She calmed down and said, "No. Never. You never promised anything, Varun. Never committed anything. I understand." And then she hung up.

We both had a sleepless night.

The next hour, there was a message. "You shouldn't have told me that you were never committed to me. At least for the sake of some respect for the time we spent together, you should have avoided this offensive proclamation. I need no explanations from you. Varun, who cares about commitments when one desires someone like living and breathing?"

And then, she made it a point to tell me, "Varun, from day one you have told me that you are alone, and your loneliness brought you to me. You wanted me as your platonic love. Now when you talk about all sorts of worldly engagements and then you are inaccessible for hours, you sound suspicious. But then, I do not want to suspect you for my sake, for my mental peace."

And the next morning, she sent an awful picture of her swollen eyes, inflamed due to continuous crying, nightlong self-abuse. She had this characteristic habit of sending me all her pictures, good or bad.

Yes, she was getting self-destructive. Her eyes were lifeless.

I was restless. Guilty.

I reasoned with myself, *I should make peace with her, I cannot afford to lose her at any cost. At any cost. After all, I had no plans of going back to my wife though we were not divorced. After Nisha's settlement, I would be free. There will be no family pressure on me to live with my wife and daughter then. In the meantime, I must meet Neelu; we had enough reticence and penitence. She is mature, she won't ask me to commit. On weekdays, we both are anyway busy with work, so on weekends, we can meet. Life would be beautiful with Neelu. We both are meant to be together. I had a commitment phobia, and Neelu wanted no commitments.*

But Neelu's approach to me changed after that night. After her swollen eyes-night, that is.

Her replies to my long messages became monosyllabic. There were no more witty or romantic messages. There were no long conversations. No debates over literature or movies. No political or social issues were animatedly discussed anymore. I was pushed back to my vacuum once again, I felt bottomless again. No heartbreakingly breathtakingly beautiful pictures from her in my inbox anymore. No sharing. No caring. No love. No, nothing.

Just, *yes.*

Or, *no.*

To anything and everything I asked.

This time I decided to be patient. Let her take her time. I should wait. After all, I had hurt her. Let her take a 'break'. I always thought a break is the best solution when one cannot take hard questions.

Months passed. Almost a year passed. There always was a response from her mobile though, to my messages. *Yes.* Or *No.*

I was running out of patience.

I had her address, which she had shared with me when we were close—she had hoped I would meet her someday with white flowers. Poor girl, she took things at the face value. Took ideas and people at face value.

On her birthday, I bought a bouquet of white roses, and one red rose, just in case! Who knows, she might accept this!

I called her before reaching her house, she had told me that she didn't like surprises. My hands were trembling while I dialled her mobile number after one year. I wanted to tell her, there was not a day, not an hour, not a moment, when I did not think of her. I wanted to remind her, in fact reiterate, about our 'three minutes' theory—that I missed her every three minutes throughout my wakeful hours round the day and night.

Anyway, the domestic help received the call.

Neelu must be studying, padhaku ladki.

"Hello! Who is there? Monu bhaiya is in the class, he cannot take the call now."

"Give the phone to Madam please."

"Madam? But she left last year, since then Monu bhaiya has been using her number. If there is anything important, you can message him. He will respond later."

"Do you have any idea where she is? Can you ask Monu bhaiya and tell me?"

"No. I am instructed not to talk to anybody about Madam. She left India last year."

I remembered the shark sweeping the Octopus away in her vulnerable moment.

I cried. Sobbed. Wept.

Yes, men *too* cry. Men *do* cry.

My Medusa, my Octopus, had her last laugh, the *Laugh of the Medusa*. Neither she herself had learnt the dating app manners, when she dated me, *Varun,the expert of dating apps*. Nor had she taught telephone manners and demeanours to her son.

On a second thought--actually, she had taught him that, precisely that.

The Wild Stream

My mother sat on the hard wooden seat along the verandah the entire evening. I lit the round charcoal stove and placed it at her feet. Massaged her feet with some heated mustard oil with cloves of garlic in it, so that her pain would subside.

But pain seemed to cling to her bones quite obstinately today, refusing to leave her. She has been speaking of her grievances against all her maidservants, one after the other, telling them over and over again how she has been '*more sinned against than sinning*' by all of them.

"I fed them, clothed them just like I would do for my daughters, against everyone's better advice! Now I am paying for my folly and no mistake. These girls and that old woman, and above all that wretch, Mami, who thinks she is nothing less than a Madhuri Dixit! Oh! I am going crazy! After all these years of taking care of them, finally police came to my house! Of all, my house!"

We sympathized with her, but couldn't help whispering that it served her right.

Mami, Mami Pradhan. The gorgeous, super-stylish maid of my mother, who was her ego-booster, oil-massager, cook, domestic-help, gossip-partner, gardener – all in one. Today Ma was cursing her.

But there is a background to her story.

Before Mami's mother joining the post of my Ma's maid, or getting all those promotions and increments after that eventful day, there were two other maids, who had troubled her so much (or at least she thought that they harassed her!) that she was losing weight every day out of stress. Sukamaa, our first maid, was a good woman, dedicated especially to my younger sister, now in the U.S., so much so that even if my toddler sister would pee in her plate , she would wash and eat her rice, would never throw it with the fear that it may harm the child. My little sister would ease herself in her lap most of the times, and it supplied laughter and entertainment to us.

"See this silly woman!"

Ma would insist, "Sukama, don't you do that. Take a fresh plate of rice and eat."

"Ma, how can you be such an enemy of my daughter? You want her to fall ill?"

Yes, she claimed that my sister was her daughter. But the fact was, she had three daughters and two sons of her own. Shakuntala, Shaila, Koili, and I am forgetting the boy's name. Koili was her favourite; perhaps she loved her as much as she loved my sister. So the year Koili was pregnant for a third time after two abortions, Sukamaa had to leave our house.

My mother was grieving, fretting, fuming.

Et,too,Sukamaa?

"Ask Koili to come and stay here, why do you need to quit your job and go there? I will anyway get another maid,but then who will give you so much money, food and saris? Your sons-in-law?"

Ma was right. She literally pampered her maids. She

was a school teacher, so she was totally dependent on them; the maids were her real home-makers.

Sukamaa left. We consoled Ma that she was not family, so forget her. Ma and all of us missed her tattooed face, tattooed horizontally and vertically all over to avoid attraction of other men towards her charming face; and her loud kisses to us, that would sound like the music of a *tabla*.

Sukamaa episode was over.

Next came Czarina.

She was street smart, a girl from the Mussalman *basti* having five brothers who were butchers; she was a hefty, strong, dark-skinned girl in her twenties. She took over the kitchen, garden, under the beds, all extreme corners of the house where Sukamaa's old hands couldn't reach.

Ma was happy, instantly.

But we were not.

Because she started eyeing our make up kits, lipsticks, *bindis* and bangles from the day one. She would stare at us when we were getting ready to go out, and sigh, then ask us the price of things that we thought she can never afford to buy.

But it was not so. After many months we discovered her affluence on that morning when police came to our house for the first time ever. Czarina had been stealing money from my Ma's school bag, which Ma called here *vanity bag*. When asked, she would reply, "Do I look like a thief ? Even if I look, I am not one. My brothers get better things for me than yours, ok?"

Czarina was notorious. My youngest sister, who was a few months old, would relieve herself on an old newspaper every morning. Ma would ask Czarina to take the shit wrapped in the newspaper and throw it in the large pit in the extreme corner of the street. But madame Czarina had a different plan. What she did was--there was Jaga Bhaina's grocery store adjacent to our house, and people used to crowd there from morning to evening. Jaga Bhaina made nice packets of dal, *gudakhu* (a tooth paste made up of opium), sugar, salt and tie them with a typical thread of jute. The packets were quite tempting. Czarina collected some thread from Jaga Bhaina saying that Ma needs some thread. Jaga Bhaina was very nice to our family, because he had a small note pad with Baba's name written on it, and we could take anything from his shop -- chocolates, puffed rice, *muan,*(a sweetened puffed-rice cake) sweets, nuts, any time. All he had to do was jot down the item and its price on the note pad. In the end of the month, Baba used to take care of the bills. Also, Ma was especially nice to him, because sometimes when she was hurriedly getting ready for her school, Czarina would report, "Ma....garlic is finished, also dal."

"Oh! This girl will never spare me. All the time she has complaints. And there is the head-mistress, Jumelia Raut, to wait for us at the gate itself sharp at 10 am! You go and ask Jaga Bhaina to give you whatever you want!"

That was that. Czarina brought lentils, garlic and some jute thread from him. Then she did wrap my little sister's shit with the same newspaper, took another fresh newspaper and covered it for safety, and tied it up with Jaga Bhaina's thread with ultimate professionalism and put the neat packet in the middle of the road. Anyone would feel that some buyer from Jaga Bhaina's shop has dropped a packet on the road by mistake and pick it when no one was looking at him. Czarina's duty was to keep the packets on the road and call us to wait and watch who was picking the packet that day. To our surprise and giggles, everyday someone was sure to look around, and then lift our shit-packet pretending as if it was actually his grocery packet which he had dropped by mistake.

We were very impressed by her smartness. Until that evening on *Pana Sankranti* (an Odia festival when people have intoxicating drinks) day, she didn't lock the back door of the house, to facilitate her brothers to enter our house in the night for a burglary.

Next morning, we woke up to the wails of my mother and to my father's anxious talks to the police about the robbery. We were in deep sleep after drinking the sherbet with *bhang*, then Czarina's butcher brothers just pushed the ajar door, entered our house, spread smoke to make us lose our senses, and stole everything from our house. Old utensils, clothes, money, jewelry, Ma's puja box and Baba's old gramophone, bed-sheets, boxes, just whatever they could lay their hands on.

The police searched the near by areas and discovered that only my father's gramophone that he cherished (and someday I am going to inherit that) and my mother's *gurubara pedhi* (box for Goddess Laxmi's puja) were thrown in the lake side. Ma says, "Idiot *Mussalman* thieves, how could they have stolen my Goddess Laxmi's box, would she have spared them?"

Both of them were relieved to discover that they hadn't harmed any one of us. We were jolly well sleeping when the theft was going on.

Thus, came to an end the Czarina episode. Czarina dynasty. (Anyway, after many years I saw her in the town during my annual visit to my parents' house. She stole her eyes and ran away.)

Ma had to take a week's leave from her school to find another maid. My second sister had to write her tenth board examination in her night suit, because Czarina's brothers had not spared her school uniforms.

Ma could manage to find a frail, shabby, poor woman, Mami-*bou* (Mami Pradhan's mother) for her maid. She had always fever, always backache; she was ever-complaining and ever-demanding.

Anyway, she was the savior, as she facilitated Ma to re-join her duty in the school. Ma was the only Hindi teacher in an Odia school, so she was much in demand. No one could engage her periods, so we were happy that our Hindi periods had been converted to games periods the whole week. Now Ma had to hurry up to finish the syllabi of all classes and make up for the absented week. She was upset. Her best friend was Urmila *mausi*, who was her colleague, our geography teacher.

"See Urmila, these maids are giving me a tough time. I pay them so well, feed them every day, still they are such ungrateful."

For a working woman, balancing between home and office is a Herculean task. Urmila *mausi* had similar problems; in her case it was created by her in-laws.

"Yes Mira *didi*, I can understand. My sister-in-law and mother-in-law are making my life hell. They came for a month, and now it's six months since they are here. Not taking the name of leaving. I am the in-charge headmistress these days, and I have to complete my syllabus for tenth class by next week. Their test exams are on. But again next week we are getting three days off for the students, because Biju Patnaik is visiting the town and our school ground will be the helipad for his chopper."

"Oh, is that so? My girls would be very happy to see the Chief Minister!"

Ma was enthusiastic. On Monday we had no classes,

no class work, and no homework. Three days off from the school! On Wednesday the chief Minister of Odisha would be visiting our town, and he has decided to grace our school, not the boys' high school, by landing in our play ground. We were teasing Baba, because he was a teacher in the boys' high school. There were many volunteers from the party, cleaning and labeling our ground, decorating the building, hiding the pits temporarily with soil, arranging a large canopy overhead under which the CM would sit and deliver his speech, cleaning rubbish from the ground, making room for water supply and food stalls where we used to play hide-and-seek, hanging colourful paper-cuts in different patterns on threads, putting two large freshly-cut banana trees at the entrance, still small raw bananas hanging on them, fixing loud speakers at four corners of the ground, one huge throne-kind-of-a-chair, red in colour, used for the brides and grooms in marriage receptions, placed at the centre for his majesty, the CM of Odisha, and the plastic *Neelkamal* chairs standing inferior around the throne, creating the binary opposition.

We were excited. Ma gave *chutti* (leave) to Mami, our maid's daughter, from watering her plants that day.

Mami was spending her childhood in our house as a woman while we, the children of the house, cherished her womanhood. She had no monotonous work like ours; no one forced her to go to school if someday she was delayed due to household work, or if she had no mood. She had no homework; she was in the kitchen, humming a tune to herself, peeling boiled potatoes, while we had to study from six to ten in the evening.

But she had, of course, a routine, not of her own creation; she had been fixed with a life of poverty that made up our lives. She had to water Ma's plants, polish our shoes, lay our uniforms on the bed, dry our clothes that her *Bou* (mother) would wash, broom our verandah.

But that day it was different.

That day we took her along and rushed to the school ground at 10 am, though the CM was to arrive at 11am.

Mami Pradhan was ten years old. But she had a tremendous sense of dignity, doing nothing that would be frowned upon in the society as just suitable to a maid's daughter. She was thin, flat chested, malnutritional and looked hardly six or seven years old. She maintained herself as far as she could, always looking good in her own terms in my old clothes that Ma gave away. She was my classmate, studying in the MCD school. Even native clothes looked fine on her, however old fashioned they might seem to others. She had that air of a refined, accomplished girl, which was purely made up, superficial. She would always struggle to be a face in the crowd, to be different, and was successful to some extent, because she had the advantage of a beaming grin, ear to ear, quite unnecessary most of the times.

Udayagiri was a small town in central Odisha, in Phulbani district. It was a sleepy town, having no character of its own. My parents spent their lifetime there, more than forty years, without any definite reason. First, they wanted to be together, as teachers, one in a boys' high school and the other in a girls' high school, both government schools, so that their children would be secure with both parents. After retirement we pleaded them to move to some other town where proper medical and higher education facilities would be available. But they never agreed.

"*Beta*, Phulbani means where flowers speak to men, '*phool*' speaking '*vani*'; see the greenery around. And Udayagiri is where the sun rises, it's like the sun-city," Baba had all excuses. But they spent their whole life with tooth aches, fever, rheumatism, with lack of medical facilities, and now they were all by themselves. Their children are away, in townships, in metro cities and two of my sisters are in the U.S., because one cannot think of a career in Udayagiri, unless one is a farmer or a shopkeeper; or at best, a school teacher.

Most people of Udayagiri belonged to the hills and most had never seen a train, a sea; forget about an airplane or a chopper. So on that eventful day, we gathered in our school ground, wearing our best frocks, applying little Emami snow-white cream of Ma under Ponds powder, and trying to look our best. Mami had taken special care to groom herself, she was looking more like a clown with that artificial black mole tattooed on her cheek and magenta coloured *alta* applied on her lips to appear like lipstick. She wore one of my old frocks which Ma had given her the previous year, which she wore only on special occasions. She had made it a point to stand a little ahead of the crowd, to catch the attention of people, and was grinning all the while, for no specific reason.

The helicopter landed at 11am on the right time, most unlikely for a politician. Biju Babu was different. He was an active and happy-go-lucky kind of a man, quite good looking, like his son Naveen Patnaik, the present Chief Minister of Odisha. Biju Babu was garlanded by the choicest beauties of the local college, best attired, perfumed, who also were awarded with the pleasure of shaking hands with the CM.

The CM went to the dais straight away and started passionately lecturing the audience. His gestures drew a suppressed murmur from the awestruck audience. In the midst of loud applause, he waved his hands and said, "Jai ho!"

"Jai ho!"

"Biju babu ki jai ho!"

"Long live Biju *babu!'*

"Jai ho! Jai ho! Jai ho!"

Instantly,and very dramatically, our Mami caught hold of a national flag lying in the ground and vigorously waved it at the party workers and the CM, out of excitement. I tried to stop her from drawing the attention of people towards us, but she was adamant. She shouted in her trilling voice *"Baju baju jai ho!" "Baju baju jai ho!"* That's what she could make out from the slogans, I mean.

A party worker of Biju babu glanced at her, a lanky girl, looking as old as five or six years, hands thin as a bird's legs, waving and hopping, in rags. He whispered something in the CM's ears.

So, she belongs to the people below poverty line, BPL; can make an eye-catching headline.

Suddenly the CM did an unusual thing. He asked one of his party workers to get that girl on stage. He did it promptly, lifted Mami in a moment and placed her on the dais, in front of the CM, the very Chief Minister of Odisha. Biju babu patted her shoulder, gently, politely, affectionately, and asked, "What's your name, *beti?"*

"Mami Pradhan," she announced proudly.

So, that was that.

"Bhaiyon aur behano! This is real India. This is the real face of Odisha! Look at this girl. Mami Pradhan. She has a dream in her eyes, even if she is poor. Poor? Who is poor? Lord Krishna ate a fistful of puffed rice from his devotee *Sudama* and they shared their fortune!

Mami is our *Sudama.* Let us all take an oath today that we, the privileged, the educated, would do our lot to support all Mami Pradhans in our villages. You have shown your great love and faith in me by casting your precious votes for our party. If you promise to shower your love in the coming general elections, I also promise you that we can create an Odisha of our dreams, where there is no poverty. *Garibi hatao!"*

"Jai ho! Biju babu ki jai ho!"

There was thunderous applause in the air. The journalists rushed to click photographs of Biju babu holding the reed thin hands of Mami Pradhan, still with a grin, ear to ear.

"God! Look at this girl, she is not at all nervous! See her guts!" our neighbor Mini *didi* told my elder sister.

"Yes, she has always been a dare devil. I knew she would do something like this someday."

Not that Mami could make out any head or tail of the contents of the CM's speech. She had nothing to do with the national or the state politics; her entire politics was her individual psyche, of catching attention of one and all. Getting acceptance was her personal agenda. Only one sentence of the CM had impressed her greatly, *"Mami Pradhan has a dream in her eyes"*. True indeed. After that day, she became the best ever dreamer under the sun.

The CM was ready to leave. Mami got tears in her eyes. *"Don't leave... don't leave....don't leave....my dream merchant"*. She was not ready to be parted with her glorious moment. It was her lifetime achievement award.

Mami-*bou* rushed to the ground as someone told her about the happenings. She dragged her daughter home, hurling her choicest abuses at her.

"Ay *Bou*, leave me alone. Let me go near the helicopter!"

"You bloody girl, go and broom the house. Ma will come home after this meeting and then shout at me that she had given you off, not me, from the household chores. I can't broom today, I have back pain."

So the king of kings, Biju babu, left, leaving behind ambitions and a truckload of dreams in Mami Pradhan's eyes.

The next day, the front pages of all news papers in the state carried photographs of Biju babu holding the hands of a BPL girl and showing a Utopian future for every poor of Odisha. The front lines were, *'Biju Babu identifies the real face of Odisha,' 'BPL girl makes history!'*

Mami managed to collect most paper cuts of the day. (Till today one can find a few of them laminated, hanging on the broken walls of her hut.)

In the evening, Ma was amazed talking to her.

"Ay Mami, why were you jumping like that in front of the dais? You wanted them to notice you and call you there, eh? What an idiot you are! If something would have happened to you? Your Bou would have scolded my daughters that they had left you alone. Do you know how these politicians are? Biju Babu is a nice gentleman, no doubt, but do you know the party workers? If someone would have lifted you? If you were crushed in the crowd? Don't do such things again, you get that? What a girl!"

Mami got annoyed; she was still basking in the glory of the morning. She rushed out of the room bouncing her pig-tail, grumbling something at Ma. Hurling a *gali* or two, perhaps.

From that day, she stopped having pigtails and managed to snatch some money from her mother's monthly salary to buy Lifebuoy soaps to wash her hair and have a pony tail, just like me. Perhaps she had a proper hair-cut too.

To add fuel to the fire, the next day two local journalists came with a mike to our house and Madame Mami was hailed.

"Mami-ji, how old are you?"

"Ten years."

"Do you go to the school?"

"Yes, of course!"

"Yesterday, the chief Minister of Odisha could identify you among all and said that you are the real face of Odisha. How do you feel?"

"Oh, I was the most beautiful among all present over there; in fact I am the most beautiful one in the whole town, so he noticed me. Someday I shall go to his house and stay there; I shall…. I shall…"

My Ma pushed her *Bou* to go and stop her. "You never know what rubbish this stupid girl is going to tell them! Go stop her. All these journalists are making a *tamasha* here, they have no other business. Those politicians left. Now we shall see them again after five years. I don't know why on earth all of you are getting such excited. We have seen it all."

But Mami became, or at least she thought that she was, a celebrity overnight. All that media attention, photographs in news papers. *"Mamiji, Mamiji, Mamiji, how do you feel? How do you feel? How do you feel?"* She was metamorphosed from an ugly caterpillar to a pretty butterfly. The ugly duckling turned into a princes charming with the magic wand of Biju babu. She felt she was more of a socialite , page-three lady now than a mere maid in our house. She had new airs. She was stubborn not to wear my old frocks anymore; thus her *Bou* gave her some finicky slaps.

"Ay *Bou*, slap me. Till I go to his house someday, you scold me, hit me. Then all of you would come to meet me with appointments. Then I won't have time."

With this new-found celebrityhood, she stopped studying with us during the evenings. Baba had made it a point for Ma that Mami could help her during the day time, but she had to sit down to study with us from six to nine in the evening, till Baba would allow us to watch Door Darshan channel on our new Surya Kiran colour T.V.

Mami started dozing and dreaming during her study hours, looking forward for that T.V. time, to get in touch with the hot and happening girls in big cities, their new hair styles and make up. She would experiment those hair styles on herself. But her new hair styles always ended up in a disaster.

So was her tenth Board examination, disastrous, as expected. She failed, never to appear in an examination anymore.

I topped the entire district, my photograph and a short interview were in the news paper, 'Small Town Girl Tops Tenth Board Examination'. Mami was least bothered about her failure. While everyone was looking at the news paper with my photograph, she said, "Oh! What's so great about being in the news paper? That to, just one photo! I was in the all the news papers before five years. What's the big deal?"

She preferred to go back to her world of dreams. Mami's dreams had become like a bird ensnared in the dreams of that man who had promised to open the kingdom of dreams to the trapped bird. Under the encumbrance of its flapping wings her moods turned out to be tender as that of women in love.

Yes, Mami fell in love in her fifteenth year. That goat-eyed boy in our neighborhood seemed to her as the prince charming of her dreams.

"Mamiji, my dearest, sweetest, loveliest one! The

chief Minster of Odisha loved (!!) you in the past! If only you agree to be my sweetheart, I shall buy you lipsticks, powders, even a sewing machine and a wrist watch. I shall wash the utensils I don't want you to do that with your hands that touched the CM. You need not touch filthy utensils! And we would look together like Rahul and Riya in Hindi films."

Madame Mami was impressed. The slumbering clocks were not awakened anymore. Time stopped there. We all got absorbed in the grim affairs of the world, in the face of which Mami's dismay over her mother's desire to keep time running seemed as meaningless and arbitrary as Lord Indra submerging some parts of the world with unending torrential rain while leaving some other parts dry and thirsty.

"Aey *Bou*, why don't you quit their house and do some other job where we can get lots of money?"

"*Hey bhagwan*! Who will make this girl understand it for good that you are a maid servant's daughter and you too are a maid!"

Had Mami left our house after those bizarre happenings years back, she would have, being so bowed down by the enormity of the errors that life can divulge, lost the enthusiasm to fight the battles for a life full of luxury. But she grew up in our house, saw us growing and achieving laurels and adding new feathers to our caps. We were, kind of, her alter-ego. My eldest sister got a high profile job in a good city. Second sister was also settled in a government school, and third sister was working hard towards her aspirations of becoming a fashion designer like Ritu Beri someday. I was good at studies, and got accolades. Two youngest sisters were happy and bright children. Our Mami never thought that she was an inch less respectable than any one of us in the society even if she never crossed the tenth board examination. So what? She was a celebrity. After all she had photographs with his Highness, the CM of the state.

Her mother would always fret and fume before my Ma.

"See Ma, this girl wants new suits every month. She doesn't want to work; neither has she agreed to marry my cousin's son who is working in the new bus-stand *dhaba* as a cook. She thinks someday she will marry a *raj kumar*. Tell me! Ma, hike my pay or may be I'll have to find another house."

Only the wearer knows where the shoe bites. It was enough for my Ma. Because, since last few years she had grown fond of Mami, she felt flattered by her. Every now and then, Mami brought *Zarda paan* for her, massaged her back, head, legs, made delicacies in the kitchen learning from the cookery shows on the T.V., gossiped with Ma about everything happening in the town, did boost Ma's ego by convincing her that she was the best and prettiest among her colleagues; she just pampered her. Ma was ageing, my eldest sister was married, second and third sisters were busy with their new jobs, I was in the hostel, and my youngest sisters were running from home-to-college-to-tuitions-to-home. None of us had enough time for Ma and her antics. But Mami was there, always at hand, ready to do all odd jobs for her, and grin even when Ma scolded her.

Ma didn't want to spare her. Mami-*bou's* annual increments became six-monthly, then quarterly. Mami got Ma's unfinished Emami face creams, *chappals* and sarees(which she would cut and stitch into suits) more and more.

Cheating ma was easy for Mami. She got her boy friends to our lounge and kitchen garden when Ma was in the school, and everybody was out; offered them tea and snacks from our kitchen, as if it were her own; she picked anything from our dressing table or shelves . If we shouted, Ma was always there behind her.

"Get a new one for yourself! Why do you shout at her? Poor thing, she is helping you so much." Actually it was the other way round, our house was helping Mami to get what she wanted. Attention.

My third and youngest sisters were very pretty, so all those road side Romeos roamed on the road in front of our bungalow and peeped in. But we were too busy to notice them. Mami was always there, to smile at them, say "Hi! How are you?" when we were not watching. Anyway, she was growing old, pimple-faced, scarred due to the broken eruptions, bald due to no oil massage (Ma said so!).She could no longer wait for her prince charming. All her boy friends had deserted her in search of newer pasture lands. She was alone and frustrated. Her mother was too old to work and provide.

One day she got married, in fact ran away, with the first man who proposed her actually to marry him. Who was that boy? Or that aging man? It doesn't matter at all, once a girl is married. But anyway, she managed to retain her age-old dreams in her eyes and found a space in her husband's home to hang her historic photographs taken years back. Even though she felt that the big dreams were no match for the small thatched house in that slum where her husband brought her, still they were alive.

Ma was upset, as expected , without her flatterer around.

Mami got pregnant the very first day of her marriage.

And it happened every year. There was very little time for her to nourish her dreams with the household chores that she had to attend to-- cooking for four kids and her husband, washing clothes of people in the near-by government quarters.

Still in her subconscious, she had the broken pieces of her lost dreams which rushed into her mind every now and then. With time, she got acne pits on her cheeks.

Springs came and left with all their flush green glory.

Anyway,she could never forget that she must do things better than sleeping beside a man in rags on a rotten mattress; and life had more in its store than washing bottoms of her kids.

"*Oh my prince! Did you send only your servant instead of coming yourself for me because I was a maid's daughter? You had touched me one day, did you forget? But don't think that I will give up.*"

Her search for the former Chief Minister Shri Biju Patnaik was on.

One fine morning, Mami left her husband's hut and her four kids at home and caught the first bus to Bhubaneswar, the capital city of Odisha, where *he* lived. Her prince, who had once touched *Ahalya* and made her a woman from a piece of stone.

She knew his name by heart. But hardly did she know that now the regime had changed. A new government was ruling over the state, and her prince had passed away since long, leaving room for his son as the head of the opposition party.

She got down from the bus and asked a rickshaw puller to take her to the Chief Minister's house.

"Why? What would you do at the CM's house?"

"Oh… he knows me well. In fact the whole of Odisha

knows it how close I am with him. Don't you know? Where are you from?"

"Oye mad woman, shut your mouth! Where are you from,eh? Knows the chief Minister! Gone crazy? Go from here! Go!"

"You don't shout at me like this, ok? Do you know who am I?"

"How do I know? Who are you? Aishwarya Rai?"

"See this photograph. This is me with him. I shall go and stay in his house. I would marry his son. The Chief Minister's son, ok? Then you can come and take some help from me if you want. Now take me to his house, hurry up!"

The rickshaw puller saw that photograph; it looked like something from the eighteenth century, an unclear figure of some politician, a blurred image and nothing else, holding the hand of a beggar like girl.

He burst into a howl, and his friends gathered. "See *bhailog*, the daughter-in-law of the Chief Minister of Odisha, and this photograph was clicked on her engagement party. He..he..he.."

Somebody snatched the photograph; it got torn into two pieces, to the utter dismay of Mami.

"Oh god! What did you do? How can he recognize me now?I was too small by then." "Oh!what shall I do now? How could you do this? You bloody fool, I will kill you...!"

They were laughing, teasing her, having the fun of their lives, juggling her photograph to each other, and she was helplessly trying to catch hold of it.

As if it was her last hope-- otherwise, again she would have to revise the mathematical table. Again the alluring alphabets have to be freed. For her, there was no other way but to make herself free of all hang-ups and spill water of the pitchers. She moved from one darkness to another great failure. A reindeer knocked her out of bounds.

In a sudden rage, she took out the stone she had kept in her cloth bag and threw at them. One of them got hurt, bled, and they pounced on her. Before anything could happen, she started running on the crowded road of the capital amid heavily loaded trucks and the busy traffic.

"I'll see all of you. You don't know who I am..."

Mami got lost in the darkness of the blackish green forest -- on the other side of the place where common men and women like us live. Perhaps she waded through the water of many streams; perhaps she broke into laughter and tears many a times, for reasons best known to her.

Mami Pradhan, the eternal dreamer, pierced through the darkness gathered in the vacuum.

Mami Pradhan was never seen again. After searching for his wife for a whole week, her husband wrote an FIR in the local police station. Mami's mother was too old and was not able to see, lying in a corner of her hut where her young daughter-in-law kept a morsel of rice and a pot of water twice a day, like she would have done for a pet dog.

My Ma had another maid, our Tintu-Maa, as usual, and she didn't like to talk about Mami anymore. That's why she was upset when the police came to meet her to get some facts and information about Mami; but in vain.

The more I thought about it, the more I got struck with bewilderment. I hadn't thought of it, ever, can a wild stream and a girl be one and the same? Are severing the wings of a bird and filching the dreams of a woman one and the same?

■

Being God's Wife
(A Memoir)

"I look up the grey cold sky
and try to feel the warmth
of my father's eye.

His grave exists nowhere
but in me
and
I am his epitaph"

Baba. Father. My father. Such a calming, heartwarming, touching, euphonic word.

Sometimes, nay, most of the times, I address my son as '*Sonu-baba*'. Baba lives in my blood's flow. Baba lives all over my home, he follows me everywhere—to the university, to the libraries, to my lecture halls, to my TV sessions, to the interviews, to my book launches. And even to the kitchen, when Sonu, my son, looks and talks like him while eating. In my basic habit of keeping things spic and span, Baba echoes, replicates. So does he, in my edginess, ambition, motivation, sentimentality and optimism.

There have always been speculations vis-à-vis a likely historical assembly between present day genetic findings and classic mythological characters, who are Demigods.

Its main attention could lie in tell-tales by exploitation of myths to analyse any such unique character around us. To understand my father,last five years I read, re-read many ancient texts, under a new light, trying to find new directions for explorations of his character. Objectively thinking about him, not as Nandini, but as a devotee of the Deity, or as a seeker, I can draw a hypothesis that Demigods actually do exist and I can prove that. The upshot of hybridization between Baba's ancestors and progeny, of modern girls like us and imaginary people of the past who could have been Demigods like Baba is a curious concern for me now. The hypotheses talk of beings of mixed human and divine origin, often in the milieu of an ordinary family like ours. Telluric hybridizing between my Baba as an ancestor of us modern humans and the daemons that supposedly existed somewhere, in some far-off land, would appear to be an elucidation of this story. I would rather talk in harmony with my present state of knowledge about a Demigod incarnated as my Baba .

Baba constantly wanted to push the envelope towards progress, as anyone can put it. He stood for women's empowerment. In a rural household of six daughters, both parents as simple government school teachers, living most of their lifetime in rented houses so that they could educate their daughters, and no luxuries for themselves—who could have thought of this kind of a life except my Baba? Baba had a big heart, he was so popular, virtuous and pious that people called him a 'Living God'. Baba smiled to such appreciations as he was above human emotions like flattery, jealousy, greed, possessiveness—in fact any such negative emotions. He lived life of a saint, he was innocent like a five years old child even when he was 75. Education and food for all, kindness to the universe—these were the goals of his life. When my parents bought a house towards the fag end of their lives, after us six girls were settled, people named that colony as 'Krushna Nagar' in the small town G.Udayagiri, after my father's first name.

Baba had a peaceful death at home, on the lap of Maa, the love of his life. He was diabetic, and unfortunately he contaminated psoriasis in a saloon when he was in his early forties. He lived with it lifelong; his blood sugar didn't allow the wounds to heal. He was very fond of us, his daughters, and he never missed having a son. In a rural Odisha village, where everyone around was worried about a school teacher having six daughters, and their prospective marriages, Baba was relaxed, because he had six 'worthy daughters'. He believed in educating his girls, making them independent, self-reliant. We lived in a narrow, train kind of house of five rooms, with relatives always around. When he could afford to buy his own house, we had flown the nest. During the last few years of his life, Baba was left alone as he got his retirement and Maa still had a few years of service. I was teaching in the local college for a few months before I left Udayagiri.

Every morning after Maa left for her school, a *petha-walla* came discreetly and handed over a few sweet *pethas* to Baba, which he guiltily consumed and skipped the hot lunch Maa kept for him in a large lunch box. He wasn't hungry when Maa wasn't around. Maa was six years younger than Baba, and those six years of her service period made Baba lonelier than ever. He got high blood sugar and acute psoriasis due to those *pethas* and unhealthy lifestyle. Soon, he took to the wheel chair. The cruel truth was, all of us had to leave the small town for our careers and marriages. Two sisters left for the U.S. Two of us left for Delhi and Chandigarh; and the two in Odisha got busy with their jobs and children, with less time left for parents. We insisted that our parents should live with us; in fact Baba used to be very happy to live with me in Delhi. But Maa had her job for a few more years, and then she did not want to leave the house she had built for herself and Baba after all those years. It was her dream home, which is understandable.

The worst part about the health care system in India is, we are so conscious about physical health, but no one talks about mental health. Baba started dementia a few years after all of us left Udayagiri. He went back to his early youth with six small girls playing in the other room. He addressed Maa by my youngest sister's name most of the times and asked her to fetch a glass of water. He spoke to Maa as if she was one of his little girls, and pretended that we were around. Maa and the maids used to smile, thinking Baba was childlike. But I found it alarming. Some treatment was also done for it, but nothing helped. High blood sugar took over, and he had a brain stroke at 76. He was in the ICU when I met him. I couldn't control my tears, I couldn't imagine the tall, fair, handsome, ever-smiling man lying helplessly in the hospital, his mouth wide open, eyes fixed on the ceiling. My heart broke. We stayed in the hospital with him for more than a month, holding his hand, caressing his forehead.Sometimes he tightened his fist, smiled, made weird sounds like a child. Most of the times he held Maa's hands and Maa talked to him incessantly, as though he was listening. I was heartbroken to see Maa talking to Baba like we talk to normal people. After a few days, he slept peacefully on Maa's lap and died a silent death.

Memory of the virtue and gullibility of Baba makes me smile today. His eccentricities were far from being commonplace. He was rather childlike in his behaviour, but rigid like a mature adult. I am reminded about an incident from 2006, when I came to Delhi as a Professor of English. He was proud of me. I asked him to visit us, and he promptly agreed. I sent him flight tickets, e-tickets. He didn't consider that as a ticket, and insisted that there should be glossy papered, coloured tickets, like the "real-real tickets". Everyone told him that he can take printouts of the e-tickets I had sent; but he was unbending. So I went to the Airport Authorities of India office and asked the officer for colourful, glossy-paper tickets, the "real tickets". He laughed. I too laughed with him. But Baba was happy receiving those by speed post. He showed those tickets to everyone. "See! My daughter has sent air tickets!" And then, in the flight, he created a tough time for the Airhostess. Initially, he asked her to open the windows once the flight took off; they thought he was joking. When he insisted on it, the girls explained that it's not possible. He was obstinate, as ever, and insisted on getting down midair and taking another flight that would open the windows for him. Poor Maa had a hard time, pacifying Baba and apologizing the crew. Once they reached my home, Maa fought with him. But he was nonchalant, he knew that he was right.

Poor Maa had several such occasions when he put her in difficult situations. Before the wedding of my second sister, Maa called the goldsmith home to take orders for the wedding jewelry. Before the jeweler arrived, Maa gave some instructions to Baba. "Goldsmiths are clever people. He will ask us to make the entire payment before he delivers the jewelry, but we will not accept his conditions. He may even disappear after taking the money. So we'll pay him only a small advance amount and pay him the whole amount after he delivers the jewelry. Ok?"

Baba nodded like an obedient child. Maa was right,

the goldsmith requested them endlessly to pay the whole amount, but Maa said we have to take the amount from the bank which will take a lot of time. Baba kept quiet. Once Maa went to the kitchen to get some tea for the goldsmith, the clever man pleaded before Baba for the whole amount. Baba said, "Beta, we cannot give you so much money because goldsmiths are clever people, and you may disappear after taking the money."

"Who said that to you Sir!!"

"My wife."

"Exactly! I was thinking that. You are such a fine person, you are pious like Gods, only Madam can think such things about us."

Maa was standing there by then with a cup of tea. She kept the teacup on the table with a jolt and left the room, banging the door from behind. She had to come to her daughters' room to cry.

The goldsmith left with only the advance money. But then, Baba had a hard time handling his wife and giving an explanation to his feminist daughters. But at the end of the day, they were always together, my father and mother. If someone asks me the definition of love, I'll simply take their names. By the way—we used to take their names jocularly as 'Meera and Jeera', though their names are Meera and Krishna. Who says proper names are non-connotative!!

We have never seen our parents having their food separately. They were always together, except for the times when they were at their workplaces. Baba would call 'Meera, Meera' round the day for every small thing, and we were assured, reassured that life was good, life was beautiful, watching *Meera-Jeera* as a team. Not that they had no differences of opinions—but both of them were ready to reconcile, resolve, reunite after an argument. Probably they never said 'I love you' to each other, during our childhood, parents never said those things to each other—we understood that. But 'love' defined them, and their love protected us.

Years back, when I was in B.A final year, I asked Baba about being a strict disciplinarian, when it came to studies and cleaning the house. Baba has a ready-made answer. He said, only a disciplined person is successful. He had anecdotes galore and quotes from classics. He said, "God helps those who help themselves". Our slippers and shoes were kept under the bed by drawing lines with permanent markers, with a specific number assigned to each girl. We didn't dare to put our slippers even an inch beyond the specified block. He put circles and dates on the calendar for every small thing, including a reminder for him to shave his beards or reminders for us to submit assignments. When we wrote letters to our eldest sister living in a hostel in Berhampur, our letters were read aloud, they were a public affair, Baba having a red pen handy to round up, underline wrong spellings, if any. That was the time when I precisely developed a tremendous love for English language. I learnt the art of writing from him, with a clear understanding of "quality, quantity and contents"—as he put it. Once I wrote my sister, "please get a nail-police for me". Baba laughed and underlined that, and corrected it to 'nail-polish'. I felt insulted and cried the whole day, my feminine ego was hurt, and I behaved in a way as if my kidney was given away to someone without my permission—today I remember that and laugh. Old habits die hard—today I find myself strictly following the values and the organized way of living—perhaps that is what makes me what I am.

During my childhood, I kind of loathed my name; 'Nandini' perfectly rhymed with the word 'kanduri', meaning a 'cry baby' in Odia. I wanted to change my name to 'Pallavi'. I beseeched Baba to change my name if he wanted me to stop being a cry baby. Baba took my hand in his hand and told, "Maa, you are born to be Nandini. *Sabko aanand dene walli Nandini,* you see!" I was convinced. I loved my name, I loved myself, and I took the responsibility given to me by Baba very seriously.

Baba wanted me to be everything that he couldn't be, due to family responsibilities. He wanted to be a Professor of English, a writer, but he was trapped into multiple responsibilities. Being the father of six girls (three of his boys died early) was no joke. Still, the center of gravity of our household was love, Baba never regretted having six girl children. He stood for women's education in rural Odisha, as I already said. He was the harbinger, almost the founder, of the local college at G.Udayagiri—he ran from pillar to post to convince the Collector, and then the Government of Odisha to introduce a college in that sleepy, small town where people had not imagined about women's education. Even today when the senior teachers of Kalinga Mahavidyalaya meet our mother or anyone of us, they have a word of respect for our Baba.

In a house of six girls, birth of a son was more than any celebration, which Baba accomplished nonchalantly, because he loved all his children equally. When my younger brother was born a couple of years after me, the entire focus of the family shifted to him. I was sent to the school way too early so as not to disturb the boy, and Baba had to get me admitted in class-I by increasing my age by thirteen months as I was not of the eligible age to get admission. Such things happened in villages, no one cared about people's age, future or career, for that matter. Anyway, my brother passed away at a tender age, even before going to school. Maa was devastated, so was Baba. An old woman, *Phulabudhi*, who used to get flowers for our daily supply, commented, "Gosh.. any one among the six girls could have died today, why the only son!! This is terrible!" Even on the worst day of sorrow, Baba hated her statement, shouted, drove her away. My sisters vividly remember that morning, and we feel so grateful to be the daughters of such a father who loved and respected us for who we are. But as it was fated, other relatives held me, the crying-asthmatic-fretting-fuming-bookish-girl, responsible for the sad, untimely demise of the only son. They commented whenever I coughed or cried or fell sick. I wanted a place to run away, a place to escape, to hide myself. Baba understood. I was hardly eight years old when he offered me his school library, he made it accessible for me, Rest is history. I spent my childhood in Hubback High School library, cataloguing, sorting, arranging books—reading each and every book luxuriously, with a Quixotical interest. My world was flooded with books, more books every single day. Today when I look at my enormous personal library in Delhi, I close my eyes and visualize Baba and me sitting on the floor in his school library, and discussing every book.

Tears roll down.

Baba had a typical sense of humour— but of course he didn't know about it. There was a Sanskrit teacher in his school, Hubback High School, who used to get drunk every so often, and tried to blabber with people. While everyone avoided him, Baba was compassionate; he even invited him home and counselled him. Once the teacher got drunk and closed his doors, excreted in the middle of his house, put incense sticks on his shit and waited. People knocked his door, but he didn't pay any heed. Finally he opened the window when Baba called him from outside.

Baba was taken aback and asked him what was going on—his answer was, "Sir, I am trying to see what happens when we combine bad and good odors, *Sugandh* and *Durgandh*." Baba managed to open the door, get the house cleaned up and from that day, he took his responsibility. After a few days, to the surprise of all, the Sanskrit teacher became a teetotaler.

I was 'Daddy's Girl'; I was proudly my Baba's beloved daughter because I was a bookworm, and I spoke English with clarity, conviction, and because I stood for justice. I remember one such queer incident. When I was in Class X, my menstruation started in the school. I rushed home. In my typical Drama Queen demeanor, I ran to Baba to show him my frock, shouting, "Baba, Baba, see I have Blood Cancer !!" (unfortunately there was no awareness, no sex education in villages at that time, and of course no Internet to keep the girls informed.) We used to watch movies where characters having Blood Cancer coughed restlessly, spitting blood into a white handkerchief. I suddenly romanticized my bleeding, though I was in pain. Baba was at a fix; he asked the domestic help to make me sit patiently till Maa came back from her school. I was traumatized with all that warm blood between my thighs, seeing my school uniform blood-soaked. Baba took the *Bhagavat Gita*, read out five chapters to me aloud-- on serenity, penitence, dedication, commitment to duty and detachment to life in an attached way. That kept my mind engaged till Maa came, though I was sipping warm water and sobbing. Today I realize why Baba did that, though I wish he had explained a bit about human body, menstruation as a normal phenomenon for any woman, hygiene and health.

Baba firmly believed in justice and fair play in examinations, in fact in the entire education system.

A spoiled brat of a rich businessman, politician in the village requested Baba to allow him malpractice in the examination, but Baba put his foot down. Maa had to bear the consequences of facing a few Memos at her work place. We grew up like this.

After Baba's retirement, Mr.Ratha, the Head Clerk of his school, expected bribe to prepare his pension papers, but didn't say that openly; he came to our place to settle the matter. He said, "Sir, *Chai-Paani ke liye kuch chhahiye*", (I need something for my tea etc!). Baba simply requested Maa to make some tea for him! He was annoyed and said, "Don't pretend. You have to make me happy by giving ten percent of the amount you will get, I'll make you happy by preparing the papers promptly." Only then Baba knew that he was asking for bribe. Baba delivered a long lecture to him about ethics, morality, quality of mercy, as expected. But then, Mr.Ratha was incorrigible. He said, "nothing doing. I am leaving". Baba lost patience, said, "This is my lifetime's hard-earned money which will be used for the education of my girls, and you are asking me to get into unfair practices? How can I give away that money to you?" Mr.Ratha misbehaved, and said, "Do what you like, you foolish, impractical man", and he was about to leave. Baba got up from his chair and gave him a tight slap. Coming few days, we saw that Maa had to face the music. She arranged some money and discreetly gave it to Mr.Ratha. Only then the pension papers were cleared. All the while Maa griped, but could do nothing to change Baba, her Demigod.

After a few days, the wedding of three sisters, including me, was fixed and Baba went to the State Bank of India to withdraw a few lakhs for the ceremony. The Branch Manager neatly packed, handed the money in packets and Baba came home. Maa and Baba sat together on their dining-cum-study-cum-multipurpose-table and chairs to count the money. Lo and behold! The Manager had actually handed over a wrong packet to Baba with three lakhs extra. In 1997, three lakh rupees were a lifechanging amount! Baba got up, asked me to accompany him to the Bank immediately when everyone was whispering to each other. When we reached the bank, the Manager was already rushing out of the Bank with two police personnel. Baba returned the amount to him, dispassionately. I practically saw the Manager and a couple of other staffs touching Baba's feet, sniveling, telling him "You are God incarnate Sir!" My eyes were beaming, teary though, and Baba told me, "Maa, if we take any money from people which is not ours, it'll ultimately go to the hospital, right?"

"Right."

Till today my Gandhian father's invisible eyes follow me, protecting me from any kind of unfair money.

Baba watched films and TV with great interest. He was the most faithful fan of Dharmendra, Hema Malini, Manoj Kumar and Rajesh Khanna. *Haathi Mera Saathi* was his all-time favorite movie. We used to sit cozily in the hall, watch Doordarshan while Baba explained us the programmes, including Krushidarshan. We watched award programmes on New Year nights, when Baba applauded to Dharmendra, Hema Malini receiving awards. Decades later, when Sridevi, Madhiri Dixit, Shahrukh Khan etc received awards on the award functions, Baba protested stridently. He would say, "Meera, see these *bokka*(foolish) people, they are not giving awards to Dharmendra, Hema Malini!" We tried to explain it to him that with changing times, new actors come up and they too deserve awards. But no! Baba never was convinced.

Dussehras and Diwalis were celebrated with aplomb

at home, thanks to Baba. Baba was very cautious that we played a safe Diwali. He had kept six neatly cut bamboo sticks where he fixed the crackers (Phuljhadiyan) in the cuts and handed over to us, while our neighbours laughed at us. It created a scene—six girls holding the crackers sticked to sticks in a row, while Baba carefully scrutinized and ensured that no one actually touched the Phuljhadiyan. It was so embarrassing for us, but then, there was no other choice for Baba's girls. Now whenever someone sends a Whatsapp message, 'Safe Diwali', on Diwali, I go back to the memory lane of playing a real-safe 'Safe Diwali'. Dussehras were full of festivity, with Baba reading out the Bratkatha, (the scriptures) while Maa made *pithas*(rice and flour cakes) in massive amounts day long. We tried to focus there, but our mind wandered to the distant drumbeats of animal sacrifice rituals by some clans, some sects, that created awe and fear. We sneaked to Baba and Maa if it was too much—and they never told us how much was too much.They were always available, never busy when their daughters needed them. In the evening, we dressed up in new dresses to go out with parents, similar pattern frocks with same fabrics for six girls, sometimes even Maa's blouse was stitched in the same cloth, if there was excess amount of cloth. One month before the celebrations, all of us went to Sahoo Vanijya Pratishthan with Baba to select one whole rim of floral cloths, maybe fifteen or twenty meters, same print same colours, and handover the cloth with measurements to the tailor, in a queue. When we grew up a bit, my third sister protested this and ensured that the patterns and the clothes were different for each one of us— to Baba's great dissatisfaction.

Baba believed in secularism, to the true sense of the term. Baba and Maa were with me in 2014 to celebrate

Diwali in Delhi, in my university campus government quarters. Baba didn't like to see that Sonu was holding the Phuljhadiyan in his hands, without the help of a stick. I tried to explain it to Sonu, but he couldn't understand how on earth a Phuljhadi can be fixed to a stick. He dismissed my explanations, laughed at me, and ran away to play with his friends—to Baba's displeasure again. So I tried to engage Baba elsewhere. I used to invite all my friends home. We cooked a lot of food with the help of female colleagues, friends. Baba was excited to see that my Hindu, Muslim and Christian friends celebrated Diwali with me, cooked in my kitchen. Baba patted my shoulder with appreciation and gave the example of Mrs.Indira Gandhi's family where there were people from all religions. A Muslim colleague's wife, Mrs.Khan, was frying Puris in my kitchen. Baba asked her to sit beside him for awhile and told, "Beta, see my daughter, she believes in *sarva-dharma-samanwaya*, she is secular. That is why, even if you are a Muslim, you are cooking in her kitchen". The lady couldn't get the essence of his innocent remarks, felt offended and left. I had to go to her house, leaving the guests, and explain it to her that it was his simplicity to say so, and he was actually appreciating our togetherness. Well, she never understood. In fact, everyone misunderstood his words, misinterpreted his intentions. Late evening when guests had left, I reprimanded Baba, "Must you, must you, always deliver a long speech on every occasion?" Baba kept quiet. He was absentminded, thinking about solidarity and secularism.

After a few years, after all of us were married and had left the village, Baba became kind of detached from us; his TV serial characters and their issues took over our issues at home. When I was going through domestic violence, miscarriages, both my parents were offhand. 'He doesn't romanticize sorrow' -- Maa put it this way if I was angry with his callousness. Whatever might be the issue, I was broken. I hated Baba for being so apathetic to my pain. That is when one of the books that Baba introduced me in his library, came handy. I felt connected to this poem:

Daddy, I have had to kill you.
You died before I had time— —
Marble-heavy, a bag full of God,
Ghastly statue with one gray toe
Big as a Frisco seal…
There's a stake in your fat black heart
And the villagers never liked you.
They are dancing and stamping on you.
They always *knew* it was you.
Daddy, daddy, you bastard, I'm through.

(Sylvia Plath's "Daddy")

I developed an acute love-hate-relationship with Baba after losing two girl children to marital-rapes, just before their birth. I looked at the fetuses both the times and wanted to hug Baba, cry aloud. But he maintained a stony silence, as if I had merely lost my toys and was crying mulishly. Baba had a weird detachment to my snags. But now I guess I should have understood, during his last few years, he remained nothing but Maa's husband. He had Dementia, fractional Alzheimer's. He traveled back and forth to our childhood after his six girls got married and flew the nest. Now I remember how he longed to check our Maths note books, ask us spellings of difficult words like 'pneumonia', 'psychology'(he always said, 'p' silent here!). Playing 'spell-the-word-so-and-so' was our favorite pastime. Baba longed for those games with me during his Dementia days—I wish, I wish I had given him some more time. I wish I would not have been running the race of life at that time as the single mother of Sonu, searching for a central government job and doing PhD, while struggling to run errands for the two of us with just a Junior Research Fellowship from Santiniketan. I wish I could have told him loud and clear—*Baba, I need you now! Save me from drowning into this bottomless pit. Hold my hand. In return, I'll hold your hand and take you happily to the lanes of childhood through Sonu's infancy, Sonu's juvenile joy.* But lot of things remained unspoken between me and Baba.

During his last few weeks after a sudden brain hemorrhage, I was with him in Apollo Hospital, Bhubaneswar, where he was in the ICU, his mouth agape, eyes moist, where he was waffling the quotes he had mugged up from the Books of Wisdom. It was therapeutic for me to take care of him there -- I don't know if he understood that. Even I heard him whisper, "God is in the heaven and all is right with the world." I wrote a poem for him in the hospital and read it aloud to him, I don't know if he could hear that.

That Foot
(for my Baba)

That foot that has walked
on thorns
all through the day for you.
That foot which has shown
you foot-steps to follow.
That foot.
That foot behind the orange sun
has walked through arches
bare foot

on fire, on water
near parapets
has cracked doors and windows
for you to enter safe.
That foot.
That foot walked, crossed the
never-ending roads
when you aspired for the colossal.
That foot. Your passport
to utopia, to dream of
new truths, passport to planets uncharted.

That foot, is walking away, weak,
parting with fantasia forever.
Will you join?

'Poetry as therapy', 'literature as witness' , 'art for life's sake' are concepts that Baba had taught me. He was a happy man, with zero understanding of adulterations and ways of the world. After months in the hospital, the doctors advised us to take him home. He was sent home in an Ambulance, that was the last I saw of him, touched his feet.

I was told, the next morning he looked happy, talked to everyone. In fact, he spoke to me and Sonu over phone, asked me to read more, write more, take care of myself and Sonu. By then he had performed all his duties, educated his daughters and married them off, built a big and beautiful house for his dear wife. That morning he had spoken to everyone over phone. So he decided, it was time for him to leave. His duties were over. He knew , he had lived a good life.

I could never gather myself to visit our home at Udayagiri after Baba; I made it a point to meet Maa in Berhampur or Bhubaneswar all these years. Last week, in mid-June 2022, I visited Udayagiri, after five years, and saw

Baba's wall clocks, watches, books, clothes, tables—all in place. Maa hasn't removed anything (Baba never liked if his stuff were misplaced!). I cried to my heart's content the whole night, I roamed all over the lonely, eerie house till the wee hours, I tried to talk to Baba. No, I couldn't find a trace of him anywhere. There was just an uncanny silence and deep, dark, intense pain in the air.

The next morning I had to be normal for Maa's sake. Poor Maa, she has been learning to live alone, and I felt she is good at it! She is doing well, and I felt proud of her. She finishes her daily dose of missing and crying for her adorable husband in the morning. Then she cooks a healthy meal for herself, takes her vitamins and supplements, wears nice cotton sarees and watches TV serials, calls her daughters regularly, reads *Grihashobha* and *Katha*, gossips with her five happily-married daughters about their in-laws and feels contented.

Over breakfast, Maa and me started telling anecdotes about Baba to Sonu. I didn't allow her to cry, I teased her, tickled her, pinched her and made her laugh over Baba's innocent anecdotes. We remembered a few incidents related to our domestic helps. Sukamaa was a delectable woman, she took care of us when we were very small. I have written a complete poetry book about her, *Sukamaa and Other Poems(2013)*. After her death, there was Zarina, who stole massively from our house with the help of her brothers; she robbed us of everything precious. Then there was one Pushavati who tried to seduce our handsome, gorgeous Baba (my sisters always say, 'our Baba looked like Dharmendra and Manoj Kumar, that is how our pedigree is so rich!') ,and how Maa threw her out. Then came Tintumaa. She was this clever woman who used to take advance money from her salary every month, but never bothered to return the amount. At the end of the month she would plead for her entire salary. Baba wrote the advance amount in a note book, but paid her the entire salary which Maa didn't approve of. Maa had a point, Tintumaa had been cheating us. After more than thirty months, one fine morning Maa decided to be very strict with Tintumaa and she put her foot down. She asked Baba not to pay her any salary for a couple of months so as to adjust the advance money. Baba was too kind-hearted to deduct the domestic help's salary. At that time Tintumaa was crying foul in the veranda. Maa picked the note book and showed Baba angrily, "See! See, how much money she already has minted from us. We have our limitations, how much more can we pay her!! After all we have six daughters to feed and then marry them off."

Baba found a way out. Yes, Tintumaa was too much. Enough was enough. She was too much of a disturbance at home. Something must be done about her! So he simply took the notebook from Maa, tore it to pieces, and said, "*Naa rahega baansh, naa bazegi banshuri.* Meera, now Tintumaa's tension is over. We have no idea, no evidence as to how much money she has minted from us. Now happy?"

Maa created a tough time for Baba the whole day, but at the end of the day she had to come to terms with whatever had happened. She had to make peace with Baba, because she only loved him, and she loved only him.

Sonu laughed aloud when Maa and I narrated this incident to him.

I saw, Maa had moist eyes. I asked her, "What happened Maa? You ok?"

She sighed deeply. And said, "I had a great life with your Baba. I have seen it all – being God's wife!!"

About the author:

Prof. Nandini Sahu, the Amazon Bestselling Author (2022), is a major voice in contemporary Indian English literature. She has accomplished her doctorate in English literature under the guidance of Late Prof. Niranjan Mohanty, Prof. of English, Visva Bharati, Santiniketan. She has been widely published in India, U.S.A, U.K., Africa, Italy, Australia and Pakistan. Apart from numerous other literary awards, she is a triple gold medalist in English literature; she has received the Gold Medal from the hon'ble Vice-President of India for her contributions to English Studies in India in the year 2019. She is the author and editor of seventeen books, *The Other Voice, The, Recollection as Redemption, The Post-Modernist Delegation to English Language Teaching, The Post Colonial Space: Writing the Self and the Nation, Silver Poems on My Lips, Folklore and the Alternative Modernities* (Vol.I), *Folklore and the Alternative Modernities* (Vol. II), *Sukamaa and Other Poems, Suvarnarekha, Sita(A Poem), Dynamics of Children's Literature, Zero Point* and *Selected Poems of Nandini Sahu(Winter-2020), Selected Poems of Nandini Sahu(Spring-2021), Re-reading Jayanta Mahapatra* and *A Song, Half & Half*. She is the Former Director, School of Foreign

Languages and currently a Professor of English at Indira Gandhi National Open University [IGNOU], New Delhi, India. Her areas of research interest cover Indian Literature, New Literatures, Folklore and Culture Studies, American Literature, Children's Literature and Critical Theory. She is the Chief Editor/Founder Editor of *Interdisciplinary Journal of Literature and Language* (IJLL), a bi-annual peer-reviewed journal in English. Professor Sahu has designed multiple academic programmes on Culture Studies, American Literature, Postcolonial Literatures, Children's Literature, Indian Folk Literature and Indian Philosophical Thoughts for IGNOU and many other universities.

www.nandinisahu.in

Black Eagle Books

www.blackeaglebooks.org
info@blackeaglebooks.org

Black Eagle Books, an independent publisher, was founded
as a nonprofit organization in April, 2019. It is our mission
to connect and engage the Indian diaspora and the world at
large with the best of works of world literature published
on a collaborative platform, with special emphasis on
foregrounding Contemporary Classics and New Writing.